EVIE
AND JACK

Glenn Haybittle

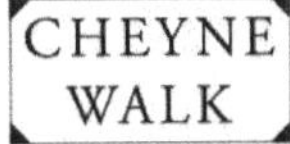

"Among the tortures and devastations of life is this then - our friends are not able to finish their stories."

Virginia Woolf

Part One

1943

1

The man in the dark glasses took her lethal pill. That tiny compound of deadly chemicals. She was told it would induce a painless death. *Bite down on it hard.* Death has always been ten seconds away, ever since she landed in France. Now something worse awaits her.

She can hear nothing beyond the walls of this inappropriately ornate room. This room that is swallowing up her entire life.

"Perhaps you recognise these, Lucie? Or should I call you Katherine?"

The chandeliers drop refractions on the polished desk like a coded message. The man, her interrogator, pushes a sheaf of papers across towards her. He looks like a ticket inspector. Wiry, humourless, vigilant. A man who scrutinises scraps of papers for anomalies.

Everything this man learns about her makes her less certain who she is.

She glances down again at the buzzer next to the lamp. She has a mad urge to press it. To get the worst over and done with. He sees her look at it. The expression on his face is another part of the game he is playing with her.

"Anais doesn't tell lies," she says.

"Perhaps you are enjoying being someone you're not because you were not happy before. Bruno can tell these things, you know."

"You're a psychic?"

"Yes. I am everything you want me to be. How you say? Piece of cake. I can be anything and everything I am told to be. I can be a grasshopper or a lion. One thing though, you don't smell French. Not even your French toiletries can change that. Perhaps you have not eaten enough garlic in your life."

Bruno is slightly overweight. His hair is receding. His moustache is comically inept, bedraggled, like something fished out of a pond. He has the self-esteem and bluster of an extremely attractive man but the appearance of a grocer.

"You are observant. But not inconspicuous. You are also diffident by nature. So you have placed yourself in a situation where your natural diffidence is justified. Your friend Lucie was less observant, less diffident but more inconspicuous."

She and Lucie shared a room at training school. She had been a bit jealous when she found out Lucie was being sent to France ahead of her. She was a better shot than Lucie. Better at climbing up trees, sliding down ropes too. "Do you believe Lucie has been captured?"

"Let's say you can go to her apartment. I'm not going to anyone's apartment. I don't care if there are flowers in the window or not."

"That's not very chivalrous of you."

"I enjoyed it when we took that corner just now and our shoulders touched. It reminded me of my first ever love, when I was twelve, and how thrilling it was every time a bit of my body made contact with a bit of her body. It was like touching all the wonder life holds. Like touching a star. Of course I am wondering if you are really married."

He is watching her slide her bogus wedding ring up and down her finger.

Part One

1943

1

The man in the dark glasses took her lethal pill. That tiny compound of deadly chemicals. She was told it would induce a painless death. *Bite down on it hard.* Death has always been ten seconds away, ever since she landed in France. Now something worse awaits her.

She can hear nothing beyond the walls of this inappropriately ornate room. This room that is swallowing up her entire life.

"Perhaps you recognise these, Lucie? Or should I call you Katherine?"

The chandeliers drop refractions on the polished desk like a coded message. The man, her interrogator, pushes a sheaf of papers across towards her. He looks like a ticket inspector. Wiry, humourless, vigilant. A man who scrutinises scraps of papers for anomalies.

Everything this man learns about her makes her less certain who she is.

She glances down again at the buzzer next to the lamp. She has a mad urge to press it. To get the worst over and done with. He sees her look at it. The expression on his face is another part of the game he is playing with her.

The sheaf of papers is no doubt another trap. She looks at the top sheet of paper warily. It is a photostat. She can't control the surprise and dismay that tugs at her mouth, rushes up into her blue eyes. It is the letter she wrote to her mother three weeks ago. She picks it up. Below is a letter she wrote to London HQ about suitable farms for an arms drop. All the mail she has sent to England in the past month is here. Mail she gave to the air movement officer, a roguish relentlessly inquisitive French man known as Gilbert. Mail he was supposed to send back to London. Mail that it wasn't thought necessary to code.

"We have arrested many of your companions. When they saw their own letters they felt betrayed. And so they talked. We have agreed to treat them as prisoners of war and not as spies. Thus sparing their lives. In exchange for information. Many have cooperated. So it is pointless for you to play the heroine. If I press this buzzer an unpleasant French thug will enter the room. It will be his job to cause you pain. And he enjoys his work. It sickens me how much pleasure he takes from his work. Do you want me to press the buzzer?"

She tries flirtation. Adopts what mirrors have told her is her most beguiling expression. "What I want is a hot bath and something decent to eat."

"All in good time. You have my word."

She has his word. He has been trying to impress this on her ever since she was led into his office. Mock interrogations at training school in England had been nothing like this. The sophistication of the Gestapo has been underestimated. She had been led to believe she would be shouted at. Blinded with skewering light. Made to stand on chairs. Made to kneel down on all fours in her underwear. None of these things have happened. It is as if this man is trying to coax her into buying something she has no need of. And he won't give up.

"Would you be surprised if I told you there is a traitor in your midst?"

She would not be surprised. It is the only explanation. She

has heard about all the arrests. Hundreds of them in a short space of time. Whole circuits compromised.

"Two traitors actually. Obviously Gilbert is working for us. But there is also someone in Baker Street. Can you guess who that might be?"

She shakes her head.

"Please take a guess. I am curious whether you have an intuition on the matter."

Her mind summons up a parade of Baker Street personnel. She scrutinises her emotional memory of each of them for signs of duplicity.

"I haven't the foggiest idea. There are many people at Baker Street I have never even met."

"But you've met Nicholas Pole?"

"Once or twice."

"He was a journalist before the war. A good friend of one of our officers. He was also a friend of Henri Dericourt, the real name of Gilbert."

She finds she can't dismiss the idea that Nicholas Pole might be a traitor.

"Your task is over. Heroics are pointless. Just give me the answer to four simple questions and you have my word you will not be hurt. Where is Marcel? What is your poem? Does Buckmaster know we are playing back his radios to him? Where and when will the invasion of France take place?"

She has not been told where or when the landings will take place though there is a rumour that they are to happen soon.

"I don't know where or when the landings will take place."

"I do. Prosper told me. He was flown back to London last month where he met with Winston Churchill. The invasion will take place in the first week of September in the Pas-de-Calais. And your task was to organise sabotage in the Calais region. As if to add weight to the idea that this is where the invasion forces will arrive. But supposing they are not arriving there at all? That you, like many of your fellow agents, have been used as part of an elaborate ploy to deceive us? To trick the Wehrmacht into moving divisions from the Eastern Front to the Calais area?"

He sits back leisurely in his chair. Removes his dark glasses and wipes them with a crisp scented square of white linen.

"Listen, I can tell you the exact location where you were dropped. You were followed from the station at Clermont-Ferrand. We could have arrested you before you unclipped your parachute. But we preferred to let you walk free for a while. Lead us to some of your friends. At the next moon we know two more agents are flying in. Anais and Bruno. Anais will go to Clermont-Ferrand to become the courier of Xan, leader of the POET circuit. Bruno is going to become a liaisons officer and arms instructor for the same circuit."

"You know far more than I do in that case."

"We have five of your wireless sets with codes and crystals that we are playing back to London. We can ask for whatever we want. Arms, explosives, medical supplies, even cigarettes and chocolate. Do you know we have even had a telegram of congratulations from the Führer himself? He wanted us to send Baker Street a message thanking them for all the arms and munitions they have dropped directly into the hands of the Third Reich. But I have my doubts. And I want to talk to you about these doubts. Either your organisation is the height of ineptitude or there's a deliberate ploy to deceive us going on. Admit, you have heard rumours there is to be an invasion of France soon."

She says nothing but she has heard this rumour several times. The French resistance were expecting the invasion from one day to the next.

"But perhaps it has all been a bit too easy for us? I have a hunch that you are all being sent as part of a trick to fool us as to when and where the landings are going to take place. Suddenly all these drops, all these new agents arriving, a huge increase in transmissions. As if something big is about to happen. But surely if something big was about to happen there would be more endeavour to conceal it? We have informed the Wehrmacht that the invasion of France will supposedly take place at the beginning of next month. And guess what? They are not interested. They will keep their armies where they are needed, not where they are rumoured to be needed. So if this is the scope of your mission it has failed. And you have all been sacrificed for nothing."

She is thinking of Anais. Her friend Anais. She is thinking there might be some truth in everything this man is saying.

"There is really no need for me to interrogate you. Because I know far more about your operations than you do. Marcel has slipped the net for the time being. But Anais will lead us to him. If my theory is correct you and your fellow agents have been used as sacrificial lambs. How does that feel – to know your country has deliberately sent you into our hands? That you are all being manipulated by your own government? I am interested what you think. How does it feel to be betrayed by your own people?"

2

Through the open window of the car the scent of dog roses and honeysuckle and wet tilled earth make her think of her poem. *And wilt thou leave me thus?* Her father quoted it to her with his mischievous half smile almost every time she left the house. Even if she was just going out to play in the garden. *And wilt thou leave me thus? Say nay! Say nay!* When she thinks of her father she sometimes feels the ghostly imprint of his palm on the back of her neck. He always placed his palm there when he wanted to comfort her. The last time she ever saw him alive he cupped the back of her neck in this way. Memories of her father plunge her down into the deepest and most receptive part of her being. In all her favourite memories he is either encouraging her to take more pleasure from the moment or helping her find comfort in the tears she cries. But all memories of her father are forbidden to her now. She feels a pulse of guilt, of resistance, at this act of betrayal against her father.

What would he think if he knew what she was doing? Papa. Daddy. That she has signed the Official Secrets Act, jumped out of an airplane at 1,000 feet, blown up a dummy bridge with high explosives, learned how to silently kill a man with her bare hands, caught and skinned rabbits in the wild? She knows the answer. He wouldn't have believed it, just as she herself cannot quite believe it much of the time.

Evie has a new father now. A make believe father. *"Didier Maupin, an electrician from Uzès. My childhood home was in Rue du Coin. Above a patisserie. My best friend was a girl called Valerie Famin."*

On her last visit home she studied the family snapshots of France. Her mother is French. The family lived near Aix-en-Provence until Evie was eleven. There was one photograph of her father standing in the market in Uzès. Caught in the act of taking off his hat. Another photo of him standing by a fountain in Paris. A photo she herself took. In this photo there is a ghostly betokening that he knows he is going to die soon.

On the night he killed himself, October 14, 1938, Evie's new incarnation, Monique Maupin, field name, Anais, was in Paris. Working as a secretary for Monsieur Dabin, a leather manufacturer.

"Remember, when interrogated, your answers mustn't be too efficiently brisk. Memory is a flawed transaction. Like all ciphers."

It was the intelligence officer who told her memory is a flawed transaction. The night she was abruptly woken up before dawn by shouting men in Nazi uniforms and taken off for a mock interrogation. (A test she initially failed: she complained in English when she was wrenched from sleep.) Some of the girls had found these mock interrogations a giggle but they frightened her. The sizzling white light scouring into her eyes. The barking of questions at her while she was only half awake, while she was caught precipitously between her real and her fictitious self. Everything a deception. Everything a game of bluff and double bluff. She had doubts that she was cut out for this work. She still has these doubts.

If you are arrested by the Gestapo, do not assume that all is lost; the Gestapo's reputation has been built up on ruthlessness and terrorism, not intelligence. They will always pretend to know more than they do and may even make a good guess, but remember that it is a guess.

Gestapo. She cannot allow the word into her thoughts without the sensation of plunging headfirst into icy water.

And wilt thou leave me thus? Say nay! Say nay!

She is allowed to remember the poem. It is one of her duties to remember it. Word for word. The poem is part of her safety.

Perhaps it was a mistake to choose this poem, which is so much part of the fabric of her authentic self. Words from the poem have been given numbers and these numbers are the key to the cipher which will conceal the plaintext of her messages.

"You know, of course, that the woman for whom this poem was written lost her head?"

"You mean it's not a very auspicious choice?"

"Well, it could be seen that way. But this is your show."

Her companion on the red leather seat in the back of the car has been quiet for a while.

"How you say? Penny for your thoughts," he now says.

The airfield has come into sight across the fields. More memories of the woman she truly is, when she was a WAAF wireless operator, first with Fighter Command, then with Bomber Command at Wickenby in Lincolnshire.

"Speak in French, Bruno," she says.

"I give you a week," he says in English.

"You have so little confidence in me?"

"No. I have very much confidence in you. I am very happy you are my companion. I am… how you say? Over the moon."

"So why do you give me only a week?"

"Before you fall in love with me? Because I am more irresistible than your Lord Byron. He walk in the beauty, like the night. I have added this to the many exemplary traits of Bruno. I too can walk in beauty, like the night. I am also very fond of children, dancing and swimming in the moonlight."

"Anais does not fall in love easily."

"I sense you are good at telling lies. I also have much experience with telling lies. I have told lies my whole life. Mostly I tell lies to myself. Have any of your lies caught up with you yet?"

Evie thinks of the dead pilot and how she turned her back on him before he died. He told her his name was Guy. But his real name was Jack. He created a false identity for himself. Just as she is doing now. She misses the moments they made together but refuses to think of him as unique. She wonders if this is a lie she is telling herself.

"Anais doesn't tell lies," she says.

"Perhaps you are enjoying being someone you're not because you were not happy before. Bruno can tell these things, you know."

"You're a psychic?"

"Yes. I am everything you want me to be. How you say? Piece of cake. I can be anything and everything I am told to be. I can be a grasshopper or a lion. One thing though, you don't smell French. Not even your French toiletries can change that. Perhaps you have not eaten enough garlic in your life."

Bruno is slightly overweight. His hair is receding. His moustache is comically inept, bedraggled, like something fished out of a pond. He has the self-esteem and bluster of an extremely attractive man but the appearance of a grocer.

"You are observant. But not inconspicuous. You are also diffident by nature. So you have placed yourself in a situation where your natural diffidence is justified. Your friend Lucie was less observant, less diffident but more inconspicuous."

She and Lucie shared a room at training school. She had been a bit jealous when she found out Lucie was being sent to France ahead of her. She was a better shot than Lucie. Better at climbing up trees, sliding down ropes too. "Do you believe Lucie has been captured?"

"Let's say you can go to her apartment. I'm not going to anyone's apartment. I don't care if there are flowers in the window or not."

"That's not very chivalrous of you."

"I enjoyed it when we took that corner just now and our shoulders touched. It reminded me of my first ever love, when I was twelve, and how thrilling it was every time a bit of my body made contact with a bit of her body. It was like touching all the wonder life holds. Like touching a star. Of course I am wondering if you are really married."

He is watching her slide her bogus wedding ring up and down her finger.

"My husband's name is Julien. He was in the 71st North African Infantry Division but I have not seen him December 1939."

"Almost four years ago."

"Almost four years ago."

"Do you have a photograph of him?"

"Of course."

"Please never show it to me. I cannot abide looking at people's photographs."

Evie Devereux, now Monique Maupin, field name, Anais, keeps thinking of the anonymous note she found in her coat pocket earlier. *Don't trust Gilbert who will be meeting you at the drop zone. Best not to trust Bruno either. Make sure it is he and not you who goes to meet your first contact. I would advise you to break with the POET circuit. There's a strong suspicion among some of us that it has been contaminated. Speak only to Marcel. He can be trusted but the Gestapo might be tailing him so be very cautious.*

A well-wisher.

3

Evie is in an upstairs room of the cottage close to the aerodrome. A man is checking the contents of her suitcase. Studying all the labels of her clothes. Some of which were made for her by a specially appointed French tailor in London. He tells her she is not allowed to take her favourite camisole which she has tried to sneak through. "Better safe than sorry," he says.

"How are you feeling?" asks Vera. Vera is compact and poised in a green tweed suit. She exudes reassurance. There is a pleasant prickling on Evie's skin when Vera smiles at her.

"I've been terribly frightened all day but somehow I feel better now. But I don't recognise myself. And this is a strange feeling."

"It's probably good you don't recognise yourself."

"Yes. I suppose it is. Because I am no longer myself. I think Monique must be braver than I am. Do you remember when you read me what one of my instructors wrote about me?"

She is eager to please but somehow always elusive. There is, in fact, something of the chameleon about her. Her decision making is, on the whole, excellent. As is her instinct for self-preservation. She is rarely rash or headstrong. Struck me at times as being almost cold-blooded. Very good at keeping her emotions in check. She is patient and deft with her hands. Physically she is perhaps on the weak side and she doesn't like being shouted at. In her favour, she is physically and mentally lithe.

"I broke a rule when I showed you that. You must not follow my example. Actually that was one of the best reports we got. You should see what they write about some of the girls."

"I've been thinking about the training. Such fun we had. I wish it was still all like that. Nothing but games. I think I only got through the courses because of my determination not to lose face in front of the men. The goading instructors."

"Yes. I sometimes envy you girls."

"You'd make a terrific agent, Vera. Always so poised. So prepared."

"We all have our façades. Here are your clothing coupons and ration cards. Marcel will give you the necessary travel permits when you're in France. Here are fifty thousand francs. More will be given to you when required. You might want to crumple them up a bit. Make them look like they have a more chequered history. And this is your *carte d'identité*."

Her new identity card sends a chill through her. The stamped photograph on the creased coffee-coloured card has a clairvoyant quality. It confronts her with her own loneliness, her own mortality. She can imagine it lying in a gutter somewhere when she is no more. She also thinks of the hands that will fumble it in the future. Nazi hands.

"I just need your signature and fingerprints."

She is about to sign her real name and only remembers just in time. She hopes Vera hasn't noticed how close she came to making a fatal error. She has spent hours practicing Monique Maupin's signature. Afterwards she presses her fingers into the pad of ink and Vera helps roll her fingers into the space provided on the folded card. The intimate touch of Vera's fingers on hers a stark contrast to the sinister sight of her fingerprints.

"And this is a gift from us. As a thank you."

It's a silver cigarette case.

She kisses Vera on either cheek. The taste of her powder stays on her lips.

"You can sell it if you ever get into trouble. Lastly the two items that are not compulsory. Your revolver. And your lethal pill."

She hurriedly puts the pill inside the transparent wrapper in her pocket. The scenario it betokens sending a chill through her.

"No need to remind you of some of the silly mistakes that are easily avoided. Look to the left first when crossing roads. And of course always cycle on the right side of the road. It's easy to forget. The French have little milk so don't specify what kind of coffee you want. Remember French women have never had the right to vote so try not to act too imperiously around men. I know I've said this before but I would still shorten your strides a little when you walk. You don't want to appear haughty. Try now."

She walks across the room. With a sense of harnessing some natural exuberance in her limbs.

Vera smiles. "Now you look as though you're walking a tightrope."

"How I walk is such a fundamental part of who I am."

"A fundamental part of who you are when you're Evie Devereux. Now you have to learn to walk as Monique. What we want is somewhere between haughty and tightrope walker. Try again."

She walks back across the room.

"Now you're walking as though you feel the whole world is watching you."

"I've got this feeling that's exactly how I'm going to feel for a while."

"One more time. And remember women don't get cigarette rations in France so try not to smoke too much publicly when you're alone. Oh and try not to laugh in public too much either. Apparently us English can never quite imitate a French woman's laugh. Can I check your handbag now and all your labels?"

She passes her new French handbag to Vera.

"How would Monique explain the presence of *Mrs Dalloway* by Virginia Woolf in her handbag?"

"I was hoping to finish it on the airplane. I'm nearly there. Nearly finished."

"I think it's for the best if you leave it behind. Just in case."

She has to leave behind the photograph of her father standing by the fountain in Paris too.

"I thought I might be able to pass him off as a French friend of the family."

"No. He looks too English."

"Does he?"

"Better safe than sorry. And what's this?"

"Oh, it's a photograph of a painting by Van Dyck of one of my ancestors."

Vera smiles. "Confiscated," she says. "It's beautiful though. She even looks a bit like you."

"Yes. My father had to sell it when he went bankrupt. He sold it to a Parisian collector. A Jewish man. Which if the stories Saunders told are true will now be in the hands of the Nazis. My father asked me to do my best to return it to the family one day. Probably he meant, marry a rich man. Then the war broke out."

"You're not going to go chasing after paintings in Paris, are you?"

"No. Of course not. But I can't help wondering what's happened to it. It's as though something of myself is woven into that painting. It used to hang in the hallway outside my bedroom. It was just about the first thing I saw when I began every new day."

Vera looks at her wristwatch. "It's about time for your farewell supper down in the hanger. By the way, what do you make of Bruno?"

Shall I tell her about the note? "Don't trust Gilbert who will be meeting you at the drop zone. Best not to trust Bruno either."

"I rather like him but I'm also glad he's not my organiser."

"You might not think it but he's jolly efficient at his job."

4

She is driven with Bruno and Vera to the aircraft in a curtained black car. She has been singled out for special attention all day. It helps her to forget who she is. The woman she must obliterate now from every transaction. She runs her tongue over her teeth. As if expecting a trace of the disguise even inside her mouth.

She has memorised her codes, her contacts, her safe houses. She has recited to herself her cover story with the anxious dutiful dedication she once learned all her lines in a school play. When she steps out onto the hard concrete beneath the full moon the swirl of apprehension and excitement she feels is not dissimilar to the high dizzying emotion she knew back in her childhood as she was urged out onto the stage in her surrogate costume, with her well-rehearsed fictitious narrative. A breeze flutters her French scarf, rustling into prominence the unfamiliar French perfume. Monique's perfume. The jumpsuit she wears with all its zips and compartments is about three sizes too big for her. The weight of the pack on her back strains muscles she usually takes for granted, as if she is battling a contrary current, as if she is wading into the sea. She is introduced to the crew of the Halifax bomber. Nice men. Boys really. They are tactile in their encouragement. She breathes in the nauseous stink of oil and fuel and scorched rubber. Smells that remind her of her life as a WAAF R/T operator. Of who she used to be. The camaraderie at the base. The gossip in the mess. The unspoken sadness when another aircraft didn't return from an operation.

She says goodbye to Vera.

"You'll write to my mother every now and again? Tell her I'm well."

Vera nods. "You can write to her as well. Gilbert sees to it that mail is brought back quite regularly. I will forward any letters for you."

Gilbert the traitor.

She turns to face the ladder. It is the loneliest moment of her life. For a moment she is lifted outside herself, a voyeur of her own experience. It's like she is saying farewell to Evie. Leaving behind everything meaningful she as Evie has created in conjunction with the world that has in turn created her. Images of that world flash before her - warm sand between her toes while walking to the sea, sitting in a blossoming moonlit garden, wearing a new outfit for the first time, reading a book curled up before a crackling sweet-scented wood fire. For a moment it's as if she is breathing on a moonlit window, writing her name on the circle of mist and then watching it slowly disappear.

Despite the heavy weight on her shoulders she feels as light and loose as a feather. A feather for every wind that blows.

The engines start up. The bomber begins to shudder and rattle with a disarming vulnerability. The dim light in the fuselage makes Bruno and the despatcher look like spectres passing into a different realm. Which is exactly how she feels. Bruno hands her his flask. Brandy. The rasp of it in her throat reminds her of standing on the balcony of the London nightclub with Guy, or Jack as she now calls his ghost, while searchlights swept the night sky.

Stop thinking your own thoughts.

The aircraft bumps forward towards the runway. Then it gains momentum and lifts its nose. She feels the force of a terrific unnatural struggle in the pit of her stomach. She finds herself lifting her hips and shoulders in an effort to help will the shuddering machine off the ground.

She sits huddled up within herself. Balanced on the edge of her tiny seat. The barrelling noise throbs through her circuitry of nerves. She leans forward because the vibrations from the fuselage wall make her feel sick. She keeps her eyes fixed on her shoes and plays with the straps of her harness. She thinks back to her first training jump. When one or two of the trainees were sick into the bucket. The smell of vomit made her feel sick herself and for a while the thought of being sick kept her mind away from the greater fear. When the red light came on it was the most alarming moment of her life. The instructor gave the order to prepare themselves. They tightened the chinstraps of their helmets and silently helped each other get hooked up. Her neighbour, Lucie, passed her the end of her static line over her shoulder. She gave it a tug and pulled about six feet of it out of the parachute pack. She saw her hand was shaking a little as she fastened the safety pin that secured the snap-hook. The instructor shuffled along the line checking their equipment. She clambered to her feet, hooked her static line to the anchor cable then crowded up in line behind number one who crouched in the doorway. Everyone was silent.

"All right, number one! Action stations! Go!"

She was impatient now to get the thing over and edged closer to the man in front with a nudge of irritation as if he was unnecessarily slowing the whole process down. One by one the strops jerked, snapped with a crack and then flapped tautly in the slipstream. Somewhere below she heard the parachutes whoosh open.

She was number seven. As she crouched by the opening she felt the blustering air whip at her bended knees and the side of her face. She looked down at a shifting tableau of chequered earth colours and felt her muscles tighten as though squeezed in an angry fist. The word of command reached her ears as if from a supernatural realm. When the instructor barked the command in her ear again she let herself slide down through the hatch. Her body screamed out in panic. There was a clotted and bursting sensation in her head as air rushed into her ears, flooded her lungs. She flailed and wavered in the slipstream like a puppet with a drunken master. Then a sudden jerk, an arresting shudder that pummelled through her shoulders. She heard the agitated flutter of silk above her head and was cradled by a gorgeous sensation of silence and detachment. The world below looked like a map, something ordered and pristine that could easily be made sense of.

As she descended weightlessly, swung gently back and forth in the high air above the tilting landscape of miniature fields and groves, her body a new experience to her, she never wanted to land.

She did three practice jumps and each time she knew the sickening fear and the immense transfiguring relief when her chute blossomed opened above her.

But she has never jumped at night before.

Think Monique's memories, not your own.

She accepts the flask from Bruno again. Remembers she has her own flask. The man with Vera gave it to her along with a tiny flashlight, a small shovel, a knife and a compass. Bruno says something that she cannot hear. She closes her eyes. She thinks with a growing sense of unreality that France is down there below. Occupied France. She pictures all the people asleep in the darkness, oblivious to her presence in the night sky above their homes. She thinks of the mysterious people down there who will soon become part of her daily life, how at the moment they are no more than shadows outside the frame of a mirror.

Don't trust Gilbert who will be meeting you at the drop zone.

There have been rumours that all is not well in France. That several circuits have been infiltrated by the Germans. That there have been mass arrests. She has heard it said that the Gestapo might now be operating some British wireless sets. That all the signs point to this being the case. Yet these concerns have been ignored by the top brass at Orchard Court. In which case the Gestapo might know she is coming tonight. Might be down there waiting for her.

She urges herself to stop dwelling on worst case scenarios.

She practices being Monique again. Recites to herself one of the stories she has made up for Monique.

I betrayed my husband Julien for another man. Why did I do that? Why did Monique do that? I was not overwhelmingly attracted to this other man. It was like a calculated act that I have no recollection of calculating. My husband then deliberately sought to get himself shot down. No, of course he didn't want to be shot down. He was not a fighter pilot. He was in the 71st North African Infantry Division. He wanted to get himself killed. To punish me. And so he got himself killed. Why did I betray him like that? There are some things we do without knowing why. Was that when I stopped wanting to be myself?

She is thinking of Jack again.

I did it because he was getting too close. Because he was going to die. Every time he was up in the air I expected him not to come back. I went through a torture of apprehension every day. I wanted to not care about him anymore. Well now I am no longer myself. I am Monique. But why shouldn't Monique too have a dark secret?

He is evidence that I am capable of betrayal.

When she thinks of her imaginary French husband she pictures Jack. Jack who told her his name was Guy. Because he, like her, had a field name. She will use Jack to describe her French husband. Merge fact with fiction as much as possible. It makes everything sound more feasible if there is some truth in what you're saying.

"If you've been caught red-handed don't tell them you know nothing. Make up stories. Waste as much of their time as you can. Send them off on as many wild goose chases as possible. If they ask for a description of your contacts describe the men interrogating you. Men don't have a clue how they are seen by women." Vera smiled when she told her that.

But she will not describe the man interrogating her. She will describe the dead man she betrayed. Betray him again. Harmlessly this time.

Stop thinking about interrogations.

She blows on her hands. Her feet are numb with cold. Beyond the steady barrelling noise of the engines she can hear some pops outside.

"Flak," shouts Bruno with a raised eyebrow. As if in reply the fuselage becomes a kettledrum for bursting pieces of shrapnel. The pilot begins taking evasive action. She is tumbled across the spar into Bruno's lap.

"Oh-la-la," he says.

The aircraft tilts and the nose rears up. She has to clings onto Bruno's arm to stop herself sliding over to the other side of the hold.

The flight engineer appears from the cockpit. He has to shout over the din.

"We're approaching the target."

The aircraft begins its sharp descent. The dispatcher opens the trap in the rear of the fuselage. She sees the shadow of the aircraft passing over fields. She sees a river. Then she sees the three twinkling lights that belong to the reception committee. *Or the Gestapo.* Three times the plane circles the drop zone. When the light turns from green to red the dispatcher throws out four canisters. He then signals for Bruno to jump.

But Bruno doesn't jump. He fiddles with his helmet. He fiddles with his straps. He pats his pockets. It is obvious to her he is deliberately delaying. *Is he scared?* The dispatcher shouts at him. The twinkling lights of the reception committee are thinning out into the distance. Then Bruno finally lets himself slide down into the night sky.

5

At the moment of separation the black body of the Halifax is an unearthly titan of raw power above her head. She keeps her legs together, her arms at her sides, her hands clutching her trousers. She tumbles away from the plane's roar of decibels. Tumbles through moon mist, star smoke. That's how it feels. The inrush of icy air sets her heart pounding.

Her body is jerked upright into a kind of secretive swaying equilibrium. The cushion of air in the canopy of the parachute above slows down her heartbeat. Swills a benevolence of peace and well-being into her body.

She can see the misted ground down between her legs. There is a field to her left with a huddle of cows but she is dropping towards a thick copse of trees. For a moment she feels like a descending angel. She feels elated. She is not frightened. She is calm and poised. The silence after the racket inside the plane is like a beautiful largely unknown part of her own being.

She pulls at one of the risers. Steering herself towards the open ground. She is wearing ordinary flat shoes, not jump boots, but her ankles have been bandaged against any heavy impact with the ground. Her handbag with all her forged documents and fake photographs of close relatives she has never met is strapped to her back. She lands on a muddy recently ploughed field close to a line of trees. She bends her knees on landing and rolls over just as she was told to do. The cows take little notice of her. A tremor of curiosity. Nothing else.

The parachute suddenly fills with wind and drags her along

on the seat of her pants. She has tight hold of the straps and the billowing white canopy pulls her to her feet. She runs towards it. She is smiling at herself because it is like some madcap mating ritual she is performing with the canopy of white silk. Finally she tames the thing into obedience.

Her only points of reference for what she's doing are her most daring insubordinate acts as a child. And she feels in her blood the same surge of exhilaration and undertow of foreboding.

The night is vast and intimate around her. It has always excited her, the feeling that she is one of the few people awake in the world around her.

She unharnesses her parachute. Just as she is wriggling out of her jumpsuit she is aware of movement about fifty yards away. A shallow mist hovers above the ground but she thinks she can make out the shadow of a moving figure.

"Well, here we are," says Bruno. He is holding his valise.

"Here we are about thirty miles from our reception committee," she says.

"Yes, the sooner we get away from them, the better."

"What do you mean?"

"You have a twig in your hair. Of course you're wondering why I took so long to jump. I was looking after you, Anais. I was also looking after myself. Let's bury our jumpsuits and 'chutes."

"You can bury the 'chutes; I need to spend a penny."

"So that's why you're so fidgety."

"What do you mean you were looking after me?"

"I had a bad feeling in my liver about our reception committee. I always listen to what my liver tells me. Let's say the details of our drop were transmitted over a wireless set that someone I trust believes is now being operated by the Gestapo. So I thought I would take an English approach. How do you say, better safe than sorry."

"Do you know where we are?"

"More or less. I'm going to take you to meet Auntie Hortense."

She is wearing a black skirt, a silk blouse and a grey jacket.

They walk along dirt tracks and narrow country roads. Both carrying a valise. She is not sure whether or not to be frightened of Bruno. A complicated argument is taking place inside her head, the aim of which is to convince herself that Bruno isn't walking her into a trap. They must look suspicious as a spectacle. On the other hand he seems to know where he is going, what he is doing.

"No talking," he says when she again wants to know what he is playing at. "Listen out carefully for the sound of a car. If the Germans infiltrated the reception committee they'll be looking for us."

Soon there is birdsong. And a stirring in the grass, an aroused expectation of sunlight. They sit down by the side of the road to watch the sun rise and smoke a cigarette. A melon-pink shimmer of light, followed by a more diffused yellow glow smudges the lower tract of grey sky. Bruno shakes his head in ironic exasperation when she says it is like the dawning of all creation.

Later a young woman cycles down the road towards them. Between the aisle of high plane trees in which birds are chirping. She jumps at the chance to wave the young woman down.

"Excuse me, we're lost. Can you tell us where the nearest railway station is?"

The woman looks at her with uncomprehending alarm.

"Ha ha," says Bruno, stepping forward. "*Désolé pour mon amie, mademoiselle.*"

Oh my god. I spoke to her in English.

She blushes to the roots of her hair.

"She is still perhaps a little inebriated from last night. She is unused to wine," continues Bruno in French.

She looks down at her shoes. Bends down to wipe away some muddy scuff marks.

When the woman has cycled off Bruno says, "I hope you're not going to try that one out on any SS officers. Though it would be amusing."

She frowns at him with a defiance she does not feel. She has always found it hard to forgive herself for making mistakes.

"Promise me you won't tell anyone. My head's all in a spin after all this excitement."

"I am a salesman of agricultural machinery. You are my assistant. That's all I'm going to tell anybody for the time being. But I now know a new thing about you."

"What?"

"That you don't trust me. I told you I knew where the nearest station is. Clearly you thought I was taking you for a ride."

"I was just double checking."

"Despite the rules perhaps it's best if you tell me what your alias is."

"You know my field name. I'm Anais as far as you're concerned. That's all I'm going to tell you. I was supposed to get my instructions from Gilbert."

Don't trust Gilbert who will be meeting you at the drop zone. Best not to trust Bruno either.

"But you have a letterbox in case you missed the reception committee. Where is that?"

"I'm not telling you."

"Ha ha. Very professional. Well, my advice is, don't go, wherever it is. At least until I've made some investigations. Can I see your documents?"

"Why?"

"Because the documents F Section send us here with usually wouldn't fool a hairdresser. I want to see how bad yours are. We have to catch a train. There might be a spot check."

"If I show you my documents you'll know what my alias is."

"You know another thing that gives you away as British is your mistrustful argumentative nature? I confess few things would charm me more than to see you naked, *Anais* - but in a bedroom with soft lighting and a window open to the moon, not in a Gestapo torture chamber."

She hands over her papers.

"Monique Maupin. Actually these are quite good. Okay, from

now on, in public, I call you Monique and you call me Georges. Georges Bouchet. Like I said, I suggest we go together to see my aunt and I'll find out how much danger we're in. I warn you that my auntie Hortense will not like you. She does not trust striking young women. She knows nothing about my clandestine activities so we stick to the story that you are my assistant. We could pretend we are having an affair to make it more plausible. No, I will rephrase that. We *should* pretend we are having an affair to make it more plausible. Also it will be good practice for you in the art of pretending."

They cross a stone bridge and enter a small village. It charms her. The pearl grey stones of the once-upon-a-time houses. It's already like a memory while she's there. Without moorings she feels light on her feet, almost reckless with irresponsibility. She is a muddle of elation and fear. The locals stare at her with a kind of grim ingrained suspicion. She reads a rations announcement posted in a store window. "One litre of wine every ten days," she says to Bruno, feeling self-conscious and anxious about her French now that she is in France.

"If you continue to reject my advances I shall soon need one litre of wine every ten minutes," he says.

They sit down for a coffee. Bruno buys some garlic sausage and chews on it as he walks. He chatters with his mouth full. Then he offers the mutilated stump of the sausage to her, which she refuses but reminds her with an unsettling blast of nostalgia of the crowded café near the aerodrome where she and her fellow WAAFs paid a shilling for sausages, egg and chips.

When they finally arrive at the station she is exhausted. On the train she keeps waking herself up because she is frightened she might talk in her sleep.

Bruno shows the little girl opposite a coin in his palm. He makes it disappear. Then produces it from his mouth. The little girl has a beautiful smile.

But isn't he supposed to act inconspicuous?

She inwardly hums with the static of her hive of secrets. With the effort of effacing who she truly is, of defying everyone who looks her way to see through her façade. But she feels certain everyone she sees knows she is English. As if she has a Union Jack flag pinned to her lapel.

The train stops by a siding where a gathering of mostly old people, women and children are being herded onto a cattle truck. She watches with horror a snarling gendarme strike a woman who is struggling with three children. She is about to say something but Bruno gives her a warning look. The other people in the carriage, she sees, are watching the scene without apparent emotion.

At Clermont-Ferrand station there is a control at the exit. There are also German soldiers. These German soldiers fascinate her. She can't stop looking at them. At the flesh and blood of them. Seems incredible that here she is surrounded by the vivid colour of uniforms and insignia she has seen on the black and white newsreels.

Her heartbeat demands a quicker intake of breath when she hands over her identity papers. She has to fight the threat of some vital force draining out of her – resolve, courage, confidence in her ability to sustain this colossal perilous implausible bluff. At the same time she struggles to believe the German war effort should find her, Evie Devereux, still as shy and shirking as she was as a child in many ways, of any importance whatsoever. The man checking her papers has a sallow morose face she cannot ever imagine breaking out into a smile. She thinks of the stranger who forged her document in London. His inky fingers, the pinpoint of concentration in his eyes. She is completely in his hands now.

He frowns and his eyes lift from the document to her face. She stops herself from risking a conciliatory smile. She remembers the warning not to stiffen her fingers, a fearful reflex these men have been trained to spot. It goes through her head that she has a gun and a new set of radio crystals in her valise. When he returns her card it is another discipline in deception to conceal the relief she feels.

"Look," says Bruno when they are outside the station, "you have to stop staring at German soldiers as if they are pterodactyls."

"Yes, I know. I can't help it. Did you see that gendarme strike a woman in the face for no reason?"

"I saw."

"Why are they putting civilians in cattle trucks?"

"They were probably Jews. I'm afraid you will have to harden yourself to many sights that will make your blood boil."

The kindliness in Bruno's eyes is the most heartening gift he has so far given her.

Auntie Hortense turns out to be the owner of a cheap hotel.

"Oh-la-la. She only has one free room," says Bruno, or Georges as she now has to call him. "And to think, only ten minutes ago, I was thinking how most of our longings go unfulfilled."

6

She lies awake in the double bed, beneath the crucifix nailed to the stucco wall. Bruno, a thicker swell of shadow in the dark room, is snoring contentedly on the floor. The strangeness of everything makes her feel weightless. This strain of trying to forget who she is. This exile from intimacy with herself. This distancing of herself from memory.

She smells with growing distinctness the body odour of the man asleep on the floor. Thinks how much complicated intimacy there is in the smell of someone's sleeping. Earlier he went out for a few hours. He left her alone in the hotel room where she had nothing to do and every sudden stammer of noise out in the street and set of encroaching footsteps in the corridor outside reiterated how much tension she is carrying in her body. When he returned he told her he'd set up a meeting for her tomorrow with Xen, her new boss. He also told her the reception committee had collected all the canisters of supplies without any problems.

She remembers a story Jack told her of how as a child he always prised out a feather from his pillow and rubbed its tip against his thumb, to stop himself from floating away, he said, to prevent himself from drifting off into oblivion. She now feels like she is floating away. As if her grip on life has been taken from her hands. She pushes back the single sheet. Swings her legs out of the bed. Sweeps her hair off her face and takes a deeper breath. She crouches down on the stone floor by the side of the sleeping man. Shakes him awake.

He frowns. Rubs his eyes. "Oh it's you. Very well. Come," he says, deadpan, patting the floor beside him. "Slip into bed with me if you absolutely insist."

"Before I left London, someone warned me not to trust Gilbert."

"Well, I don't trust Gilbert. He's a showman. He can't look a person in the eye. What pretty feet you have. Will you pass me a cigarette please?"

She lights him a cigarette and one for herself.

"Let us say Gilbert *is* working for the Germans. In that case the Germans will already know the address of your safe house. Just as well, then, you're sleeping here and I have the pleasure of seeing you in your pyjamas. I do not want to offend you but at present you are almost worthless to the Gestapo. They want information. More than anything they want Marcel and his wireless set. Eventually you would have led them to him. As things stand though they've lost you. Thanks to me."

"They might be following Xan. They might have followed you after you met with him today. They might be lurking outside at this very moment."

"They might be. That's why we have to break with all the original arrangements. In the meantime you may well have to shake off a Gestapo agent trailing you tomorrow. This will be good training for you. To shake off a tail. You did this in training, no?"

"Yes. I spent a whole day trying to lose the man tailing me and failed."

"You are a woman. You can stop and look in every shop window you pass. Keep an eye open for the reflection of any well-dressed man. Or else a man so insignificant looking that his insignificance is odd. By the way, this person who told you not to trust Gilbert did he tell you not to trust anyone else?"

Even in the half light, even without looking at him, she is aware of the hint of mischief in the line of Bruno's lips. It suddenly dawns on her.

"It was you, wasn't it? You wrote the note."

"Very good, Anais. You are getting more astute by the day."

She can't help laughing.

"Yes. I suppose I can console myself with the thought that I'm getting more astute by the day while the Gestapo are removing my teeth."

"If you are arrested you have my word I will shoot Gilbert myself. In the meantime I have to go to Orléans and you have to go to Paris. Otherwise what is there for us to do? Sit out the war pretending to be the salesman of agricultural machinery and his secretary having an affair? Sponging off Aunt Hortense?"

"Hortense isn't your aunt."

"No. I've only met her once before in my life. But the less you know, the less you can pass on."

"I was led to believe I was entering an efficient network with the task of exchanging information vital for the war effort, of helping to organise a well-coordinated resistance to the Nazis. Instead I find the only piece of information I have is that your aunt Hortense isn't your aunt at all. Well, thank heavens Herr Hitler doesn't know that."

She is aware of Bruno grinning at her in the half light. "That kind of sarcasm will give you away as English straight away," he says.

"Well it's all a bloody shambles, isn't it?"

"That, wouldn't you say, is the nature of war. Life now is largely a question of improvisation. Of quick wit and moving stealthily through darkness. Think of yourself as an actress with no script. Think of every minute of every day now as a creative challenge. I fear you are like all the English. You want everything to be tidy and subject to your will. Like in a grocery shop. Now then…" He moves his face towards her. Puckers his lips.

She laughs. "Now you look like a hungry fish."

"You're not going to kiss me?"

"No."

"Then can I go back to sleep please?"

7

She tries to take everything she sees in her stride - the rippling red and black swastika banners draped over the municipal buildings, the German soldiers milling about by newsstands and outside every café, the Nazi propaganda posters pasted to walls, the military vehicles accelerating and stammering on the roads. To pretend it's all normal, like walking down the Kings Road on her way to a hairdresser's appointment. Her effort to appear outwardly nonchalant reminds her of the strain of descending midnight stairs without making the boards creak. Every moment deepened and electrified by the tension she carries in her mind and in her body. Several times she has idled in front of shop windows to assure herself she is not being followed.

Discreetly she studies women of her age. How they walk, what they look at, their makeup, their hairstyles, whether they smoke, the gestures they make with their hands. She worries about her shoes. They are too elegant, too well-made. She notices most people ostentatiously ignore the German soldiers as if they are invisible, irrelevant, unworthy of attention. However it surprises her how many faces she deems capable of duplicity; how few unmistakably kind faces there are in the world.

Her heart is beating a little too urgently as she approaches the chemists where she is to meet Xan. She has left her pistol behind. She carries nothing incriminating in her purse except her fake *carte d'identité*.

A short elderly white-coated man with thinning brown hair and a mole on his chin greets her from behind the counter.

"Special delivery for Madame Cochet," she says, the code. He leads her behind the counter and into a backroom. A man wearing dark glasses, grease and oil stained blue overalls and a beret is pacing back and forth.

"Well, you're certainly an improvement on the fat frumpy thing they gave me last time," he says. He leans in and kisses her on either cheek. "Your figure anyway is lot more impressive than your parachuting skills. I hope you realise three men risked their lives to greet your arrival in France. I wasn't there but I heard Gilbert in particular was annoyed. Luckily for you he's gone to Paris. Bruno tells me you insisted on redoing your lipstick before jumping."

"Then Bruno's lying."

"Is that so?" He removes his dark glasses. His eyes are fidgety, bloodshot and puffy. "Anyway, you're to be my courier. First thing you have to do is go to Paris. We're getting you the necessary travel permits. By all accounts the situation in Paris isn't good. Lots of arrests. Sounds like we have more than one traitor in our midst."

"So I might be walking into a trap?"

"That's the case just about every day here. To be honest, I don't think women are suitable for this kind of work. Too flighty, too easily distracted and flustered. You're to take this new set of crystals to Paris where you need to make contact with Madeleine. In the meantime I've brought you some work to do."

He unfastens the rucksack from his shoulders and swings it over to her.

"All needs washing and a couple of the shirts need mending." He winks at her and pats her bottom. "You go out first. I'll be in touch."

Evie is so angry she forgets to check for suspicious looking characters when she leaves the chemist. She forgets to check if anyone is following her. She can still feel the intrusive touch of his hand, burning like a wasp sting. All her attention is centred on Xan's ugly rucksack which she holds angrily by the straps.

8

She arrives alone in Paris. Hungry and thirsty after the long train journey, much of which she spent standing in the corridor leaning on the window rail. When she joined the line to have her papers checked at Gare du Lyon there was a moment when she felt she might be losing her nerve. She has new papers now, given to her by Xan, and was mistrustful of them. She also has 200,000 francs sown into the lining of her jacket and a new set of crystals in her bag, required to change the frequency for Madeleine's wireless set.

Now she wants to walk. She does not want to go down into the underground tunnels. The address she has been given is apparently just around the corner from the Gestapo headquarters in Avenue Foch. There is an insistent voice in her head telling her not to go there. Gilbert knows about this planned meeting. *Don't trust Gilbert who will be meeting you at the drop zone.* At the same time there is her pride urging her forward. Her deep reluctance to give Xan more ammunition for treating her with disdain. Her mission is to establish whether or not Madelaine, a wireless operator, has been arrested. And, if not, to give her the money and the new crystals.

"Why can't Gilbert do this?" she had asked Xan whose face was flushed with fury because she hadn't done his washing and sowing.

"Because he's got enough on his plate, that's why."

Streets and buildings, she sees, have been given German names. She is now able to take for granted the Nazi banners draped over buildings and the German soldiers. This new order feels settled, as if Paris will forever be swathed in Nazi flags, submissive to Teutonic men in crisp grey green uniforms and sinister insignia.

She hasn't eaten since leaving Clermont-Ferrand. Every time she passes a café with its wicker chairs outside she looks with envy at the people eating. The baguettes women carry under their arms or in their bags taunt her with all the allure of forbidden fruit. She is too nervous about using the ration coupons, especially in a city as nonchalantly sophisticated as Paris. Stupidly she hasn't asked anyone how the coupons work. Her shyness, her stagefright, when called upon to exhibit a worldly self-assurance is another thing she has brought out of her childhood with her and been unable to shed. She knows it might be dangerous to show her ignorance of how the coupons work at the counter of any shop. So she can't eat.

After walking for almost an hour she is lost. It's another part of the anxiety she feels not to show her dismay on her face. She struggles to keep up a façade of sophisticated nonchalance. As she is waiting at a zebra crossing she catches sight of a face behind the glass of a bus which knocks all the breath out of her. For a moment she is convinced she has seen her father's ghost. Afterwards, she realises it is more the expression on the man's face than the face itself that brought her father so vividly to life before her eyes. An expression of deep concern which he seemed to direct at her. It was like a moment of transcendence, a warning from the spirit world. She realises fatigue was making her careless. She is immediately more alert to her surroundings. Which is why she notices the parked black Citroën in the road where Madeleine's contact lives. There are two men inside. A tremor establishes itself in her thighs as she approaches it. She knows they are Gestapo and that in all probability they are waiting for her. As she walks past she feels their eyes on her, like insects drawing blood from the nape of her neck.

Act as though this street is of no importance whatsoever.

She steels herself not to look at the bakery, above which is the apartment where her contact lives. The strain of not looking, of not increasing her pace. All her antennae listening for the sound of a car door opening, slamming shut.

Now she has to make sure she is not being followed. But, inside her head and body, it's as if she is alone at night in a creepy house and every faint noise reaching her has sinister stalking intent. She is so keyed up she stops in her tracks and turns round. Something she has been warned never to do. But she can't stand the suspense. There is a man in blue denim holding a toolbox walking towards her. Otherwise there is no sign of anyone suspicious in the vicinity. She asks him for directions to rue de Passy and is reassured by his innocently helpful manner.

Her instructions if there is a problem at the apartment above the bakery in rue de la Faisanderie are to go to a bookstore in rue de Passy. Her password here is, *Avez-vous des exemplaires neufs?* The woman should answer, *Non, que des exemplaires d'occasion.*

Evie enters the shop. Her heart thumping. She walks directly up to the woman behind the counter. "Have you got any new copies?" she says, asking the coded question without thinking.

The woman pats her sculpted crisp hair before looking at Evie with undisguised disdain. The woman is squat, thickset, with thin angry eyebrows. "New copies of what?"

Only now does Evie realise she should have picked up a second hand copy of any book and taken it with her to the counter. She is stumped. Her mind goes blank. The only book she can think of is *Mrs Dalloway.*

"Oh, silly me. I meant to say, have you got a new copy of *The Hunchback of Notre-Dame*?"

She emerges from the bookshop with a copy of Victor Hugo's novel wrapped in brown paper. The scorn with which the woman treated her has infected her, made her feel grubby and insecure. Her longing now is for the comfort of the familiar. She thinks of the photograph of her father standing by the fountain. When a man pedalling a bicycle taxi appears she flags him down and asks to be taken to the Place de la Sorbonne. With the sun warm on her face she is able, now and again, to enjoy Paris for the first time today. She begins to notice the flowers, the familiar landmarks and vistas, the couples walking hand in hand along the quays, the barges on the river; she begins to ignore the Nazi banners and propaganda and uniforms. So much of her childhood haunts these streets that her real self grows ever more clamorous for recognition. As if it is a futile sham that she can pretend to be anyone else.

She arrives in Place de la Sorbonne and feels like a ghost visiting a familiar landmark. Memories swarm into her head, as if keen to betray her. Two moments, six years apart, coalesce – her father standing by the fountain, a memory she has always sought to keep whole and detailed, and now she arriving at the same fountain. Time suddenly seems like a conjuror's trick. As if only an extra effort of attention on her part might bring back her father and make the Nazis disappear. The sudden swell of emotion makes her feel conspicuous. As if the brickwork of her identity is visible behind the plaster of the façade.

On the day she took this photograph she and her father were staying in the Select Hotel, by the side of the Sorbonne. Despite the warnings not to stay in hotels, she books a room here for the night.

In her room on the fifth floor she sits on the bed looking at her trembling hands. Hands that have safely handled explosives, hands that have held and fired guns, hands that have learned to silently kill. Her hands have been trained to protect her but equally they might betray her, she thinks, unable to stop them trembling. She has to concede that Xan is probably right and that she isn't cut out for this work.

Later she realises there has been a fundamental flaw in her execution of a bogus identity. The trick is not to act innocent but to convince herself at all times that she truly is innocent, something, she thinks, we all do all the time in our lives. She thinks back to when she played with dolls as a child and how absolute was her belief that the dolls were alive and possessed an autonomous personality. She needs to find again that leap of imaginative immersion.

She strips naked in front of the full length mirror. She has always felt separate from the sight of her naked body. And yet at the same time it is the principle cypher of how she identifies herself.

She has only made love once in her life. With Guy, or Jack as she has learned to call him, in Mrs Savage's guesthouse. For a moment she knows a memory of the quickening on her skin brought about by Jack's raking fingers. Maybe were she still a virgin she would be less convincing as the married Monique Maupin. It makes her smile that Jack has provided her with an experience familiar to Monique and thus perhaps helped her impersonate Monique with a shred more authenticity.

PART TWO

1940

1

He recites the names on the stones out loud. "Susan Duckworth," he says, wondering when was the last time anyone spoke her name in the world. She died in 1903. Aged 56. He likes best the blackened and ivy shrouded headstones tilting at drunken angles but they do not suit his purpose. He looks up at the face of an angel with unfurled wings. His appraisal of her more sexual than aesthetic. She does not attract him. He thinks he would not like her as his companion in death. Then he knows a moment of unease. As if he is guilty of a blasphemy. As if punishment now awaits him. He didn't know he was so superstitious. It perhaps does not augur well that he is so superstitious.

Seeing as I'm about to rob the dead.

He walks down a path where there are newer gravestones. The sly hiss of the gravel shifting beneath his feet. He reads the inscriptions. The quotations. Still he cannot find a citizen of the dead and buried who answers his need.

Then he sees a bouquet of white lilies tied with a red ribbon lying beside one headstone. He looks around to make sure he is not being watched. He steps over a succession of graves to read the inscription.

BLESSED ARE THE PURE OF HEART,
FOR THEY SHALL SEE GOD. IN LOVING MEMORY OF
GUY WENTWORTH. DIED 20TH NOVEMBER 1939,
AGED 21 YEARS. REST IN PEACE.

Guy Wentworth, he says to himself.

*

"Morning sir."
"Call me Guy."
"Yes sir."
The man has a smirk in his eyes. Both of the two men do. The fitter and the rigger. A private joke they share, no doubt at his expense. The sleeves of their shirts rolled up. Standing with their hands on their hips by the side of the starter trolley. Like his jury.

He jerks at the parachute slung over his shoulder. One of the men is a huge grim faced chap with observant blue eyes. The other is a scrawny man with sunken shoulders, jug ears and a nervous smile.

He feels their eyes on him as he puts on his parachute. The searing critical scrutiny of their interest. The wing commander and several of the experienced pilots are sitting outside the dispersal hut. They too will be watching him.

Imagine if you had to make love to a woman for the first time with a group of sardonic men watching your every move.

Come on, Jack! You've flown a Tiger Moth, you've flown a Harvard; how much more difficult can a Spitfire be?

He thinks of the girl he saw earlier. Struggling a bit with the weight of her kitbag as she disappeared into the guardhouse. He only caught a glimpse of her. In a brand new tailored WAAF uniform. The line of her thigh against the cloth. But he somehow recognised her as an element of the inevitability in life. Because he could still see her after she closed the door behind her.

As jauntily as the knot in his stomach allows he levers himself up onto the wing of the Spitfire and settles himself into the cockpit. He catches a glimpse of himself in the mirror. Doesn't quite recognise himself in the helmet and the unfastened oxygen mask hanging down. But he very much approves of himself in the uniform. He can't help seeking himself out in any reflecting surface. The peaked hat, the lovely slate blue of the battledress.

He studies the controls while one of the ground crew straps him in. The big burly chap with the small staring eyes.

"First time in a Spit, sir?"

He nods.

"Once you're up there you'll feel like her wings are your own, sir. Isn't that right, Stan?"

"She'll show you who you really are, sir. Behind all the masquerading."

He looks a bit uneasily at the younger scrawny man.

"What do you mean?"

"Just wait and see, sir."

He sees there is nothing personal in the man's remark. He is glad of the display of kindness in these two men who he thought were his enemy. He glances over at the dispersal hut for a sign of his other detractors. Sure enough there are four pilots in chairs all looking his way. They have all been distant with him. Ever since he arrived at the squadron.

I am not like my father.

Fuel on. Primer pump. He eases forward the throttle. Waves at the two men to remove the chocks. He pulls the door shut. He is alone now. Where he is most happy. He settles himself into his solitude. Discovers he likes this cockpit.

Magnetos on. Engine start and booster coil on. The engine roars into life with a keenness he isn't quite ready for. A devilish flame from the exhaust stubs. The smoke trails away in ribbons and whorls. He acquaints himself with the aircraft's exhilarating pulse. He feels her feed eagerness and adrenalin into his own bloodstream.

There's a hiss as he releases the brakes. Drops of moisture fly past the cockpit in the slipstream. She begins to hurdle over the grass.

Bloody hell, this baby can move.

He glances over at the wind sock. Manoeuvres her so she is gunning into the wind. He tweaks the rudders against the torque. Applies more throttle. And still more. The high nose impairs his vision of the ground in front of him. It feels a bit like he's being made to run at full speed blindfolded. She is sprinting off and it's as if he is hanging onto a saddle. All his muscles tight with the concentration of keeping up with her. The tail lifts off the ground. He feels suddenly lighter in his seat. He is bounced up inside his harness as a bump on the ground flings her into the air. The wings wobble before settling themselves.

Throttle back to climbing power. He feels like she and he are engaged in a battle of wills. There is a resistance in her to being tamed. She is like a living thing with her own pulse and design. She is more sensitive, more wilful than any other machine he has flown. He pulls back the throttle a tad. Soaring up towards the sky smoke, the sky surf. He looks down at the shrinking and expanding world of southwest England below. A miniaturised Chichester Cathedral to his left, a toy replica of Arundel castle to his right, so small he could put them both in his pocket, like childhood toys. The rolling Sussex downs are flattened out into a chequered tapestry of browns, golds and greens. Over to starboard is the glittering sea.

He pumps the wheels up. It's harder work than he expected and it's difficult to synchronise his right hand on the crank and his left hand on the stick, like that party game when you have to rub your forehead clockwise and your stomach anticlockwise. He still feels a little on edge. Still feels she is trying to throw him from the saddle.

The airspeed indicator shows the needle at almost 300 mph.

She takes him up among ethereal mountain ranges of cumulous cloud. A world of cleanliness and new beginnings.

There are entrances through the clouds like secret pathways into deltas of blue sky. He makes a game of pretending the clouds are physical obstacles to be avoided. Then he is alone in a vast blue world and the rolling bank of cloud below him is like a veil separating two dimensions. He looks along the length of the curving wing, at the glint of sunshine there. He is falling in love with this machine as if she is a girl. She grants him easy access to all the bold elation of which his body is capable.

Never has he loved his life so much.

Through the pageantry of breaking cloud the earth looks like a childhood memory. Something still and finished and remote.

The altimeter reads 8000 feet. He turns on the oxygen.

Shame you can't fly without wearing this damn mask.

He does a series of acrobatics. Imagines the WAAF with the heavy kitbag is down there somewhere watching him. He wanted to ask her to give him something of hers. Something for luck. A pair of her knickers, he thinks with a smile.

Never mind that I didn't. I'm bound to see her again.

He is delighted with his slow roll. He tries an upward roll. Two upward rolls in quick succession. A spin to the left. Then he puts her into a steep dive. He shouts out loud to relieve the pressure in his ears. He eases out of the dive and climbs back up to 7000 feet.

A little more top rudder coming out of the roll, old son.

He loops the loop. Then decides to perform the manoeuvre that most terrifies him. The high speed stall. The starboard wing drops. There is a violent shudder and the entire aircraft shakes and clatters. The Spitfire with its dead engine begins a madcap plummeting fall. He looks down at the English countryside spinning in circles like a giant gramophone record. The whirl of detail on the ground gains in definition. He carries on spinning down until the altimeter shows 500 feet. Then he pushes the stick forward and kicks hard on the right rudder. She obeys him without complaint. Her dizzying precipitation towards the ground is over. He peels back up into the higher air.

The sudden crackling and voice in his ear almost makes him jump out of his seat. It's as if God is speaking to him.

"Spearhead Red 3, this is Shortjack control. Are you receiving me?"

Who the devil is Spearhead Red 3?

"Spearhead Red 3, this is Shortjack control. Are you receiving me?"

You bloody idiot. Spearhead Red 3 is you.

He looks at his watch. He has been up in the air for almost two hours.

I thought it was about twenty minutes.

Then he looks down at the red cockpit lights. At the fuel gauge.

You bloody fucking idiot.

He decides not to answer Shortjack. He will say his radio was U/T.

"Spearhead Red 3, we have three bandits over Maidstone sector. Are you receiving me?"

Where the hell am I?

He sets the gun button to fire. Just in case. Peers anxiously above and below and behind for signs of marauding enemy aircraft.

He drops her nose. All of a sudden the vastness of the sky frightens him. Makes him feel vulnerably tiny but also glaringly conspicuous. She tears through streamers of cloud until below he sees a map of England. In no time at all he is down to 3000 feet. He recognises nothing down there.

Right, you've got to put this baby down as quickly as possible. What we need is a nice flat field.

He slides back the hood. Breathes in the clean air. He sees a cluster of cottages. A church. Two young boys running down a road, arms extended and slanting, pretending to be Spitfires. A small farm. A farmer with a white horse and plough.

Righty-o, we'll put her down in one of these fields.

Cows begin careering off to left and right. The ground rushes by and rises up beneath him. He throttles back. There is a large house. A marquee on the lawn. Then he can't see anymore. The nose obstructs his vision of the immediate future.

The wheels, you bloody idiot. You've forgotten to put the wheels down.

They said it's better not to put them down in emergency landings. Too late now anyway.

He clips a hedge. Hits the ground with a terrific bump. Slams on the brakes.

"You do realise that the machine you've wantonly damaged today is a damn sight more valuable than you are?"

He stands to attention in the Station Commander's office. He has a black eye. A grubby pink plaster on his cheek.

"In fact I'm beginning to wonder if you're not completely and utterly worthless, Wentworth. What exactly do you think you're playing at? Has anyone told you we're at war? That there's a chap out there called Adolf Hitler who wants to destroy as much of this country as he can? And here you are giving him a helping hand. Anyone would think you were secretly a German come to sabotage our squadron. I know what you are though, Wentworth. You're a bloody imbecile. You've turned the squadron into a public laughing stock."

He had landed fifty yards from a brigade cocktail party. Members of the press had been invited. One took photographs of him standing bruised and cut beside his aircraft that had churned up the lawn and come to a halt on the edge of an ornamental pond carpeted with water lilies and algae.

"I'm grounding you for a month. And you're bloody lucky that's all I'm going to do. Now get out of my sight."

"Yes sir."

He liked and looked up to the Station Commander. He wanted more than anything to earn his respect. Now it's as if his past has caught up with him yet again. The curse of his father. His sin visited upon him, his only son.

When the door is closed behind him he feels like joining the German air force. Feels like joining the bloody Luftwaffe.

2

He gets off the train at Norwood Junction. There are lots of children with mothers and small suitcases on the platform. The mothers all look puckered and overwrought. He remembers when he was a child on this platform. But the memories he has of this station are all unwanted. Like beggars jostling and supplicating him. Daytrips by train to the beach at Littlehampton when he was a little boy. Special treats provided by his grandfather and grandmother. There was a current of excitement running through the bucket and spade he held in his small fist, the fishing net. Knowledge has dirtied these memories. Knowledge that his childhood, compared to most, was one of thrift and struggle.

He is not wearing his battledress. He is incognito. Disguised as himself. Jack Cave. It is raining. Outside the station everyone is shrivelled up beneath an umbrella. He passes two army privates. They are completely alien to him, inhabitants of a different world, like kids he saw when he was a kid who didn't go to his school. He looks about warily. The downcast dirty nature of everything makes him feel he has just had to dry himself with the soiled towel of a stranger. The ugliness of these streets, the poverty of these dwellings. There is a barrage balloon overhead, hanging there in the grey drizzle, almost directly above his old school. He walks down the road where the Barton brothers bloodied his nose when he was twelve. For a year afterwards he returned home from school by a long circuitous route to avoid the Barton brothers. Then he enters the street where he and his pal Tag forced Nancy James to drop her knickers in the garden shed behind her house. He felt unclean and despicable for a week afterwards. Terrified too. That she would tell and he would be sent to prison. He saw his first used condom here too. Remembers the awed complexity of his emotion still. How sex took on a whole new dimension of mystery. How it was no longer simply something we had in common with animals.

The front door of the small terraced house is open. He is greeted by the familiar smell of boiled vegetables and escaping gas. His grandmother is knitting in the armchair in the front room. There's an unlit cigarette hanging from the corner of her mouth. She never lights cigarettes. She just likes to have something in her mouth, she says. And this way one cigarette lasts her a week, she says.

"You're all wet," she says, smiling. An ironing board, the fabric torn and yellowing, leans against the floral wallpaper.

"That's me."

He leans down and kisses her cheek. Wrinkled and papery like the petal of a poppy.

"Where have you been anyway? We were worried about you."

"No you weren't, Nan. You never worry about anything. It's your modus operandi."

"Get away with you," she says. What she always says when she doesn't quite understand what he means. His grandmother has a brittle chirpy voice, pitched on one essential note of jeopardised stoicism. It never changes. "When are you going to get married anyway?"

"I'm only twenty-one."

"I got married when I was eighteen."

He can't believe his grandmother has ever done an impulsive thing in her life. She is like the inside of the kitchen cabinet. Disinfected shelves. Neatly stacked crockery.

"I suppose you'll be wanting a cup of tea."

"I'll do the honours."

"Your grandfather's in the kitchen. Doing his football coupon thingies."

His grandfather is standing by the window. Watching the rain. He catches a glimpse of all the vulnerability in his grandfather standing there watching drops of rain slide down the misted glass. It makes him shy on his grandfather's behalf. He looks down at the football coupon on the table.

"Huddersfield York City won't be a draw."

"Oh, you're back. The prodigal son. Damn rain. I was hoping to sort out the air raid shelter in the garden today."

His grandfather approaches him, dodging and weaving, throwing a punch he is expected to parry. His boxing routine. He taught him to box when he returned home with the bloodied nose after the Barton brothers set on him. Bought him a pair of leather boxing gloves. He recalls those gloves now as an oppressive presence in his bedroom. Remembers too how he always burst into tears the moment he was involved in a fight. He was always surprised by the tears. He didn't understand what their purpose was. They just arrived without a noticeable emotion, like a nosebleed.

"Where you have been, young Jack?"

"Can't say, I'm afraid. I'm working for the War Office. All very hush hush. In fact you mustn't tell anyone. If anyone comes here asking about me tell them you don't know where I am."

"You'd better not be pulling my leg, Sonny Jim."

"Wouldn't dream of it. You'd box my ears."

"There was a man who came looking for you."

"What did he want?"

"He gave me something to give to you. He said he knew your father."

"My father?"

"That's what he said. War Office, eh? Good for you. Glad to see those brains of yours aren't going to waste. And what does the War Office have to say about the situation?"

"What situation?"

"Hitler. When's he going to attack?"

"Soon. Very soon." He winks at his grandfather. Makes him smile.

He fills the kettle. Lights the stove. The chipped white cups all have ringed brown stains at the bottom. His nan's eyesight is failing. She who was always so house proud. For whom cleanliness was a morality of sorts.

"So where's this thing this man gave you?"

"I'll go and get it."

He stands by the window on the threadbare carpet. The same carpet he used to arrange his toy soldiers on. He looks at his name on the large brown envelope. His name that is no longer his name. It taunts him, tells him he will never be able to be anyone but Jack Cave. And brown envelopes never augur well. The blue ink slightly smudged.

"Aren't you going to open it then?" says his nan, with the unlit cigarette still gummed to the corner of her mouth.

His fingertips are tingling when he rips open the envelope. There are two drawings inside. On crisp smudged and stained paper torn at the edges. Portraits in pencil of two men. Two soldiers in uniform. Neither of these men is his father though. At least he doesn't think so.

Dear Jack,

I didn't know your father personally but I took an interest in him after his death. I managed to come by the two drawings here enclosed. They were done in the trenches somewhere on the Somme. I forget exactly where now. One trench looked very much like another. I was told he caught the likeness of these two men fantastically well. Apparently he did many drawings. Sad to say his sketchbook vanished. I made every effort to find it.

Probably you have a poor and very unfair idea of your father. I dare say you have only the brutal facts. But from what I could gather your father was not a coward. He simply reached the end of his tether as many of us did. I was told he talked about you a fair bit. You were only two or so as I recall and he only ever saw you once.

Probably you are asking yourself why it has taken all this time for me to make myself known. Truth be told I was in rather bad shape when I returned from France and I needed to put away all thought of that dreadful time. Perhaps because I've grown older and now there's another war which you will be called upon to take part in I felt it incumbent on me to set the record straight regarding your father.

Please feel more than welcome to pay me a visit. I feel it is my duty to share with you as much about him as I've learned.

Yours Sincerely

Peter S Woodburn

"It's from a man who knew my father."

He had been eleven when his grandfather sat him down and told him his father had been shot as a coward. He had three fights the next day at school.

"These are his drawings. I didn't know he could draw. They're jolly good."

"Listen to him with his jollies. Gone all posh now, have we?"

"Didn't you find any drawings among his things?"

"There were some drawings but I threw them away. I thought it was morbid to keep them lying around. I threw them away when I was sorting out your poor mother's things."

"Bloody hell."

"You watch your tongue, young Jack."

"Sorry."

More than once his grandfather had taken his belt to him. For stealing money out of his grandmother's purse. For stealing sweets from Mr Cronk's shop. For forging a sick letter to his PE teacher at school because he was ashamed of his scrawny undernourished body which his classmates made fun of.

Up in his bedroom there are his model airplanes and his childhood scrapbook swollen with photographs and drawings of airplanes. He has always wanted to fly. Fly away from the thrift and monotony of his home life.

3

"Jack?"

He looks up from his book. He is sitting in a green leather armchair beneath the fragment of the tail of a Junkers JU 87 hanging on the wall of the dispersal hut. The compelling menace of the black and silver swastika. "Yes?"

"Guy, what do *you* mean, yes?"

"Ha ha. Not content with gatecrashing the Brigade cocktail party Guy is now gatecrashing your name."

"Sorry. I was miles away. My people sometimes call me Jack as a kind of a nickname."

"Your people? And who are your people exactly?"

Angus doesn't like him. Angus can't look at him without lifting his chin in rebuke, without narrowing his blue eyes in disdain. Angus is his nemesis here. More his enemy than any German. Angus questions the truth of just about everything he ever says. So in a way is the most perceptive pilot in the squadron. Otherwise his standing has gone up considerably since he crashed-landed his Spitfire at the Brigade cocktail party. He is teased about it in continuation. He has a reputation now for being impulsive and rebellious. Which he rather likes and plays up to. How easy it is to mould oneself to other people's ideas.

He also has a new roommate. The old one, the best friend of Angus, is dead. He was shooting a line for some girl. Pranged the steeple of a sixteenth century parish church.

He feels a bit guilty because he never liked Ron. Ron was surly and condescending. Benedict, who now billets with him, he likes a lot. Benedict was reading history of art at Oxford before joining the RAF. He was full of praise for his father's two drawings which he has pinned to the wall over his bed. They were the first things Benedict noticed.

"I wish I could draw. I wouldn't even mind this tiresome war if I could draw."

It's the first time he has ever heard praise for his father from an impartial source.

"I had my heart set on going to Venice after Oxford. How far to Venice do you reckon we could get with the fuel in a Spit?"

"All the way. We just wouldn't be able to get home after."

"Perfect. What do you say, we take off for Venice at 00:15 hours. Hide there for the duration of this wretched war. God, how I hate the bloody Germans. What a race of humourless bullying philistines they are. How dare they interrupt my life. There's one thing to be grateful for. That we're not German. Fawning over that preposterous little shoeshine man. I ask you."

He is no longer grounded. The Germans have begun attacking naval convoys off the English coast. Rumour has it they are preparing a full-scale attack. Wing Commander Leslie Wilson, who is likeable in his dry reserved way and calls him PB and Benedict Lord B because he deems them the closest thing to Shelley and Byron they have in the squadron, takes him and Benedict up every day for some formation flying and unofficial combat practice. Benedict is a deft and graceful pilot at acrobatics but he lacks any aggressive instinct. He himself is sometimes reprimanded for lapses in concentration.

"I know literally you have presently got your head in the clouds but you do have to be more grounded when you're flying, PB, odd as that sounds."

Today, all of the squadron, except him and Benedict, are on standby. Angus makes another jibe at him as he is leaving the dispersal hut.

"Why do think Fungus loathes me so much? I don't like not being liked. It makes me feel there are things about myself I know nothing about."

"I take it as a compliment when I excite dislike in someone I have no admiration for. It's not as if Fungus has a double first in Classics. He looks like an insurance salesman. He's probably jealous of your good looks. You are rather striking you know."

He thinks the same of Benedict. He enjoys being paired off with Benedict in the eyes of everyone at base. Benedict has a confident effete way of conducting himself, a clipped resonant voice, as if he is always projecting himself out to a larger audience. Being with Benedict increases his self-esteem notably. Gives him a more romantic idea of himself.

They are walking towards the NAFFI when his heart skips a beat. "That's her," he says.

"Who's who?"

"The girl I told you about."

"Your muse? Where?"

He gives the faintest nod of his head. "Coming towards us."

"Crikey. I know her. Or rather I went to school with her brother. Her father committed suicide last year. Lost the family fortune. Including a beautiful Van Dyck painting. Her name's Devereux. Evie I think."

She is walking past the stack of sandbags of a gun emplacement.

"Excuse me," calls out Benedict. "My friend and I were wondering if we could try on your cap."

She hesitates, smiles, then carries on walking towards him and Benedict.

"You're Benedict St Aubyn, aren't you?"

"Officer Pilot Benedict Harold Frederick St Aubyn at your beck and call. And this is Officer Pilot Guy Wentworth. Don't know any of his other names yet. Oh, except his people sometimes call him Jack."

"I like the name Jack," she says. "Not that I don't like the name Guy," she adds.

He smiles. An inane smile, he feels it to be.

"I must say that uniform suits you. Doesn't it, Guy?"

He nods. He looks at her navy blue shoulder bag. He is intimidated by the sense he has of her being a whole world, a new world, a thrilling and deeply challenging world.

"I'm training to be an R/T operator. Except it's more PT than RT at the moment. Lots of touching toes and swivelling hips."

He knows there is a witty rejoinder to this remark but he can't for the life of him find it. He blames his deprived background for his shyness. The crackle of interference that scrambles messages before they can be broadcast. He looks at the faint swell of her breasts beneath her tunic, at her hips in the narrow skirt and then down at her feet, her lace-up shoes. He tries to imagine her without her shoes and stockings.

Clouds move urgently across the sky. The passing of time up there seems to have speeded up. In time with his heartbeat.

"We were just going to the NAFFI for a coffee. It's on Guy if you want to join us."

He stands beside her at the counter. Her shoulder is brushing his shoulder. He is gratified that she doesn't edge away. It's as if she likes the brush of his shoulder. The coded message his shoulder sends forth.

"So it may be your voice we hear instructing us to pancake," says Benedict to her.

"You never know. It was my voice they liked. Can't think why. It's just an ordinary voice."

"It's a beautiful voice. Especially that breathless quality it has, as if you've run all the way to meet one. Don't you think, Guy?"

He nods. For the first time he is a bit jealous of Benedict. And he wants her to go away.

What's the matter with me?

It's that something about her peels him down to what is raw and authentic in his nature. He has stolen the history of one of his former roommates at training school for Guy. He has an archive of about thirty biographical details with which he parries probing questions. But he doesn't want to be Guy with her. He wants to be Jack. And he is caught in a no-man's land between

Guy Wentworth and Jack Cave. And so he wants her to go away.

When she has gone off to PT instruction Benedict says,

"I have to say, you did not do very well. Unless there are ploys for seducing women I know nothing about. Which wouldn't surprise me in the least."

While she was by his side he wanted her gone. Now she is gone he wants to run after her. He has given her the wrong impression. He could not have given her an impression that is more out of kilter with how he feels. The desperation he feels to redeem himself in her eyes and in his own makes him unable to return to the moment.

"I think I'm in love."

Benedict raises an eyebrow in humorous disdain.

Tell Benedict the truth.

That I'm a fraud? That I've treated him with scorn by tricking him with a pack of lies from the word go?

He'll enjoy it. The vaudeville of it. He's not a social snob.

Perhaps he is on the verge of outgrowing Guy Wentworth. But Guy Wentworth now holds him prisoner.

The air raid siren starts up. For a moment he thinks it's just another facet of his mental confusion. People on the base are now mirroring the clouds above. There is a brisk alertness about the sudden need to find a hiding place.

4

"Rise and shine, sir. Four o clock."

It's Jenkins, his batman. Shaking him by the shoulder.

"I've brought you your tea, sir."

He squints up at the kindly face of Jenkins. Extraordinary that someone waits on him, shines his buttons, makes his bed and refers to him as sir. He always has to conceal his wonder.

Then knowledge dawns on him. That this might be the last morning he ever wakes up on.

He sips at his hot tea while Jenkins wakes Benedict who groans and curses and then breaks out into ironic song. Benedict immediately makes him feel better about everything.

"The day of days," he says. Gazing at his own face in the mirror. Standing at the washbasin in his stripy pyjamas. Barefooted on the linoleum floor.

"Do I want to get out of bed?" says Benedict.

"You tell me. I did it."

He always washes with cold water. Splashes it up onto his face. Thinks even this habit might give away his lowly origins. He doesn't like soap. Doesn't need to shave more than once a week. At school he was the last in his class to put forth body hair. A source of shame at the time. Now he is glad. A past shame that became a future blessing.

Benedict pads across the room in his green silk dressing gown. Toothbrush in his mouth.

He stands looking out of the window. At the dawning of the day of days. Then he pulls on his trousers. With so little sleep the skin on his legs is overly sensitive and prickles at contact with the cloth.

The parched tightness in his throat. The hollow churning in his stomach. He and Benedict are on ops today.

It hadn't been a drill yesterday. His ears are still ringing. He, like everyone else, has been taught to recognise German aircraft. Models of them hang from the ceiling of the briefing room. There is a poster of their silhouettes and capabilities on the wall above the washbasin in his and Benedict's room. Silhouettes of the various Luftwaffe aircraft he is expected to shoot out of the skies. The Stukas yesterday had dived down screaming so low that he was able to see the black crosses edged in silver on the fuselage. The living incarnation of something he had only seen before on newsreel. A kind of wondrous apparition for a split second. Like beholding some prehistoric bird of prey. A heaving explosion behind him had ended that emotion. He and Benedict thrown to the ground in a flummoxing sprawl. Showered by turf. After which everything sounded distant, as if arriving from the far end of a tunnel, as if arriving from another dimension.

There had been six casualties, including two WAAFs.

Please not her. Please not Evie.

In the mess later, after the raid, the pilots who had been on ops all looked shattered, dead eyed. There were no jibes from Fungus. He sat stroking his pencil moustache and staring into the fireplace where there were no embers. A pilot was missing. Another of Fungus' friends.

Stay his enemy. Everyone he befriends gets the chop.

He and Benedict walk together through the mess hall and the stale acidic vapours of the anteroom into the dining room. Greetings consist of little more than brief eye contact. One or two men are eating toast. Despite it being the day of days, despite the strained subdued atmosphere, he still knows a moment's pleasure at being paired off with Benedict in everyone's eyes. He and Benedict sit down at a table with Charlie and Tom. Charlie's father is a plasterer from Catford; Tom's father is a Lord from the Shires but they are the best of friends.

"Morning boys," says Charlie, making no attempt to hide the mesh of chewed toast between his lips. Ginger-haired Charlie is the showman of the squadron. He strides about, loose-limbed and jaunty, like a boxer entering the ring. He exaggerates all physical gestures. Especially touch. Treats objects with either rough-handed disdain or the sleight of hand of a conjurer. Charlie fought in France during the evacuation of Dunkirk. He has shot down more German aircraft than anyone in the squadron. He tells stories of German fighter pilots strafing civilians. "The Germans are evil-hearted bastards who shoot at women and children. That's what you need to remember when you're up there."

Charlie has given him and Benedict advice. Told them what to do and what not to do.

"Skill, composure and steadiness of nerve will play a big part in your chances of survival. But there's no getting away from the fact that luck will play a bigger part."

How much luck does Charlie have?

He has formed an instinctive idea of how much luck each pilot in the squadron has to play with. The fount of this knowledge is mysterious. As is its veracity. Except for himself. He has no idea how much luck he has to play with. And he worries about Benedict.

The steward clears his throat and announces that their transport is waiting outside. He walks out into the early morning air still holding his piece of half-eaten toast. Charlie winks and throws an arm around him, walking in step. He is grateful for this show of affection. He who has never enjoyed being physically fussed over. He climbs into the back of the truck.

The smell of wet foliage. The stillness. So precarious and close to the root of life's beauty and mystery. He savours it as he is driven around the perimeter track. Headlights on.

He enters the dispersal hut. Says good morning to the orderly who sits at the desk within reach of the black telephone. There are some pin ups of actresses tacked to the walls. Pouting and showing off their curves. He thinks of her. Thinks of Evie. Imagines the warmth of her body beneath bedclothes. Such a far cry from the lonely overwrought atmosphere of this makeshift outpost. He waits until Angus has moved away before looking at the flight board and the order of battle. He and Benedict are numbers two and three to Leslie in Green Section. This suits him fine.

There is an unfinished game of chess on a table. A black bishop lies on its side. Absurd to read anything into this. As if it is a message from an oracle. He walks over to his locker. Takes out his flying kit. Pulls out the bulky parachute. He doesn't like setting eyes on the parachute. Terrifies him the thought of falling from the sky. Almost more than dying. He has had no training. More than once he has pictured the moment. The frantic scrambling out of the cockpit of a machine he has lost control of. The silk canopy not opening when he tugs at the ripcord.

Fifty yards away the various ground crews, removing the covers from the twelve aircraft and preparing the starter trolleys, are like phantoms in the mist of the arc lights. It's still too early for birdsong. The world seems embryonic. Not yet quite born. He walks across the grass and clover. The dew settling on his flying boots. Parachute slung over the shoulder of his sheepskin jacket. A thumbprint of moon up in the sky. The sky that is bereft of either light or darkness.

Stan, his fitter, is climbing up into the cockpit of *his* Spitfire. He is possessive of his aircraft. Feels a pang of irrational indignation every time he catches sight of Stan in *his* cockpit. As if he has caught Stan sitting at his desk, rummaging through his private correspondence.

"Morning sir," says Ed, the giant rigger. As ever there is a film of sweat beneath his receding hairline. But there is an unspoken bond between him and the giant rigger now. A growing affection.

The airscrew of Benedict's Spitfire a few yards away begins to flick at the air. The engine splutters into life. Shooting out a finger of flame. Soon it is joined by the mounting roar of the engine of another Spitfire. A crescendo builds as one by one the aircraft judder into life. The ground begins to shake. The grass all around is blown into a tilting ballet and dew is flung up into the air.

When Stan starts up the engine of his aircraft the barrelling noise feeds exhilaration into his frame. The engine note sharpens in pitch. Stan gives him the thumbs up and climbs out of the cockpit.

He immediately feels more confident when he is in the cockpit. He hangs his helmet on the stick. Plugs in the R/T lead and oxygen pipe. Goes through the routine of checks. Fuel, oxygen, break pressure, trim. She is now ready for him when the word arrives to scramble.

"Monopoly?" says Charlie when they are all back in the dispersal hut. Charlie throws the box down on the table with deadpan ebullience. Snatches off the lid with uncalled for violence. Throws it to one side as if he never wants to see it again. It is Charlie's way. His caveman impersonation. But it is an act because to fly a Spitfire you need the sensitive dexterity of touch of a concert pianist. "Right, I'm banker. And I'll take the battleship. Tom?"

Tom blows up his corkscrewed fringe of hair. There is something of the urchin about Tom, a mischievousness, a grubbiness too, as if he doesn't like washing.

"Do we really have to play Monopoly?" asks Benedict.

"Angus. Monopoly?"

Angus looks up from his paperback, *No Orchids for Miss Blandish.* "How about Bridge? Except I bet Percy Fish here doesn't know how to play Bridge."

Why don't you just punch him in the face?

5

The telephone, when it rings, seems directly wired up to his nervous system. It sends a high voltage shock to his heart. Despite the fact that he has been anticipating on every nerve the summons of the telephone for the past hour. Monopoly money falls to the floor as he gets to his feet. He feels the draining of blood from his face must be a spectacle that centres everyone's attention on him. Ashamed, he avoids eye contact even with Benedict. He feels that it is only he who is terrified.

Think of her. Think of Evie.

He barely hears the shouting of the telephone orderly. Something about Dover and 20,000 feet. He is running with the others across the grass to his aircraft. The others have become strangers. Of no help to him whatsoever. He is alone. Never has he felt more vulnerably alone. It helps a bit to run though. He wishes he could carry on running all morning.

He feels like an impostor when he reaches his Spitfire. Not at all like a warrior prepared for battle. As if all the training has been a trick. All his forces are engaged in concealing his fear. The worst thing of all is that his fear should be noticed. As if it is unnatural. Freakish. Evidence that he belongs in a funny farm. No, the worst thing of all would be that he discovers himself to be a coward. Like his father. Though perhaps his father wasn't really a coward. He has not had a chance to meet the man who knew his father. Wonders now if he ever will. Ed and Stan are like transparencies at the edge of vision. It takes an effort of will to bring them into focus. Stan climbs down from the cockpit. Ed moves the starter trolley away.

He puts on his parachute. He notices concern on the face of Ed. He tries to suck up some saliva into his bone-dry mouth. His tongue like an alien thing, a swollen tumour. He has never really looked at his aircraft as a war machine before. Thought about its ability to withstand bullets. How flimsy and frail the fuselage seems all of a sudden, like a toy, how thin and delicate the lovely elliptical wings.

Already several of the Spitfires are taxiing. Turning into the wind. He is dillydallying.

Come on, Jack. Pull yourself together.

But he can't think straight. He looks at the controls. The controls he has to entrust his life to.

"God be with you, sir," says Ed. And there's a kindness in his eyes that makes him feel less alone as Ed leans into the cockpit and helps strap him in.

He puts on his helmet and mask. Checks the oil and water temperature. When he gets himself comfortable in the cockpit and the engine starts up and begins throbbing its intent into his blood he feels a little better. He feels he might actually be able to go through with this.

The aircraft, his aircraft, is like a friendly enveloping animal presence. R/T on. He looks out for Leslie who he sees is waiting for him. He needs to position himself to Leslie's right. Brakes off. Throttle eased open. He gives Stan and Ed a last farewell look. Taxis up alongside Leslie and Benedict. Breaks on.

"Okay, off we go."

Leslie's aircraft, his magnet, begins to move.

Breaks off. Throttle open. He listens attentively to the note of the engine. Increases the throttle. Brings the pitch up. There is the familiar surge of power, of willpower. She is now bounding across the grass and the momentum performs an alchemy on his fear, transforming it into nervous excitement. The aircraft itself is a rousing battle cry. The tail lifts off the ground. The sensation of lightness and abandon. Of the world being his oyster. Leslie and Benedict are both off the ground. He follows, a little way behind.

Clears the hedgerows. Soars up through the early morning haze above the cornfields. Glances down at the expanding lay out of the airfield.

At three hundred feet the squadron has already formed into a textbook formation.

So far, so good.

Every minute in the air is bringing him closer to the reality of being shot at for the first time. He looks across at Benedict. He can't see much of his face because of his mask and helmet but there's something about the shape and tilt of his head that he recognises as unmistakably Benedict.

It begins to get colder.

"When you sight a formation of bombers below keep your eyes peeled above. Don't get over excited and rush in. Because next thing you know you'll have a couple of ME 109s swooping down from behind the sun. They use the bombers as bait. And remember the trick to success is always to turn inside your opponent." He constantly seeks advice from Charlie. Charlie has a reputation for engaging in head-on attacks. He just flies straight at his foe, guns blazing. "Scares the shit out of 'em."

He enters some cloud. Loses sight of everyone. Condensation on the windscreen. Ghostly scribbles. Impairing visibility a little. When he emerges from the clouds he can't quite believe how far he has drifted away from the formation. They are gnats in the distance. At least he hopes it is his squadron.

"Green leader to Green two. Stop dawdling unless you want to make a sitting duck of yourself."

He is Green Two and he is made to feel inept.

Wasn't my bloody fault.

The cloud layer at 15,000 feet like some ghostly arctic landscape. A tumble and swell of snowy surf. The sky above is perfectly clear. Sunlight flashes sparks off his fuselage. A break in the clouds to the southeast gives him a startling clear view of the curves of the French coast in the distance.

"Eagle leader, this is Sapper. Hundred plus towards Eastbourne at angels twelve. At angels twelve. Vector 180. Over."

"Okay Sapper. Message understood. You heard everyone. Climb up hard through angels seven steering vector 180."

Leslie's voice over the intercom is deadpan.

Wish I felt that calm.

And what does he mean a hundred plus? Twelve of us against a hundred plus.

He plugs in his oxygen. Lowers the seat a fraction. Turns on the reflector sight. Switches the guns to fire. Prop pitch from fine to coarse.

Anything else?

Don't waste ammunition. You've only got fourteen seconds of firepower to play with.

Climbing up steeply, higher into the brightening sky, he senses some movement ahead. He sees a flurry of black dots that soon become smudges and then silhouettes. Stark above the stacked clouds below.

"There they are. Bombers at ten o'clock. Snappers at three o'clock."

He has his first sight of the enemy. About two miles away a formation of thirty or so heavy bombers. About 3,000 feet higher to starboard a swarm of fighters. The sight of so many aircraft in the sky is breathtaking. Like something on a biblical scale. There is nowhere to hide. Only a few wisps of cloud now in the brightening sky. It's like going over the trenches. Like the moment he imagines broke his father. Yes, his mouth is dry and his stomach is hollow but for the first time he knows a new emotion. A note of indignation. The sight of these arrogant German invaders brings some aggression into his blood.

"Righty-oh, Eagle Squadron. Let's give these Jerries something to think about. And you two new chaps, try to stay close and throw your aircraft around like crazy. Don't steer straight and level for two seconds. Sections line astern."

He tucks in beside Benedict.

"Okay chaps. Charlie, after you. Tally ho."

He watches Charlie roll over and bank to the right. Followed in perfect synchronisation by Angus. One by one the squadron peels off – Tom, Jamie, Archie, Mark, Jimbo, Leslie. It is an impressive sight. Now it is his turn. Down he goes. Followed by Benedict.

It is hard to keep Leslie within his sights when so much is happening. He is hunched forward in the cockpit now. Every fibre of his being jumpily alert, his head swivelling from left to right, eyes straining above and below, constantly glancing up in the mirror.

The quickness and sharpness of his vision, the speed of his reflexes, the deftness of his touch at the controls. These are the qualities he now needs to keep him alive.

He singles out one particular bomber as a target. Realising that at the same moment some German fighter pilot is probably singling out him. This is how it works. You pick a victim at random. No not at random. You look for a sign of weakness or hesitation. The Heinkel he has chosen seems like the calf in the herd somehow. It is a hunch. Something he feels transmitted across the stretch of sky between them.

Right, you smug Nazi bastard.

He swoops down towards his prey, anticipating every action before he makes it. As if he is at the controls of the German bomber too. The Hun begins diving and weaving. Isolating himself from the formation. Vapour trails disperse and reappear in its wake.

He's panicking.

He follows it down, gaining on it quickly. He has time to marvel how intimately he knows his kite. He can make her do whatever he wants with commands he has no need to think about. No tracer comes from the Heinkel's guns. The gunner is no doubt being thrown about by the desperate manoeuvres of the pilot. He feels a bit sorry for the man. In imagination he has already shot the blighter down. He is breathless with the impatience of getting the thing in his sights. He shouts at it. Willing it to obey his will. To make a fatal error. He begins to make out the rear turret. He grows in confidence. He ignores all the confused chatter over the intercom. Has stopped listening. Then he is aware of something amiss. Sees a twist of smoke ambling leisurely towards him until all of a sudden it spouts red spots and zips by lightning fast with a hiss and a flash, curving just wide of his cockpit.

Up above, you idiot.

The ME 109 is enormous for a split second as it fills the frame of his vision. Then it breaks and veers off. He swivels his head, straining his neck to see where it has gone, what it is going to do next.

Am I conspicuous as a novice at this lark?

He immediately disregards his prey. He breaks hard, half rolls and goes into a steep spiral turn. The engine and all the rivets holding together the thin sheets of metal encasing him scream out in protest. A shudder goes through the wings. He is aware of dust and tiny bits of debris raining down on him. His head is pressed down into his shoulders by a terrific force. He can feel the strain in the straps of his harness. Another aircraft flashes by his cockpit. His thumb instinctively presses down on the trigger. The noise is like something sturdy and compact being tidily ripped apart. Through the ghost haze of smoke drifting back into the cockpit he sees it is a Spitfire he has shot at. There are so many aircraft in the sky his instinct is to fire the moment he sees any flash of metal through the windscreen. He had not bargained on this extra strain of distinguishing friendly kites from the constant skittering of enemy aircraft.

Out of the corner of his eye he sees a Spitfire on fire. A trail of black smoke in its wake. A parachute opens down below.

Hopefully not Benedict. Or Charlie or Tom.

He cranes his neck again to see if there's anything on his tail. *Shit.*

The yellow nose of the ME 109 is no more than fifty feet away. He is aware of puffs of greyish smoke around its wings and then there is a dull thud. Something has hit the fuselage of his Spitfire.

He throttles back viciously. Turns up and over. Hoping the Hun won't be able to pull up in time. That he overshoots.

He has gained a bit of leeway but his persecutor is still on his tail. Though a little above now. He throws the Spitfire around the sky. Turning in continuation. As steeply as he can. The barrelling force against his face and neck bringing with it a blackness into his eyes, into his mind. He shouts at himself. *Don't you dare black out!* He thrusts himself forward into his seat. The bastard is still stuck to his tail. Copying his every move. He can almost feel the smugness of the Nazi pilot. Convinced he's got another kill to tell his mates about later.

Do something completely unexpected.

Like what?

He is filmed in sweat. His feet on the rudders ache. The ankle joints. He puts the nose down. The speed at which he is hurtling over the world seems to defy all laws of ordinary existence. He glances at the gauges but without registering what he sees. He performs the tightest turn he has done to date. The aircraft shudders and screeches as if about to combust. Again he is on the point of blacking out.

"Fuck off, you bastard," he yells at the top of his voice.

There's an overwrought Jack and a calm Jack. The calm Jack is Guy.

He goes into another quick series of spiralling turns. The strain in the straps of his harness. The blood sucked from his head. He comes up into the sun and is blinded for an instant. He has antennae now for this German behind. He is like a dark presence in his own mind. There's a kind of psychic wavelength between them. He knows an instant before it happens that the German is going to fire his guns. A quick blast.

Missed, you bastard. Surely you must be low on fuel by now, you German sod.

He can sense a faltering in the German fighter. A slackening of resolve. Or is it wishful thinking? His confidence in his aircraft has grown. It is just a tad more agile than its German counterpart. Or so he thinks.

He dives down. Flat out. The aircraft plummets in a heart-hammering vertical fury. Down towards the English countryside. There is a village church down below. He can see the gravestones. A bus that has stopped. A game of cricket. Boys in whites, statuesque, with upturned faces. A man, a woman and a little boy. The woman is looking up at him. Her hand to her mouth.

The ground is rushing up to meet him. He swallows hard. All his muscles in a vice. He levels her out at six hundred feet. Blood thumping in his veins.

He cranes his neck, searching the higher sky for his foe. He knows another moment of panic when he is nowhere to be seen. He looks frantically to left and right, below and above.

Where the fuck has he gone?

He can't believe it. The sky is empty. It's a beautiful summer's morning and there isn't a single aircraft to be seen anywhere. He feels elated. Tension, anger, terror, resignation, elation. All within the space of five minutes.

Don't get cocky. You've still got to get home.

The ground below reels away as he rolls her onto her back. Upside down, tiny bits of debris rain down on him again. He pulls through hard into a half roll. Throttle open and off he soars.

Keep your eyes peeled. You're on your own now.

He likes being on his own. Has never in his life liked it so much. His blood is singing with the relief and elation of it. Soon he picks out the lighthouse at Dungeness.

Ed and Stan are waiting for him when he brings her down. He can see they are glad to see him safe.

"Ben?"

"He's back sir. Shaken up but safe."

"Charlie and Tom?"

"They're back too, sir."

He can barely concentrate on what the intelligence officer is asking him. No, he has no kills to report.

"Charlie got a Heinkel and a ME 109. Leslie another Heinkel.

And Angus got a probable on a Heinkel too. Bloody good morning's work on the whole. Well done, Wentworth."

Well done for what?

The elation has passed. He is a bit ashamed of how little of his ammunition he has expended. One short burst at a Spitfire and that was it. Ed and Stan will see how little ammunition he has expended.

Benedict is asleep in a deckchair outside the hut. He looks five years older than he did at breakfast.

Charlie puts a cigarette into his mouth. Tom gives him his shy conspiratorial smile.

He is given a bowl of porridge. A mug of cocoa. Then, three hours later, he is running across the grass to his Spitfire again.

6

"Leslie told me not to worry myself too much about scorecards. Definites, probables and possibles. That it's not a competition. Thing is, I'm not sure I was worried about it before he brought it up."

"But you are now?" asks Benedict.

They are side by side, sauntering unsteadily on their bicycles. Charlie and Tom doing the same twenty yards ahead. The sun setting over the sweep of gold and green fields behind hedgerows.

"A bit," he says.

"First thing my mechanics ask is, any kills sir? As if I've been out shooting grouse. And when I shake my head they shift uneasily on their feet and look at me as though I've just been diagnosed with TB. Interrogation time with Polly and his pencil and clipboard isn't much different. Then there's Jimbo shooting a line about how much more collateral damage he's done to the bloody Luftwaffe and the condescending look of Fungus when he sees I still haven't got any burns or scratches on my face."

"Awful thing is, there was a part of me today that secretly hoped Fungus wouldn't make it back."

"Only a part of you? My whole being craved for nothing else."

He's being flippant. He doesn't mean it. But I do.

"He's started calling me Fishy now."

"He knows you call him Fungus."

"You call him Fungus too."

"But I went to Harrow."

"You're all such bloody snobs."

"Bred into us, dear boy," says Benedict, ringing the bell of his bicycle. "To be honest I won't give a fig if I get through the entire war without a single kill. My prevailing character trait has always been a penchant for taking evasive action. My one and only girlfriend once told me I reminded her of a lighthouse. I'm pretty sure she didn't mean it as a compliment. To tell the truth, most of the time today I forgot I even had guns. Too much else to think about. Except for this one moment when I had Baron von Nazijackboots tally ho-ing on my tail. I've never in my life wanted to give anyone his comeuppance so much. I had no idea I was capable of such anger. And there was I believing I was incapable of ever surprising myself. One thing about war, it does provide revelations."

"The anger. It helps when your back is up, doesn't it? Bloody arrogant bastards. Thinking they can come waltzing into England. I don't think I've ever felt so passionately English as I did today. There it is spread out down below. Our country. Our people. Beautiful and benign." At the end of his speech he imitates the Prime Minister's voice. Mocking himself.

"Most of the time I was too busy being terrified to indulge in flippancies like passion and anger."

He loves Benedict all the more for admitting to being frightened.

"Don't you feel sometimes that it's just us against the Nazis?"

"You and me?" says Felix with a grin.

"More or less. Or, to put it another way, do you ever get the feeling there's a well-equipped organised army down on the ground, ready at a moment's notice to heroically repulse an invasion? Because that's not the feeling I get. The feeling I get is that we're just about the only obstacle now preventing Hitler from hanging swastikas all along Whitehall."

When he's not talking his mind obsessively replays the combats of the day. He studies his performance with critical detachment. Sees things he didn't see at the time. Rectifies his mistakes. Forms a clearer idea of the enemy aircraft's capabilities and tactics. Understands how he can improve his chances of survival. Develops a better idea of how he will perform this or that action. Is almost eager to put his more refined understanding of the choreography of aerial battle to the test.

Outside the pub Charlie is crouched down beside one of the many bicycles propped against the trellised white façade of the building.

"What you up to, young Charles?"

"Letting down Jimbo's tyres. I'm going to bet him five bob I can race him to the river and back."

Inside the crowded pub the station commander buys him and Benedict a drink.

"I dare say you both have a better idea of what makes you tick now," says their commanding officer.

"Alcohol, sir. But I've known this since I was sixteen," says Benedict.

"Like father like son. How is dear Clive?"

"A bit annoyed there won't be an Ashes series this year but otherwise very well."

"So, any kills today boys?"

"Not a sausage."

"Not to worry. No rush. Your moment will come."

"Are we always going to be outnumbered about fifty to one? Jolly unfair, sir, if you don't mind my saying so."

"Up there," he says nodding towards the low wooden beams, "it all boils down to who sees who first. If you ask me, that is. Keep your eyes peeled. That's why you young 'uns make such good fighter pilots. Quicker reactions, better eyesight. I'm too old now for this malarkey. Bloody Germans, eh? You see, that's how people behave when they have a chip on their shoulder. No chips on your shoulder, Wentworth, I hope. Humility. It's a great asset, you know."

Does he mean my humble origins?

"Yes sir."

"Sorry I had to breathe some fire on you, Wentworth. Bad day and all that. Good to see you've become a credit to the squadron. Might drive down to London after last orders here. If you want a ride mum's the word."

He is happy to be back in the station commander's good books. Father approval.

He and Benedict join Charlie and Tom at a table in the corner. It is snug in the yellow light of the shaded table lamps behind the blackout curtains. Like a secret world. The wreaths of cigarette and pipe smoke beneath the low ceiling create almost an atmosphere of memory. As if they all are being remembered years later.

"How do you manage to make a drink last so long?"

"I was just thinking, how do you manage to drink so fast?"

"Oh look! Your muse is here."

The feeling is not dissimilar to when the telephone rings in the dispersal hut. Sudden lurch of the stomach, giddiness in the head, mouth sucked dry of saliva.

Jack intercepts her before she reaches the bar. Buys her and her friend a drink.

"Who were you today?" she says.

"What do you mean?"

"I was on shift in the control tower. We sit at our bench listening to all your voices coming through the loudspeaker. Were you operational earlier?"

"Green Two."

"You were told off for dawdling."

"You've got a good memory."

"We all had a laugh about your dawdling. The FCO placed a bet that you'd soon be returning with engine failure…"

"He thought I was a coward? I don't think I like your FCO."

"He's a decent enough taskmaster. We joke around a bit to ease the tension. Put faces to the voices."

"Did you put a face to my voice?"

She smiles and nods. "It's automatic. We always try to picture what we can't see, don't we? One of the girls believes you can tell everything you need to know about men by the way their hair sits on their head. So we picture hair."

Never has it been so important what someone thinks of him. He watches her moisten her top lip with her tongue.

"Anyway, we girls defended you. We had you down as a romantic type. Lost in the clouds."

"I wasn't lost exactly. But you'd be surprised how quickly order changes up there. Today at one point there were about a hundred kites in the sky. I went into a spin to evade this Jerry fighter and the next thing I knew the sky was absolutely empty. Not a single aircraft in sight. It was like a conjuring trick. A conjuring trick by God."

"I'm not sure if I envy you or thank my lucky stars that my feet are always on the ground. My father used to tell me I was always lost in the clouds."

"Used to?"

"He died quite recently."

She avoids his eyes. Lights a cigarette. He can't stop looking at her hands. Such beautiful long tapering fingers. A serpent ring of Russian gold on her little finger. It's as if she multiplies his susceptibility to tender feeling by ten.

"So what's it like. Being up there in God's territory?"

"You leave behind the world of boundaries. And I've always hated boundaries."

He means his background. He senses she knows this and there's a wobble between them for a moment, like a blast of slipstream.

"Me too. Sometimes this war makes me wish I was born a man. No I don't wish that. I like being a woman. But I wish women were allowed to do men things. Quite a few men here look down on us. They think we're only here to find an eligible husband."

"You already are doing men things to some extent. WAAFs drive lorries. There's even a couple of WAAF pilots too. Granted they aren't allowed to engage in combat. But the way things are going, who knows? We were so heavily outnumbered every time today that it's a wonder any of us got home. Luckily the Huns don't seem over keen on fighting."

"Don't they?"

"I wish I hadn't said that. Asking for trouble really. Now the collar of my shirt is chaffing the back of my neck," he says.

"Awful how superstitious war makes us, isn't it. I was machine gunned the other day. I was on my bicycle, going to the village. A cluster of starlings suddenly took to the air before I heard anything. I just assumed it was one of our Spitfires. It wasn't. I saw the yellow nose just in time. Threw myself into a ditch at the side of the road. The noise of the bullets was like the frantic bashing of a snare drum. I had been unkind about someone earlier in the day. I felt what happened to me was a punishment for this unkindness. It's probably time for me to leave. Nearly ten o'clock. Rather unfair we women have such an early curfew. More evidence of the inequality between the sexes."

It is exciting to hear her use the word sexes.

"We could cycle back together."

"Actually a friend of mine has promised me a lift in his car. Angus. I've known him since I was a little girl. We used to have baths together. Which reminds me… "

She rummages in her bag. Pulls out a bath plug which she holds out for him to see. "Just making sure. They always go missing, the plugs. So I've stolen one. Bath. That's what I'm going to do when I get back. If there's any hot water."

Can she guess I'm picturing her naked?

She stands up. Offers him her hand. Once again there is an exchange of body awareness between them. A current they feed into each other.

He looks down at the table in search of something of hers he can put in his tunic pocket. A memento of what has been the best night of his life. Nothing except for lipstick-stained cigarette ends and dead matches. He doesn't want burnt out things.

"Will you give me something for luck?" he calls out.

But she doesn't turn around to face him again.

Benedict, he only now notices, is up on a table. Dancing to music only he can hear. Dancing on his own but as if with an imaginary partner. Nearby, Tom is doing the hokey cokey with his trousers around his ankles. The Station Commander seems to be enjoying himself too. Charlie has his arm around the girl Evie arrived with. A plump ebullient girl with half bleached crinkly hair and freckles, like Charlie.

He watches Evie leave with Angus. Then he goes over to Benedict. He looks up at him on his perch.

"Everything okay?"

"In a blue funk," says Benedict.

"Oh?"

"Keep feeling I'm about to be bounced."

"Well you're not. Not at this precise moment anyway."

"Hatchets?"

"Hatchets?"

"Night club. Piccadilly."

"We can't go to London. We're on standby at four o clock."

"CO's orders. Won't sleep anyway. Keep seeing yellow nose Hun darting down onto my tail." He makes a machine gun noise. Almost loses his balance.

"Come on. I need to talk."

"Don't want to talk. Know you're just going to rabbit on about how bloody wizard Miss Evie bloody Devereux is. If you were really my friend you'd be drunk."

"I didn't make her laugh enough. In fact I didn't make her laugh at all."

Outside Tom is climbing up the façade's rose trellis. He's bad-mouthing Hermann Goering. As if the newly appointed Nazi Reichsmarschall is up there hiding behind the chimney stack.

Tom is on standby at dawn as well.

7

Out in the grey early morning air, dew soaking into his boots, he watches Benedict up in the cockpit of his Spitfire taking in deep draughts of oxygen through his mask. He can smell the alcohol on Benedict six feet away.

"Better?" he calls out.

"Actually, yes. I feel like a Christmas balloon that's just been blown up. Certainly beats Alka-Seltzer. Someone should market this stuff for hangovers."

He turns to Benedict's two mechanics. "Just as well we've got nothing more important to do today than fight for our lives, eh?" he says.

"You'll both be fine, sir."

Back in the dispersal hut the telephone rings twice in quick succession. Both false alarms. One call is from an irate WAAF. She demands to talk to Tom.

"It's Cinderella. She says you ran off with one of her shoes last night," the telephone orderly says. "And that she wants it back."

Tom sits slumped down in the armchair. He is quiet and shy when not drunk. Quiet and shy with a dishevelled air, a sheepish smile and a devilish low laugh.

"Tell her Prince Charming is otherwise disposed," says Leslie. "But I'm not overly amused, Tom. Same goes for you, Ben. Look at the bloody state of the two of you. You both stink to high heaven of booze." He picks up a scuffed cricket ball. "Here, catch." Benedict reacts too late and flinches as the seamed and scuffed red ball lands in his lap. "What does that tell you?

Basically you've just copped it. I suggest the pair of you go out and clear up your grogginess with some more oxygen."

"I'm afraid Pilot Officer Vane-Temple doesn't appear to be in the immediate vicinity at present but I will certainly pass on your message. Would it be correct to deduce that you require the restitution of one shoe?"

Jack walks outside. The atmosphere of hangover inside the hut is out of kilter with his mood. He strolls about on the wet grass. Deliberately not looking over towards the control tower. Aware of nothing else.

Can she see out of the window?

The order to scramble arrives within the hour.

"Guy. Not you as well?"

He stops in mid stride. Mystified. He turns to look at his flight commander.

"What about your Mae West?"

Shit. You bloody fool.

As he takes off, circles the aerodrome, tucked in behind Green Leader (Leslie), and quickly gains height it is like his first ever solo flight all over again. Everything is a marvel. The sense of elated detachment he feels as he rises up through the cloud base into the clear air. Higher than the sun. The unreality of gazing down at what looks like an unearthly kingdom of drifting white islands.

In his head he is describing his sensations and the visuals to Evie.

Stop bloody daydreaming.

He has not been conscious of controlling his machine for some while. He checks the altimeter.

Oxygen time.

He smiles at the recollection of Benedict earlier. Looks over across at him. Catches his eye. Can see the ironic long-suffering expression even behind his mask. How well they already know each other. His headset emits a burst of crackling.

Evie will be listening to this.

He hopes Leslie will call on him to say something. So she can hear his voice.

Fat chance. You're still the novice here.

"Sapper to Green Leader. One hundred and fifty approaching Dover at angels fifteen."

"One hundred and sodding fifty plus?"

It's Benedict. Except he doesn't realise he's transmitting. He can tell by the private contemplative sound of his voice. Sure enough Leslie reprimands him.

"Heartfelt apologies. Addled brain cells and twitchy fingers have been given a stiff talking to."

Jack switches his guns to ready. Checks the oil pressure and temperature. Then sits up alert in his seat. Straining his eyes out into the far distance.

The leisurely drift of the clouds is like the epitome of peace. And then it's as if heaven suddenly spills over into hell. He can see them now. Black pencil scribbles on the blue transparency over the sea. Pencil scribbles that soon become a swarm of insects and then a black armada of unspeakable menace.

"There they are. You know the score. Green and Red sections, get in among them and panic them out of formation. In and out as quick as possible. Blue section intercept the 109s. And remember these bastards are probably going for our airfields. Possibly *our* airfield. Our friends. Okay lads. Tally ho. Repeat. Tally ho."

He pictures Evie in the control tower. A sitting duck. Then he forces himself to clear his mind of everything but the task at hand. He follows Leslie down. As he does so he is aware of a fiery glitter diving down out of the sun towards him. The glitter soon reveals itself to be a dozen or so 109s. The tight formation of bombers is like an obstacle course. Huge ugly lumbering things he sweeps past. The sinister black cross flashing into his field of vision. Trails of white smoke streaming out from their guns and exhausts. He fires his own guns. More to feel the heartening savagery of their recoil in his bloodstream than with hope of hitting anything. Out of the corner of his eye he is aware of flames and a trail of black smoke. The tremendous strain on his eyes as he tries to look everywhere at once. The varying high pitches of noise. The metallic clamour. Some of the bombers are veering away or going into dives. He avoids collisions by what seems a hair's breadth at times. A part of his mind is trying to register details he can report back to the intelligence officer. Enemy tactics and numbers. Then he knows a moment's annoyance with himself for taking it for granted he will see the intelligence officer again.

Humility. It's a great asset.

And he is back in the pub. Momentarily with the Station Commander. And then with Evie.

Snap out of it, you fool.

He spots two 109s circling into position on his tail.

They're going to have a go at me.

He looks around for a sign of Leslie and Benedict.

Damn. Lost 'em.

Half roll to starboard and down in a tight spiral turn. Done with barely a thought. No time to think. His old instructor would have been impressed. Always told him he thought too much. *Let the aircraft flow exclusively through your hands and feet.* More strength required in his grip on the control column as his speed increases. He heaves back on the stick. He glances up in his mirror. With dread. Sure enough, the bastards have followed him round. Grey smoke and flashes of white light shooting off from the two yellow noses.

What will they least expect I do?

Before he has answered himself he forces a screaming turn out of his machine and hurtles directly towards the two yellow nosed ME 109s with his guns blazing.

Charlie tactics.

He is shouting his voice hoarse. It is the bravest or most foolhardy thing he has ever done in his life. A new achievement. Except he doesn't recall any conscious moment in which he made the decision.

Then he has dropped ten thousand feet in the blink of an eye. There is that wondrous bewildering moment again. The sky is empty except for a long smoke trail high up to port. He can't quite believe it. But he scans the sky in every direction and there is no trace of an aircraft anywhere.

Soon he is flying at 5,000ft over the white cliffs of Dover.

Don't want to be the first one home. Doesn't look good.

A devout Catholic called Jamie Groves has the reputation for most often being the first one back. Just shrugs his shoulders and grins whenever it's mentioned. So he's nicknamed Godspeed. Six feet four, mop of straw-coloured hair, clumsy as hell with his lurching stoop, gesticulating like a tipsy orchestra conductor, he always passes out after his third drink. Falls fast asleep for the rest of the evening.

He counts three returned aircraft on the ground.

Godspeed and Fungus are inside the hut. Talking to the intelligence officer, Roger. Or Polly as he's nicknamed, in his rimless glasses with his sceptical frown as if life is a maths problem he can't quite solve.

Angus says, "Well, he's a bloody fool getting into the state he did last night. What did he expect?"

Tom or Ben?

Godspeed, real name Jamie, turns to him and, in his Oxbridge accent, asks, "Guy, did you see Leslie or Ben go down?"

Angus is looking at him as if he is to blame in some way.

"No. I had two 109s on my tail when I came out of the bomber stream."

Soon Charlie and Tom arrive. And then the others. All except Ben and Leslie. The general consensus is that Leslie managed to bail out but that Ben didn't. Charlie is kind to him. Brings him a cup of tea. Keeps him engaged in conversation. When the telephone rings he sits up erect in his chair. Every fibre of his being startled into hope. The hope that it was Benedict who bailed out. It is more than a hope. It feels like a fundamental need of his being. As if he won't able to carry on if Benedict has gone. But it is only the Air Controller.

He keeps glancing over at Benedict's name on the flight board, scrawled in chalk. As if to reassure himself it is still there, still hasn't been wiped off.

Within two hours the squadron is up in the air again. On their way to intercept another hundred plus enemy aircraft fifty miles out to sea off Great Yarmouth. He is wingman to Charlie now in B Flight. Bastards, he thinks when he sees the formation of German machines. Fucking bastards. He fires his guns with more malice. Values his life a little less perhaps. Blacks out twice. Comes to one time upside down. Disorientated. A moment of panic. More and more he realises the centre of his gravity is in the seat of his pants. It's there he is most intimately connected to his aircraft, from there he understands her every mood swing. A Dornier swings into the bead of his gun sight. He presses down hard on the red button. Feels in the seat of his pants his machine lose a tiny bit of speed as the guns make their bracing shredding noise. Next thing he knows he has three Messerschmitt 109s on his tail. Fighting for his life again. They must be low on fuel because they give up after a while. And he is alone in the sky once again.

The aerodrome has been attacked. The controller tells him to land with due caution. He sees the signs of damage as he swings round in an arc in preparation to bring his machine down after his third sortie of the day. Tiny figures with shovels standing around craters. A burnt out petrol bowser. When he's taxiing towards dispersal he sees the control tower is missing all its windows.

Please not her as well.

He feels as though he will burst into tears if anyone shows him even a flicker of kindness.

"Half a dozen Stukas," Ed, the rigger tells him. "Couple of Spits frightened the bleeders off. But there's an unexploded bomb near the Waafery. That's got their knickers in a twist."

"Any news of Ben or Leslie?"

"Not to my knowledge, sir. Not yet."

He doesn't go to the mess for tea. He goes to his room. Benedict's green silk dressing gown is still lying in a heap on the floor. His book, with its marker, is by the bed. Benedict has reached page ninety-five of *Mrs Dalloway*. Benedict reads it out aloud when they are both in their beds. Strings of beautiful words burning themselves into the air like benign tracer fire. He refuses to think of Benedict in the past tense.

All the strength is drained out of his legs. He sits down on the bed and lets the tears come.

8

He can't hug him, kiss him, press all his body heat up against him. Because it's not the done thing between males, no matter how close the friendship, no matter how many secrets they have shared. The surge of thanksgiving, the rekindling of wellbeing cannot be channelled into any adequate physical gesture.

Benedict, in borrowed stripy pyjamas, is propped up in bed. One of several beds in what might be the ballroom of an elegant country house that has been turned into a nursing home. He can't hug him so he shakes his hand. Tosses his green silk dressing gown and *Mrs Dalloway* down onto the bed.

"Thanks. I've been wondering about Mrs Dalloway."

"You haven't lost your looks. So what's the damage then?"

"My left foot has apparently declared a twenty four hour ceasefire. Three splinters of cannon shell pierced my left boot. After the rest of the blighter had made a hole at the bottom of the cockpit. I feel such a fraud. Not to mention a bloody idiot."

"What happened?"

"Don't suppose anyone has a flask? They've got nothing but milk here. I thought milk was supposed to be like gold dust. No wonder. It's all been stockpiled in this place. Tom? Any alcoholic beverages up your sleeve?"

Tom grins. Scratches his mop of black hair. "Nothing doing."

"Come on, tell us what happened." He can't believe how happy he is to see Benedict alive again.

"Learned a lesson, didn't I."

"Stay away from spirits, stick to the watered down beer?" says Charlie.

"Beware of hubris. I must have had such a smug look on my face. I thought I was in the ascendancy. Thought *I* was the orchestra conductor. I was already imagining Polly wiping his glasses on his sleeve with a deeply sceptical expression as I reported my first bull's eye. The slumbering leviathan firestarter was fattening in front of my eyes. It was just about to drift into the bead of my gun sight when I felt this tremendous angry shove in my back. Astral debris flying up into my face. Windscreen covered in muck, like black sealing wax. Smoke all over the shop. When I think of it now it's like slapstick comedy. Okey-dokey, Benedict, I said to myself. Parachute drill. Buggered if I could remember anything that chap Horace or Homer or whatever his name was said. Then it struck me just how insane the thing I was about to do was. Jumping out into the sky eight thousand feet above the earth. I don't actually remember much after that. Until I saw these two sheep looking up at me. They had this kind of amused beatific expression in their eyes. As if they had ordered my arrival for their afternoon amusement. Then I noticed I was missing a boot. And what was worse there was a burning pain in my foot. I landed rather gracefully, if I do say so myself. I was trying to remember the procedure for disencumbering oneself of a parachute when two doddery old home guard chaps came panting and wheezing towards me. Rifles raised. One of them had a coughing fit when he stopped running. The other one told me in very slow loud diction that I was under arrest. As you can imagine I was still rather dazed. But when one of them prodded me with his rifle I told him to bugger off. And eventually I was brought here. Tomorrow the splinters will be removed by the medic at base. Back on ops the day after. Though you and Leslie will have to make do without me tomorrow."

"Leslie bought it," says Charlie. "Actually everyone thought it was Leslie who bailed out. Not you."

He had forgotten about Leslie. Some of his renewed well-being dribbles away. There is a moment of awkward silence. Then a strident squeaking noise that makes everyone turn around.

A nurse is pushing an effigy of a man in a wheelchair. All the personality has been burned from his face. His eyebrows and lips are no longer there. He has no hair. His skin like something plucked and raw. His eyes stare out of cut-out red sockets. His hands clamped to his chest. Bandaged in white lint. His feet too are covered in white lint. He looks like the first few strokes of a charcoal drawing.

"Take a good look, fellahs. I'm a mirror for what might well be in store for the lot of you."

"Hurricane pilot," says Benedict. "I'd probably look like that if I had been flying a Hurricane today. Did you know the overload fuel tank of a Hurricane is beneath the instrument panel? Instant inferno right under your nose if it's hit."

Charlie springs abruptly to his feet. One of his no nonsense moments. "Time to toast Leslie," he says. "Otherwise when we get there they'll all have drunk all his kitty."

"Hang on, Guy. I've got something for you."

Benedict calls out to a nurse. "Could I trouble you to bring me back that copy of *The Tatler* you kindly lent me earlier, nurse? Something I want to show my friend here."

"When she brings it discreetly rip out page twenty five. Little piece about your muse signing up for king and country. Fetching photograph of her too. How did it go last night?"

"I didn't make her laugh enough."

"Believe it or not I do remember you telling me that."

"So you're okay?"

"Shaken me up a bit. I'm rather dreading getting back behind the controls of my kite. Stupid, isn't it? I love flying. Oh, thank you very much, nurse."

9

"Someone got out of bed the right side today," says Jimbo, sitting in a deckchair outside the dispersal hut.

"Got a date tonight," says Angus.

"Remind me again, when's tonight? Isn't that after we've been outnumbered about ten to one by enemy aircraft at least another three times, enemy aircraft that deploy smarter tactics than anything we've been taught and have more powerful guns?"

"Got to count your chickens sometimes in life."

"I feel like I'm being stalked by a shadow every time I find myself taking tonight for granted. Who with? Your date."

"A girl called Evie. Known her since I was a child."

Jack pretends he isn't listening. Isn't interested.

That's the end of that then. She's way out of your league anyway.

There was a photograph of her family home in *The Tatler*. Larger than the entire road he grew up on. It was a photograph that was unkind to his hopes. All but dashed them. He keeps seeing the house he grew up in. Its sallow routines of thrift. Its supernatural distance from the world she grew up in.

He is wingman to Charlie in Red Flight today. The sun is edging over the horizon when he runs with his parachute slung over his shoulder to his machine. Soon he is up above the green and gold crops. The green and pleasant land. He begins humming. Unaware his R/T is on.

"That's the spirit Red Three. But if you're going to do the next verse, in tune would be preferable."

"Sorry," he tells Charlie. He tells himself he hardly cares whether or not Evie might be listening.

The Controller gives them constant updates over the R/T. His measured clipped voice, as if offering housekeeping tips. Another hundred plus. Heading towards the Thames Estuary.

He begins to strain his eyes for a glimpse of ominous dots in the sky.

When they appear and quickly grow in size it is a terrible and mesmerising spectacle. Stretching thin his capacity for comprehension as if a sinew is about to snap inside him. There are too many to count. Though the intelligence officer will expect them to be counted. He reckons fifty bombers in two tight formations. And an escort of around fifty fighters. At least today he and his squadron are above the fighters. As long as there isn't another Nazi squadron hovering higher up in the haze somewhere.

He presses the emergency boost override. Lowers his seat behind the windscreen. Guns on ready.

Charlie streaks down at full throttle into the formation of bombers, head on. Weaves through them like a cat twisting in and out of railings. Objective is to hit the leaders and panic the entire herd out of the watertight discipline of their formation. Charlie hits one of the leaders. Jack sees bits fall off the nose and sees smoke as he swoops down with his thumb on the gun button and is aware he in turn is being shot at and instinctively ducks down in his seat and soars back up into higher clear air. Maybe he has hit one of the bombers too. He's too intent on watching for enemy fighters and avoiding a collision to take note. Up above he spots three ME 109s half roll and come swooping down into the fray. There is a constant babble of agitated voices over the R/T. But how are you supposed to concentrate on voices in the midst of this mayhem? When he turns and dives back down towards the stream there are a few bombers that have been panicked away from the pack. He chooses his prey. Reminds himself there are bombs on board his target and these bombs will kill his countrymen if he doesn't shoot it down. He needs to feed more aggression into his system. Needs to think of these Germans as evil bastards. And that right is on his side. Once again when he's manoeuvring into position, can see the swastika coming into focus on the tail, is about to get the beast in his sights, he senses menace in the air. It is communicated to his skin as if by an invisible wire. It is then communicated to him over the R/T by Charlie. "Bandit behind you, Red three. Break sharpish."

Sure enough he has been singled out as prey by a ME 109 pilot.

Here we bloody go again.

He has to ignore the bomber. Swings away to port. Diving to gather speed. There is someone on his tail who wants to kill him. He can feel the determination of his adversary in the slipstream. He pictures a set heavy jaw and bullet-hard eyes devouring the intervening distance. One lapse in concentration now and he will be dead. Chilling thought. Thank heavens it is not his thoughts that guide the aircraft. It is something just beyond the reach of thought. What an artist would call inspiration. A choreography of instinctive flourishes.

The German copies everything he does. As if he can sense it in advance. Like some demon doppelganger. Blackness wells up behind his eyes every time he goes into a steep turn. The rhythm of his heartbeat accelerated to a crescendo. Now and again tracer flashes past his cockpit. He breaks to the right, into the glare of the sun.

Now you see me, now you don't.

When he turns away from the sun's dazzle he sees he has gained another couple of vital seconds.

The German begins to dive away from him.

What the hell is he doing?

Chase him my little beauty.

The predator becomes prey. He is on the German's tail now.

They are alone together in the sky. Except for some vapour trails being etched on the blue transparency a couple of miles away, as if God is writing a letter.

He's making for those clouds out at sea. Where the bloody hell did they come from? Have these bloody Germans got some kind of weather machine now?

He follows the ME 109 down into the cloud. A conjuring trick. It has vanished. He doesn't like the sudden diminishing of visibility. Anything could suddenly pop out from anywhere now. And he feels exhausted. All his joints aching. The places where one bone is joined to another.

Time to go home, Jack.

Okay, Guy.

Towards the coast he spots something below. He drops down to investigate. It is a Heinkel 111. Completely alone. He looks around for any sign of nearby activity. Nothing. He half rolls. Plunges down from his great height. With the suspicion that this is too good to be true. He keeps looking above and behind. His pulse is galloping. His hand trembling with excitement. He has to inwardly shout at himself to calm down.

He has been spotted now. The bomber begins to weave. He keeps an eye on the rear turret but he is not being shot at by the gunner. As he swoops down astern he realises why. The rear gunner is dead or badly wounded. He can make out flecks of red on the perspex. He fires a couple of bursts at the port engine.

Surely that hit him.

Yes, there is some smoke. He pulls up on the other side. Looks back over his shoulder. The smoke has blackened. Oil smoke. The beast is wounded. This is all too easy.

To lighten its load the Heinkel releases its bombs. He sees them spin elegantly earthwards. He looks down at England below. Open ploughland with a few farm buildings scattered. He doesn't hear the explosions. But he sees a mist rise up from the ground.

As he manoeuvres himself for another attack it occurs to him that this is now virtually calculated murder.

No it isn't. There's still two gunners who want to kill you.

But his resolve has slackened. He has too much time to think about this. There is no aggression in his system. He is tired. He has been thrown about inside his harness for almost half an hour. The oxygen mask is irritating his face. He feels like letting them go. As a thank you for Benedict's return to life.

Why not just let the thing get back to Germany? A damaged bomber won't be good for Nazi morale.

He decides to have one more crack at it. The starboard engine this time. Decides the crew can always bail out.

Look out. Up above!

He sees a swooping streak of glitter in his mirror. Is about to take evasive action when he notices the RAF markings. It is another Spitfire. It takes what was going to be his trajectory. Sprays the Heinkel with bullets then breaks underneath as if to admire his handiwork. The nose of the German beast drops. It begins slewing to the left. Losing speed. The black smoke thickens and some flames can now be seen. As the Spitfire attacks again he sees from its markings that it is Angus.

He's stolen my kill, the bastard.

Serves you right for being so bloody indecisive.

He leaves Angus to it. Makes for home feeling tense and dissatisfied. To add insult to injury Angus somehow arrives back at the aerodrome before he does. He walks into the dispersal hut in time to overhear Angus claiming the bomber he himself incapacitated.

"A Heinkel 111. About three miles north east of Maidstone. Crashed into a field. Saw it plain as a day."

"Witnesses?"

"Yep. Fishy here was stooging around in the vicinity."

"Fishy? You mean Guy?"

"Yes. Guy."

"Can you confirm, Guy?"

"Confirmed."

"What about you, Guy? Hit anything?"

Angus scowls at him before walking away.

"No, nothing again."

He glances over at the board. Sees Godspeed's name has been rubbed out though he can still see its outline beneath the chalky smudge.

10

He strips off his uniform and dives naked into the river. The shock of the cold water brings his heartbeat closer to his chest. He breaststrokes out to where the pool of sunlight gilds the water. Parting the duckweed and river muck. For a while he floats on his back. Basking in the blessing of the sun's heat.

As he was cycling between the hedgerows to this spot he saw the squadron returning to the aerodrome. One by one. He counted eleven Spitfires. One missing. He recalled the parting look of Benedict this morning. Trying to ascertain if there was any suggestion of finality about it. Benedict's ambition is to at least make it to the end of *Mrs Dalloway*.

He swims until he can no longer see his heap of clothes on the bank.

Twenty-four hours leave and he stays at the base. He contemplated going home. Back to Anerley. Its squalid grey Victorian geometry, queues at the bus stops, queues at the chemists, children in threadbare clothes with runny noses. Its taunting reminder of how pinched his prospects are. The loose floorboards beneath the worn carpets. More than anything he needs to believe luck is on his side. He wouldn't be able to sustain that belief in his childhood home. The latched gate, the cracked concrete and tiny square of parched grass in front of the house. The yellow stains on the porcelain in the bathroom. The smell of escaping gas from the heater in the front room. It would infect him, his new fighting self with its relentless undertow of resignation.

He swims further upriver. Until he can hardly believe his eyes. Level with him on the grassy riverbank but as if occupying some dreamspace is Evie.

"I came here to be alone," she calls out. Her voice sounds beautiful over the water after the relentless drone of engine noise in his ears.

"Sorry."

He sinks as though being tugged down by tentacles beneath the surface of the water.

Is that making her smile?

He stays under the water for as long as he can.

"Come back." There's a smile in her voice.

Up he comes. Suddenly remembering he is naked. Completely starkers except for the dog collars around his neck. He looks down at the surface of the water. The spectral outline of his naked body beneath the water.

How much of me can she see?

"Those flowers suit you," he says. He means the radiant blue wildflowers growing in the tall grass by the trees behind her. She has taken off her cap. Let her hair down.

"You make me wish I had brought my bathing costume. Next time."

I make her wish…

"Just what I needed," he says.

"Not on standby today?"

"Finally got a day off."

He is compelled to keep himself afloat on the spot. Buffeted by the gentle current. He can't swim in case he gives her a flash of his nudity. So he's stuck here. He begins to feel a bit awkward. He can't see a way in which this situation will resolve itself.

"Do you want some tea? I've got a flask. We'll have to share the cup though."

"I'd love some. Only problem is, I'm not wearing any clothes. They're down there, about half a mile away."

"I brought a towel. To sit on. You can borrow that. I'll close my eyes."

"Okay."

"Righty-oh. Eyes closed."

There she is, in her WAAF uniform, sitting at the water's edge, hugging her knees, with her eyes closed, as if waiting for the revelation of a surprise. He has to stop himself from getting excited as he swims over towards her. He slips on river mud as he is half out of the water. Almost loses his balance. He is sure she opens her eyes a fraction at the disturbance. He wishes he wasn't quite so thin.

He wraps the blue and white striped towel around his waist. It's not RAF issue. Must be hers. Something of hers pressed to his naked wet skin.

"Aren't you worried someone might steal your clothes?"

He takes the cigarette she offers. Her hand brushes his as she lights it for him.

"Don't say that."

"Saying things makes them happen? I always thought it was the other way round. Saying things aloud makes them not happen."

"I'll remember that next time I'm shouting at the pilot of a 109 to bugger off back to Germany. I'll tell him to keep chasing me instead."

He's made her smile again.

The sun makes the drops of water on his navel glisten. He catches her glance at them.

"Can I tell you something?" she says, serious now. "Perhaps you can give me some advice."

"Okay."

"Well, one of the girls I room with brought a man back last night and it's created an enormous fuss. I came here to clear my head. Left to myself I'd ignore it. Even though it was frightfully embarrassing. Trying not to listen."

He mirrors her smile. But he has never made love to a woman and has to fake a worldly demeanour he does not feel.

"Problem is, some girls in the room next door heard. You

know, tell-tale noises. And they want to report her. In fact they want me to lead the protest. Thing is, she's my friend. And so is the pilot in question. Puts me in a pickle. I really don't want to rat on my friend but how can I claim to have been oblivious when I was only six feet away?"

"They were making a lot of noise?"

A wide smile brightens her eyes. "Isn't it all ridiculous? We're treated like schoolchildren. Why shouldn't there be love? We might all be dead tomorrow. Angus could get shot down today."

"Angus?"

"Whoops. That was supposed to be secret. Still, I suppose it will all come out sooner or later. Yes, Angus was the man involved."

He can barely keep the grin off his face.

"And I was partly to blame. I arranged to meet him for a drink last night but I took my friend along because she rather likes him. The plan was I would plead a headache and leave the two of them alone. Which is what happened. Except I hadn't expected things to move along quite that quickly. But I won't do it. I will not tell tales."

"Why not say you were exhausted and didn't hear a squeak. Benedict slept through the air raid the other night."

"The girl who most wants to report my friend is called Peggy. Do you remember when we were talking about superstition and I told you I was strafed after harbouring unkind thoughts about someone?"

He is overjoyed she remembers their conversations. That there is now evidence he has an existence inside her.

"Well, those unkind thoughts were directed at Peggy. I can't help it but I really don't like her. Chiefly because she doesn't like me. She's like one of those fairground mirrors. Whenever I look at her I feel grotesque. I'd always hoped identity was something one could rely on more. Hideous how easily all one's outlines can be smudged beyond recognition simply by an unkind glance. But exciting too. What about you? Do you know who you are?"

PART THREE

1943

1

"The woman in white is dancing barefoot in the meadow of bluebells. I repeat, the woman in white is dancing barefoot in the meadow of bluebells."

"I can picture that, can't you?" says Evie.

Leopold, with his dishevelled blonde hair and attentive blue eyes, in his short grey trousers and grey jersey, manages a reluctant smile. As a rule he views smiling as a sign of weakness. Leopold is holding a piece of a jigsaw puzzle. Leopold is twelve years old.

"Grandfather Maurice has forgotten his walking stick again. I repeat, Grandfather Maurice has forgotten his walking stick again."

"And that. Poor Grandfather Maurice stumbling out of his garden."

"Are these messages for you?"

"Of course not. And don't look at me like that."

"Like what?"

"Full of suspicion. I just thought it would be fun to listen to them together."

She walks across the kitchen to turns off the wireless. The

large echoing kitchen with its whitewashed stone walls. The unfinished jigsaw puzzle is on the table, a table that can seat twenty guests.

"Me and my friend used to send messages to each other. We did it by thinking really hard when we were apart and alone in our beds at night."

"Was this Adela?"

"How do you know about her?" he says accusingly.

"Your mother told me about her."

"My mother doesn't know anything about her."

"She knows she was your best friend and that you miss her."

"She doesn't know anything. No one does."

"It's nothing to be embarrassed about. Just the opposite. In fact, Adela's a very lucky girl to have inspired so much trust and affection in you."

"How can she be lucky when the police came to our class at school and took her away? The things you say don't make any sense."

"I heard you stood up in class and tried to stop her going and then told the teacher he was a cowardly slave and wasn't fit to teach children history." She can't keep a smile from her face, a smile brimming with pride for him and his gesture.

"That's why I was expelled. I don't even understand what a Jew is. Adults are supposed to be wise; I think they're stupid. War is stupid. Why does Adolf Hitler or Marshal Pétain care where Adela lives? She's just a little girl."

"I know and I couldn't agree with you more."

"Why do you want to live here?"

"Why not?" she says.

"It's boring. Every day is exactly like the day before. It's like being a hen, living here."

"Where would you like to live then?"

"Everyone does that with me."

"What?"

"Tries to turn talk into some kind of fantasy adventure. It doesn't fool me."

"I'm not trying to fool you."

"You would if I was a Nazi."

"Yes, I would if you were a Nazi. What about the war?"

"What about the war?"

"Well for most people every day isn't exactly like the day before. They wake up not knowing what to expect. They can't take anything at all for granted."

"You mean it's because of people like me that there is a war?"

"No. That's not what I mean. How did you get that idea?"

"Because sometimes I wish that I'd wake up and everything I saw would be different. But not even the war comes here."

"Thank heavens."

"I don't believe in heavens."

Leopold's head is almost perpetually thrown back, slowly rotating back and forth on his sinewy neck like a cat looking for comfort. This gives him a dissatisfied air of looking down at the world. He has the most expressive eyebrows Evie has ever encountered. She always feels seen through when he looks at her. He has muscular dystrophy. His every physical gesture is like a balancing act of sorts. As if the forces that hold his body in equilibrium are no more than whims. She has read up a bit about muscular dystrophy. Apparently it impairs the ability of nerve cells in the brain and spinal cord to communicate with each other. She sometimes tries to visualise this breakdown of order taking place in Leopold, beneath his skin. There is something about him that compels her to look beyond the surface of things. The disarming honesty he demands at all times perhaps.

"I'd decided not to talk to you today if you came down with your hair piled up on top of your head."

She laughs. "You don't like my hair like this?"

"No. You look like a peacock."

"Okay, I'll remember that. I don't want to look like a peacock."

Leopold fits another piece of the jigsaw into its allotted place. A black piece with flecks of white. Part of the whale's back. The whale is emerging from the sea.

She and Leopold stand by the table in the kitchen of the house called Compagnac. Compagnac is her safe house.

"Will you help me build a fire tonight?" He doesn't look at her and his voice is both shy and matter of fact as if his request is of little importance. Evie knows it's of the greatest importance.

"What kind of fire?"

"A fire outside."

"What about the black-out?"

"Why would the Allies drop bombs on our house?"

"It's not the Allies I'm thinking of; it's the Germans and the Milice. Why do you want to build a fire anyway?"

"I promised I would."

"To Adela?"

"Yes. So she will know I'm thinking of her."

"That's lovely, Leopold."

"It's not lovely. It's just a promise."

Xan, she knows, would have one of his nervous fits if he knew she was lighting fires in the garden of her safe house.

"Okay," she says. "We'll light a fire for Adela."

2

Palms clamped to headphones, she slowly turns the dial. The hiss and crackle in her ears sounds like the language of some spirit hinterland.

She is in a barn. Sitting on a milking stool beside a cart loaded with hay. Two rabbits in wire-meshed cages to her left. A towering stack of firewood to her right. Through the open door she can see the benign dips and hollows of ploughed fields and vineyards and meadowlands. She is bare legged in a simple floral print blue dress. Stray tufts of hay tickle her bare legs every time she changes position. The delight of not wearing stockings. Her body breathing more freely. To feel the close proximity of her nakedness is one of the joys of summer afternoons. She slowly turns the dial until she finds the frequency Marcel has given her. It's a wonder that her messages will soon arrive coded in England. Like the concept of prayer. Like being a child again, kneeling by a bed and sending some plea up into the sky.

In training she was able to send nineteen words a minute.

"All right, you've had your fun. Shove off now," says Marcel. Marcel is the real wireless operator. He holds out both hands in a camp gesture. Breathes out an ironic exasperated sigh on which she can smell fried onions. She hands him the headphones. Watches him run a hand tenderly over the crumpled sheet of torn paper on which he has coded all the messages she brought to him. *Raymond Boscardin disappeared believed arrested stop sabotage instruction proceeding well but political unrest amongst men stop more have joined the communists stop need at least a million francs urgently to pay men stop attack on Michelin factory will go ahead as planned stop arms and explosives therefore required now at Elephant stop BBC message Adela Leopold is still building fires for you stop adieu.*

The day the RAF schedule to make the drop in the field codenamed *Elephant* the BBC will broadcast her message. *Adela, Leopold is still building fires for you.* She pictures the wonder on Leopold's face when they sit listening to it together on the wireless. It's the moment she most looks forward to. More than ever she needs moments to look forward to. The most unsettling part of her work here is the risk to which she subjects the people she stays with. She hopes it isn't foolhardy of her to quote Leopold's name in a BBC message.

She goes out into the courtyard, stepping around the hens, walking towards the green tomato vines with their first faint splashes of red. Wherever she is now she has to plot out an escape route before she can relax. Today she doesn't have to worry because any approaching vehicle can easily be detected long before it winds up the stony road to the farmhouse. She watches the women on the slopes pruning the vines, her thoughts beating themselves out to the rhythm of Marcel's fastidious way of tapping out the Morse. This new language she has learned for the exchanging of secrets.

"My fifty third transmission." Marcel, sharp featured, thin, dark haired, wearing riding breeches, takes hold of her by the waist and waltzes her around in a circle.

"You're counting?"

"What else is there to do?"

"You could help prune the vines."

"And get dirt under my fingernails, darling. Not on your Nelly. So this Raymond individual. Is he about to bring down this house of cards we all live in?"

"How can I know?"

"Who he is, exactly?"

"One of the regional chiefs."

"It goes against my nature to trust people. Especially people I've never even met. I thought the idea was, trust no one. That was one of the aspects of this work that attracted me. No one told me I would be entrusting my life to a rabble of grubby and highly excitable communists and farmhands."

"At least Bigwig trusts you. He doesn't trust me." Bigwig is what she and Marcel call Xan.

"That's because he doesn't like you, darling. It's patently obvious. To begin with word was, he was very pleased with you. Then, all of a sudden, he changed his mind. Shall I be indiscreet?"

"Yes please."

"Bruno told him the first thing you did upon arriving in France was to converse with an entire village in English."

"I spoke in English to one woman. Not an entire village. It just slipped out. I could kill Bruno."

"He had me tell London in a sched. Bigwig I mean. Not Bruno. Bruno worships the ground you walk on. That he thought you were unsuitable for work in the field. A security risk. That you were flirting with all the men. London said to give you a bit of time, which made him spit and curse at London."

"He doesn't like me because he tried to kiss me."

"I knew it! And you rebuffed him. You've tinkered with his monumental vanity. You absolute heroine. I love you even more now." He leans forward and kisses her lightly on the mouth.

"This is our secret. I don't want anyone else to know."

"I think the reason he has put you solely in charge of this next drop is in the hope that you botch it in some way. Then he'll have the excuse to get you sent back to England."

She turns her back on Marcel. Walks off across the courtyard, her face flushed with anger. Walks blindly into one of the snuffling pigs and curses it.

"Don't you go upsetting Goering and Goebbels," he says. These are the names Marcel has given to the pigs.

"If he's willing to sabotage an operation to get rid of me surely he's the one who's a security risk."

"The man is a nervous wreck. He's been out here too long. He's going to get nabbed soon. I can sense it. He doesn't like me either, you know. Bruno told me he refers to us as the spoilt debutante and the preening nancy boy. Can't you just picture his face when he says that? That horrid little pinched mouth of his quivering, like aroused genitalia. And then his hand will go straight to his balls followed by a vigorous tug at his belt. By the way, have you heard about the new Gestapo torture device? A tiny room with an asbestos floor which they heat up to hellish temperatures from beneath. I've imagined it. To begin with you'd dance around like a lunatic and provide a great deal of amusement for the agents watching through the grill. Then you'd try to stand on tiptoes because the soles of your feet would not be able to bear the pain. Then the skin on the tips of your toes would be burned away and the pain would be unbearable so you'd probably lie down and rest all your weight on your elbows and the heels of your feet. Then…then you'd probably pass out and your face and hair would get burned and you'd come round in agony."

"Stop it. We won't get caught anyway."

"Let me see your palm."

"No," she says and smiles.

He snatches hold of her hand. Twists her wrist round. "You have a good long lifeline. This makes me happy. You will live to be about ninety-two. Look at mine. It's interrupted at about the half way point. As if I'm going to die and then miraculously be brought back to life. Can I tell you a secret?"

"No. The less I know about you…"

"Yes I know all about that. The rules. I think this is the only job I could do in the war because there aren't any rules. Not really. I have to report to the high and mighty once a day of course. But otherwise the only orders I have to obey are mine. Anyway, I'm going to tell you a secret whether you like it or not. There's a boy who works for the Gestapo I mean to fuck."

"Don't you dare!"

"That SS uniform." He makes an expression of encroaching orgasm.

"You're joking, aren't you?"

"Yes, I'm joking. Marcel is joking too. He detests the Nazis almost as much as I do."

"How different are you from Marcel, Marcel?"

"Oh we have quite a few things in common. You do realise that all the cover story charade we have to learn by heart is an utter waste of time. No doubt it's an edifying pastime for some aspiring novelist in London thinking all this stuff up. But it'd take the Gestapo an hour to expose our stories as third rate fiction. Do you know the papers London sent me here with were six months out of date? Luckily Bigwig spotted the errors and got me some new ones. So you see, I make myself up as I go along now. And so far, so good. Don't try too hard to be someone you're not, Anais. That's what will give you away."

"Just speaking French all the time has changed the way I feel about myself. Sometimes now I think it would be an effort to become again the woman I was before I became Anais."

"We think of identity as embedded within, like the heart and the lungs, but it's more like a surrounding atmosphere that can be subtly altered by every new foreign agent with which it comes into contact. You need to allow for that when you're acting the part of someone you're not. You need to be fluid. What do you think about when some fascist dogsbody is checking your papers? Some oily mean-mouthed member of the master race. I look the man in the eyes and silently say to him, I am tricking you. I am exactly what you have supposedly been trained to decipher. A secret agent working for the British government. I am also homosexual and at this precise moment I'm visualising your genitals. But you needn't worry because I find them no more attractive than your face or your personality. That's what I think. It involves no effort to think the truth. All my facial muscles are perfectly relaxed. Before, I found I was exerting myself to conceal the truth, especially when they do that thing they've been trained to do – the scowling officious stare with no trace of the milk of human kindness in it. The effort of concealment was making me appear suspicious."

"I often feel dizzy with the sliding back and forth of this identity and that. And that they must be stupid not to spot it, all this sliding back and forth."

"Yes, sometimes it can feel like being in an elevator that goes down when you have ordered it to go up. Okay, you keep Goering and Goebbels company while I do some alphabet juggling and find out what London expects of us now."

3

She is walking with Leopold through the streets of Clermont-Ferrand. She wants to buy him a new pair of shoes. It's the first time she has been with Leopold among crowds of strangers and she is struck by how much attention his affliction attracts, the unusual angle his head sits on his neck and its gyrations. When two German soldiers ostentatiously laugh at him it requires effort on her part not to slap them. But she realises Leopold has not noticed the derision of the Germans; his attention is drawn to a poster on the wall ahead. An ugly caricature of a bearded, beak-nosed Jewish man with typeface: Le Complot Juif Contre L'Europe. Leopold leaves her side and rips the poster from the wall. He screws it up and tosses it in the gutter.

Her first instinct is anger at him for so rashly subjecting them both to danger. She catches the eye of a woman walking towards them who has seen what Leopold did. She cannot read the emotion on the woman's face. She cannot convince herself this woman will not hurry to catch up with the two German soldiers and denounce what she has seen.

She takes his hand. "I know you were thinking of Adela and you're angry but…"

Leopold frees his hand from her grasp. "There aren't any buts," he says.

"Et maintenant voici quelques messages personnels."

"Why are we listening to these stupid messages again?"

"Wait and see."

Leopold is often dismissive of what she says. He likes making a point of establishing his independence of her. But his body constantly betrays him. He is forever sidling up to her. Allowing his body to make contact with her body, as if it is an accident of so little importance that he feels no need to rectify it. As he is doing now, his thigh pressed against her leg. It's the first time in her life she has realised how much comfort her body is capable of providing. The first time she has truly felt it as a gift she can give. Since being in France she has learned more about herself in two months than she did in the previous two years. It's ironic, she thinks, that the fictitious Monique has helped her own herself more fully as Evie.

She can't wait to see the expression on his face. She is more excited about this than the scheduled parachute drop itself.

The stream of repeated messages is endless. Leopold is growing bored.

"Where are you going?"

"Where do you think?"

"You're not going anywhere." She takes hold of him, hugs him to her breast. He makes a few annoyed noises but she holds him tight and his body relaxes into her embrace.

Then the voice on the radio. "Adela, Leopold is still building fires for you. I repeat, Adela, Leopold is still building fires for you."

Leopold looks up at her as though she has just walked on water.

This is the field she found. The field she told London about. Code named *Elephant*. It feels like her field. Already an intimate and pivotal part of her biography. A flat field in the midst of a thickly wooded area. A haze of moon smoke canopying the sweep of long grass. She pictures herself as a grandmother returning to this field. Telling grandchildren that this is the field. The field I found. She stands by a tree on the edge of the field. Holding a flashlight. She it is who will signal the code letter to the pilot. She is wearing a beret. Woollen mittens. A blue coat. Tonight she makes no attempt to dress like the local women. Tonight there is a Sten gun slung over her shoulder.

Bruno is by her side. He too is holding a flashlight. He wears a rucksack from which he has produced a bottle of Armagnac. He too has a Sten gun slung over his shoulder. It is the first time she has seen him with a weapon, seen him prepared for battle. She is unable to take the sight of Bruno with a weapon seriously. As if it is another of his comedy routines. She wonders if he feels as unbelievable to himself as she feels to herself. She looks at her watch.

All day she has been praying for clear skies. And there is a clear sky. The sense of wonder when she and Leopold heard the message broadcast by the BBC is still in her blood. *Adela, Leopold is still building fires for you.* A message whose meaning only she and a dozen other people in the world would be able to decipher. It was almost a mystical experience to suddenly hear these words spoken into the rustic kitchen by a disembodied voice. As if an angel had spoken. Had spoken to her personally.

She has given orders to the six French men who are hidden amongst the trees on the perimeter of the field. To stand at one hundred yard intervals at the edge of the field. One or two of the older men made it plain they did not like taking orders from a woman. The young boys were fine, excited, like her, but the older men were stiff with impotent resistance in the dark. As if this business of taking orders from a woman was the latest humiliation to add to all the others inflicted by the Nazis.

Now she is straining her ears up at the sky. The big blue black sky with all its flickering stars. Every so often she hears the hunting cry of some night creature. Reminding her of the dangers the shadows in the woods might spawn.

Bruno takes another swig from his bottle of Armagnac.

"You're sure you won't partake?"

"It's bad luck to celebrate something before it's happened."

"Who said anything about celebrating? You English are such puritans."

"Ssssh. I think I can hear it."

The distant drone she thinks she heard disappears.

The disappearance of the faint droning noise has left behind a hollow. An echoing place within her own body. Then a breeze rustles the leaves in the tree overhead and the low ebbing hum returns. More like the gentlest of caresses at the back of her neck than a sound. She takes a step forward, out of the shadow. Strains her eyes up amongst the stars. Feeling she is known up there, as she did when she was a little girl looking up at the stars.

The rumble of the engines seems to come up through the ground. It trembles up the length of her legs. A silhouette appears in the sky. Takes on definition. She can see a flicker of flame from the exhaust stubs. The RAF markings on the fuselage. She signals up the letter C in Morse. When it is directly overhead the entire field is trembling with the pulse of its presence. The letter is shone back as it veers away. The men around the field flash their torches up at the sky. A sequence of twinkling lights with a message.

The crack and rustle of the parachutes opening beneath the moon settles a pause up in the sky. They look like blossoming magnolia flowers. Glazed an ethereal white by the moonlight. Hypnotic in their leisurely graceful descent. She counts them. Eleven. One missing. They contain a million francs, Sten and Bren guns, rifles and pistols, ammunition, two new wireless sets, grenades, plastic explosives, limpet mines, magnetised bombs, detonators, fuses, chocolate, coffee, corned beef and cigarettes.

She is distracted by some shouting. She looks across the field. There are far too many men all of a sudden.

"What's going on?"

"Either communists or Germans disguised as communists," says Bruno.

Bruno's face is suddenly awash in white light. She can see

individual bristles on his chin in this sudden clarity, this sudden revelation of light. Then an explosion throws her into Bruno's arms. The mental shock of it rather than any gusting rush of displaced air. A brighter explosion of light opens up the woodlands. A white transparency is ghosted into being between the aisles of trees. Like candlelight in a cathedral. Then there is another explosion. Louder this time. She ducks and lifts her arm in a curve above her head. There is one explosion after another. She throws herself to the ground. A crescendo of blasts that makes her want to scream.

"That'll be the grenades," says Bruno.

There is a whistling in her ears. Her eyes are sore with tears. The smell of the earth, of the day's sunlight, the night's moisture on the soil, is replaced by the stink of smoke and cordite. The acrid smoke drifts across her face. "What do you mean?"

"The twelfth canister. Parachute didn't open. They will have heard that explosion for miles around."

She strides over into the mist of black smoke towards a man she does not know. He is holding a rifle.

"Who the devil are you?"

"We're requisitioning these supplies on behalf of the FTP."

"The hell you are."

All around the field there are men pointing guns and shouting at each other. There is a tug of war with a container.

"Who told you about the drop?"

"Never you mind."

"But I do mind. It was that bloody radio repair man, wasn't it?"

"What are you people doing exactly? Seems to me you do nothing. We need guns and we need explosives. What's the point of you having them if you don't use them? You British aren't much better than the Nazis. You sit back letting our Russian comrades …"

She steps forward and slaps his face before he can finish.

"Don't you dare insult my country," she says. She is thinking of Xan. Of the secret smug satisfaction he will feel if tonight is a shambles.

Bruno steps forward. "Listen. The Germans will have heard the explosions. Conclusion, unless we get out of this place now, we make a present of all these arms and our lives to the Germans. Is that going to help the war effort? You can have some Sten guns and rifles. Nothing else. The rest we need for an urgent mission. Take it or leave it."

"Who says he can have Sten guns and rifles?"

"And the cigarettes and coffee," says the man.

"That's what you most want, isn't it? And the money of course. You're no better than a band of brigands."

"Anais. Let me handle this."

There is a lull in the shouting and fighting. Weapons are no longer pointed. She walks off towards the van. That's where Bertrand, the radio repair man, is supposed to be.

The door of the van is open. Bertrand isn't inside. But the keys are.

When she returns to the field men are beginning to organise the transportation of the containers.

"It was Bertrand," she tells Bruno. "The traitor. He's vanished. I've told Xan Bertrand isn't to be trusted. And he ignores me. So Xan is to blame for this fiasco tonight. What did you agree to?"

"We can live without what I've let them have. Now we need to get away from this field as soon as possible."

She feels dissatisfied. Like the director of a play whose cast bungled too many of their lines.

She walks off to help with the removal of the containers. The metal container is too heavy for her to lift.

"Men's work," says one of the older men. One of those who was hostile earlier. But he smiles now. She has brought him cigarettes, coffee and chocolate. And money. She has become a sort of guardian angel.

4

She puts the wireless set in the basket above the rear wheel of her bicycle. She looks at the two rabbits in the wire-meshed cage and they look back at her. A shine of brightness in their eyes that touches her. She wonders how they see her. In a silver grey buttoned dress trimmed with white. Hair swept back off her face by a mother-of-pearl clip. The bogus wedding ring on her finger. She finds herself identifying with their predicament. The cage angers her. Why not risk the wrath of Monsieur Filou who she can't see, who must have gone back inside the house. She feels some superstitious compulsion to release these two animals from their cage. So what if she deprives Monsieur Filou of a meal or two? She has brought Monsieur Filou real coffee and chocolate. She has given him money. She could make it look like an accident. She kneels down in the dust and hay and opens the cage. More fearful at this moment of Monsieur Filou spying on her than the Gestapo. The two rabbits seem reluctant to leave. Then they hop off in a leisurely fashion. Three or four hops at a time before stopping and sniffing at the air.

Eight kilometres she has to cycle with the wireless set. On her bicycle that makes a jarring squeaking noise. Often she has to stand up to pedal. Her heartbeat increasing every time she approaches a new bend in the road. If she is searched no story will save her. Nevertheless she still has to invent a story. Every day she has to invent a new story to explain why she is doing what she is doing. The overriding objective of the new story will be to protect Leopold and his mother. She cycles in the midst of sunflower fields. She enjoys the sun on the back of her neck and freewheeling down the downhill sections of the road. With the British wireless set in her basket. Sometimes it is a wonder to her that she is not more frightened. Especially when she is cycling through the streets of Cournon-d'Auvergne and there are men in uniform who look up at her as she pedals towards them.

"I thought you weren't going to risk broadcasting from your apartment again? I thought you said the detector vans were closing in?" she says when Marcel lets her into his apartment.

Marcel lifts an eyebrow. He opens the suitcase she hands him and begins unravelling the long coiled wire antennae over the floor. The shutters in the houses opposite are all closed. She stops herself from imagining someone spying through the slats.

"They'll be closing in all the more today. This message Xan wants me to send will have me on air for about an hour. Which is why you're going to stand guard at the window. Xan, by the way, is asking that you be replaced. He's livid you made a gift of thirty Sten guns to the communists."

"It's Bertrand, the radio repair man, who brought the communists. I warned Xan not to trust him but he ignored me. Don't send that bit of the message. I don't want to return to England."

"They probably won't take any notice. Anyway, I've grown fond of you, Anais. I think I would like you to return to England. I would like to know you're safe."

"No one's safe, no matter where they live. One of my school friends was killed while trying on shoes in Selfridges."

"Time for sentry duty," he says.

She stands guard at the window. Two women in house dresses stand talking outside one building. Further down the street a little girl skips along the pavement in front of her mother. She watches Marcel change the quartz. Soon Marcel's relentless tapping begins to irritate her. She keeps looking at her watch. He has been on air for forty minutes. Then she sees the van. The van with the circular listening device fixed to its roof. She yanks in the wire at the same time as warning Marcel. The grey van stops outside Marcel's apartment building. Marcel is still tapping the radio key. Four men emerge from the van. She steps back from the window.

"Strip down to your slip."

"I'm not wearing a slip."

"Look, we pretend we're lovers. Can you do that? We'll make out we were in the midst of some afternoon hanky panky. Make a mess of the bed. Or perhaps better still, take off all your clothes and get into the bed."

"I can't face the Gestapo naked."

"Yes you can. And if you're naked, caught in the act, it'll explain any nervousness you show."

Marcel gathers up the wireless set and the antennae and the spare crystals and everything else incriminating and disappears into the bathroom. She doesn't know where he will hide it all. She has to trust him. She can hear the shouting of German men and fists pounding on a door downstairs. She tears off her clothes. Throws them haphazard over the floor. She pulls the shutters closed. Marcel returns and strips down to his shorts. They listen together to the footsteps climbing the stairs. The brutal hammer blow on the door. "*Deutsche polizei!*"

The two men in long leather coats wielding pistols push past Marcel. Both men are uncommonly ugly, humourless, bloodless, mean-mouthed and bristling with zeal. They flood darkness into her mind, confront her with a finish line, the riveting eyes of these pasty-faced hollow men. The light is turned on. One of the bulbs flickers in the wall mounting and finally expires. The uglier of the two men marches over to the bed and rips the sheet from her grasp. He has the face of a man who rarely gets what he wants from life and deeply resents it, who wants revenge on a world that has denied him his desires. She doesn't try to conceal the fear or even the loathing she feels. At the same time it's as though he has shorn her of all Monique Maupin's fakery and stripped her down to the naked English girl she truly is. His eyes worm over her naked thighs, her naked breasts. He must be able to see how urgently her heart beats behind her ribs. She is aware of Marcel's calm voice demanding an explanation. The man throws her her dress and demands to see her papers. The muscles in her hands pulse with the memory of breaking a human neck as she was taught how to do in training. Her hands want to break this man's neck. Once again Monique has led her to a revelation about herself as Evie. She suspects she might be capable of killing this repulsive man, given the chance. His small deep set eyes with barely any lashes are like searchlights on her face. She feels small and unbelievable and defiant all at once. He hands her back her papers with a chill of disdain. She remembers what Marcel told her. Inadvertently finds herself swimming up into her eyes as herself, Evie Devereux, British parachutist.

While the two men search the apartment she thinks of all the people whose fatal secrets she might betray if she can't stand up to torture. Kindly Monsieur and Madame Pellon who have the weapons stored in their barn. Monsieur Filou whose son died fighting the Germans and whose wife drowned herself on hearing the news. Most of all she thinks of Leopold and his mother. The floor seems to sway beneath her feet, as if she has just stepped off a merry-go-round. It's then she feels the ghostly imprint of her father's hands on the back of her neck. At first she fears the sudden proximity of her father's ghost will bring tears. But instead, it fortifies her resolve. The floor stabilises beneath her bare feet. When one of the men goes into the bathroom she is able to not betray a whisper of emotion, to not risk a glance at Marcel.

5

She walks with Leopold through the vineyards. He walks with his hands linked at the back of his neck. His head cocked, like a crow.

"My boss is going to send me away."

He is silent. She knows when he is in the grip of emotion because the contortions of his neck become more unruly. He stops now and twists his head back at an almost impossible angle. As if he wants nothing more to do with the future.

"I shouldn't be telling you this. I shouldn't be telling you anything. But I can't help it."

He reminds her of Guy, or Jack as she has learned to call him, because of the ease with which he encourages her to speak truths about herself. The flow of intimacy he effortlessly creates. His gift of sidling up so close. He's like the son she and Jack might have had. In a different life.

"I don't want to leave." She wonders if this is true. The relief she felt when the two Gestapo agents left without arresting her is still a dizzying lightness in her being. The hug she gave the almost naked Marcel after he closed the door on them perhaps the most heartfelt gesture she has ever performed.

"I'm never going to let anyone tell me what I have to do," says Leopold. "Why should I even wash if I don't feel like washing? What difference does it make?"

"Might make you smell bad," she says.

He flinches with a pained expression when she runs a hand over his arm. The expression on his face both beseeching and hostile.

"I don't care if I smell bad. Another reason for people to look at me and pretend they're not looking at me. Anyway you must be weak. Letting someone else tell you what you have to do."

"It's the nature of life."

"I hate nature."

"You're right. I shouldn't leave. I haven't done anything wrong. Add to that, my boss is a petty and vain man."

"I suppose you think I'm petty and vain too?"

She laughs. "No. In fact I wish you were my boss. You'd do a better job than him."

"Except I'm still a child."

"So is he. In fact, the whole war is childish. It's men wanting to turn life into a childish game again."

"Is that what you'd say to Hitler if you met him?"

"I might do. Fat lot of good it would do though."

Leopold is going to draw her. He has always refused to show her his drawings. He says they are just something he does when he doesn't have anything else to do. When he's not poring over his stamp album. He is going to draw her in his and Adela's secret place. She feels honoured that he is taking her to his secret place. Beyond the vines they climb up a steep slope matted with high bramble and thorns. She is wearing short black socks, not stockings, and the thorns sting and scratch her legs.

"I had to do things like this when I was training to come out here."

"Things like what? Climb a hill."

"Survive in the wild. We had to catch rabbits and kill them with our bare hands and skin and cook them. Bathe and sleep under the stars in the middle of winter."

"I'd rather jump out of an airplane."

"Would you? It's the most terrifying thing I've ever done. It's like staring death in the face for a moment. And the most trusting thing you'll ever have to do in your life. I'm a bit like you. I don't find it easy to trust."

"If I had a father would I know more what I'm like?"

"You know yourself better than I did when I was your age."

"When your father died did you stop knowing who you are?'

"A little bit, yes."

"I bet Monique isn't even your real name."

"Who are you, the Gestapo?"

"Would they torture you if they caught you?"

"They won't catch me."

"They might do. They might be following us now."

She swivels round and, shielding her eyes from the sun, gazes out at the peaceful landscape. The field of sunflowers they walked through earlier would now fit on the palm of her hand.

He slips near the top and allows her to pull him up by the hand. They stand side by side high on the ridge of a ravine. The riverbed is almost dry. Huge polished stones reflect the sun's glitter back up into the air.

His secret place is a cave by the dry riverbed. She sits on a polished white boulder at the entrance. While he draws her with a pencil stub. His tongue darts out continually as he draws. His mouth hanging open. She decides she will ask Marcel to send a message to London. Giving her side of the story. She will not leave Leopold just because of the hurt vanity of another bullying man.

"Can I see?"

"Okay."

"That's absolutely brilliant, Leopold."

He screens his pleasure. Makes every effort to hide it.

"I've got drawings of Adela if you want to see."

"Yes please."

There are dozens of pencil sketches of a pretty young girl in various poses. In all of them her eyes are averted, in all of them she looks like she is about to slip away.

"These are fabulous, Leo. Did Adela like them?"

"I guess so."

"I wish I could hear what you talked about together."

"Why?"

"Because I can tell from these drawings you shared a beautiful friendship. Did you tell each other all your secrets?"

"Sometimes. Who do you share your secrets with?"

"I'm not allowed to share them with anyone. Perhaps though, even before the war, I was never brave enough to share my secrets with anyone."

"It isn't brave to share secrets."

"Oh yes it is. It's one of the bravest things a person can do. I bet Adela has taken a lot of courage from you and that courage will help her wherever she is now." She thinks that were she granted one wish at this moment it would be to return Adela to Leopold. Her hatred of the Germans and all the collaborating French population receives a fresh supply of kindling. Then an explosion echoes along the ravine. For the first time she notices two birds of prey circling up in the cerulean blue sky. Before long, the sound of men shouting reaches them. Accompanied by what she now recognises as gunshots.

"It's a boar hunt," says Leopold. "Look, the men have goaded the boar into a corner."

She can just make out the cowering animal further along the ravine, beneath the high bridge. A group of men carrying guns are throwing stones at it. The stones tear red smudges from its dark fur. Repeatedly, it charges only to be struck and knocked off balance by another large stone.

6

Bruno is holding the jar with the snake inside when they arrive back in the enclosed courtyard of the farmhouse. The black serpent with its staring slit yellow eyes, arrested in the act of baring its fangs.

"What's its name?" he asks Leopold, tapping on the jar.

"Why does everything have to have a name?"

"Good point. I keep expecting it to come back to life. To finish what it was on the verge of doing."

"It won't ever do that because it's dead."

"I hear you're a master chess player. I'll give you a game one of these days."

"If you want."

"What's that you're holding?"

"A drawing Leopold did of me."

"Can I see?"

She holds it up.

"Good job the *Milice* don't know how good you are at getting a likeness. They'd hire you in a jiffy."

Bruno replaces the jar with the snake inside on the shelf, takes her hand and ushers her out of hearing of Leopold, towards the solitary fig tree in the courtyard.

"Xan has been arrested. I saw him chatting to two men outside the Café des Amis. I was about to attract his attention when I sensed something was wrong. Maybe it was a fluke. A spot check. Perhaps they don't even know who he is."

She feels guilty for every bad thing she has ever thought and said about him.

"Even so…"

"Even so, what?"

"Precautions."

"We're not going to Orange tomorrow?"

"We're still going to Orange tomorrow. But you've got off lightly. You only have to carry one suitcase of high explosives. Xan wanted us to take two each. But that would make us look like a shifty pair of black marketers. We'll catch an earlier train. And we'll get off before Orange. If Xan talks they'll probably take him to the station to identify us. Hopefully they'll be waiting for us when we've already left. How did he seem yesterday when you saw him?"

She has been looking forward to recounting Xan's self-righteous tirade ever since leaving him. *"Look, I'm in charge here. I decide who I do and do not talk to. Just because you come from some high and mighty family…Hundreds of people's lives depend on me. Do you understand that? This isn't a game. When I give you an order I expect you to obey it. Discipline and security have to be maintained. I felt like having you arrested. You're lucky I didn't. You have Bruno to thank that I didn't. You carry out this mission with the explosives the day after tomorrow and then that's it. That's my final word."*

"He said he wanted to have me arrested," she says, no longer able to send him up.

"I know. He's flipped his lid a bit. Hell hath no fury like a man scorned."

"Who told you?"

"Who do you think? Marcel can't keep a secret for more than ten minutes. Sometimes leads you to think he might have chosen the wrong profession. I have to say I felt rather geed up by this news. At least it isn't only my advances you swat away like a feeding insect. Anyway, I've told Marcel to clear out and I think you should leave this house. I've already left mine. Which is why I've come. Tonight you'll be staying with me in my new home."

"What about Leopold and his mother?"

"You should warn them too."

"She won't leave here. This is their home."

"Then let's hope Xan is thick skinned."

While Bruno waits on his bicycle in the courtyard she takes Leopold's mother aside. Runs through the story she wants Leopold's mother to tell. It doesn't sound very convincing. They both know this as they look across at each other over the kitchen table.

She can't find Leopold anywhere. He is hiding from her. Instead one of the dogs follows her out into the courtyard. A big shaggy beast with doleful eyes. She leans down to stroke its dirty black and white fur. There is a look in its eye that makes her not want to leave. She looks back, up at Leopold's window above the solitary fig tree in the courtyard. She looks at the snake in the jar on the shelf outside the gatekeeper's hut. She looks at her watch. An hour and a half until curfew.

"Ready," she says to Bruno, mounting her bicycle.

7

She enters Clermont-Ferrand station two minutes after Bruno. Wristwatches synchronised. Eyes peeled for Xan. She is carrying a suitcase full of explosives. Boxed explosives fitted with magnets. The weight of the suitcase jars the joints in her shoulder. She has to feign ease and nonchalance. She carries the suitcase past a cluster of SS soldiers. They are laughing. Only they enjoy attracting attention to themselves. Everyone else makes themselves as insignificant as possible. As if they are ashamed, either of themselves or of each other. One of the soldiers tries to catch her eye. Again it is a wonder she is not more frightened. To not be frightened she has to forbid herself imagination. She has to hide crouched down in a small sealed part of her mind. She runs through today's story. The mundane reason why Monique Maupin is catching a train from Clermont-Ferrand to Orange. She can see Bruno on the platform. Through a shroud of smoke. She is to follow him onto the train but give no indication of knowing him.

When she climbs aboard the train Bruno is standing in the corridor. She enters the carriage outside which he stands. There is one free seat. Opposite a woman with two small children. She smiles but the woman does not smile back. These little mysterious snubs that can be so disheartening. She heaves the suitcase with difficulty up onto the string reticule of the luggage rack. Neither of the men in the compartment helps her. She pushes it into place beside Bruno's suitcase. She is about to leave the compartment when a man offers her his seat. This act of generosity throws her. She knows she shouldn't stay in the compartment with the suitcases but can think of no reason why she would refuse the offer of a seat.

Often during the journey she looks at the reflection on the greasy glass of the long window of the train compartment. It's like another world, that reflection. As if she might see herself there suddenly perform a gesture she would never do as herself.

The train is approaching Lyon station where they have to change trains when the two Gestapo agents appear in the corridor. She pretends not to watch as they study Bruno's papers. Bruno's impassivity is impressive. He appears perfectly relaxed while the man in the fedora hat interrogates him. The woman opposite catches her eye. Evie does not smile this time.

The two Gestapo agents enter the carriage. Not even towards the children do they show any sympathy. One of them brandishes a bronze badge at nobody in particular. Hat pulled down over his left eye. Double-breasted grey suit. The sight of the swastika makes her want to curl up her hand into a fist. Dig her nails into her palm. Her palm with its long lifeline, its coded map of her fate. She stifles an urge to yawn, to sigh, to take a deeper breath. Knowing they have been trained to watch out for every sign of discomfort. She empties her mind while they question the man next to her.

"Papers."

She looks up. At the bored expression in his eyes. He asks her questions. She tells her fictitious story. Aware of some strands of loose hair at the nape of her neck.

"Who do these suitcases belong to?"

"That parcel is mine," says the man next to her.

"Open it please. What about these two?"

No one answers.

The woman opposite looks at her. She waits for the woman opposite to tell the Gestapo man one of the suitcases is hers. But the woman says nothing.

"Who do these suitcases belong to? You, answer me." The

German grabs hold of the tie of the man sitting next to her and yanks at it.

The man points at Bruno. She expects him to point at her too. But he doesn't. Instead his shame fills the carriage like a sour smell.

"These are yours?"

"I've never seen them before in my life," says Bruno.

His smile is a mistake, she thinks. It's the most unconvincing lie he has ever told.

"Open them."

She looks at Bruno. He is making the decision whether or not to shoot the two men. It's as if he has spoken the thought aloud so sure is she that this is what is going through his mind. If he shoots the two Gestapo agents they will have to jump off the moving train. *Don't think of contact with the ground as the end of the event; continue your fall as you hit the ground. This goes for jumping out of high windows and moving trains too.*

But Bruno doesn't draw his weapon. He doesn't draw his weapon because of the two children. She wants to scream at him. *Shoot them. Kill these diseased men. The children won't be hurt.*

Bruno balances his way into the carriage, ignoring her. For the first time she can remember there is no trace of a smile in his eyes, no mischief latent on the line of his lips. There is tension around Bruno's mouth now. He no longer looks impassive. He squeezes past the man unwrapping his brown paper parcel.

Surely he's not going to casually just open the cases.

She realises there is nothing she can do except wait for this situation to play itself out. All the training, the unarmed combat classes, the mock attacks on dummy foe, the guns fired, the knives bloodied and there is nothing she can do.

Bruno reaches up to the rack. His shirt comes loose from his trousers as he stretches up his arms and she sees a wisp of hair on his pot belly above his belt. It is her suitcase he hauls down. Inside, covering the detonators and explosives, are a change of underclothes, a nightdress and a pair of stockings.

Bruno holds the suitcase in both hands. There is no room in the compartment to open it. He mentions this to the agent. There is a wobble in his voice, like a loose tooth.

Why has he chosen my suitcase?

"You, Madame, leave the compartment with your children."

The situation acquires an element of farce as the woman gets to her feet and there is not enough room in the compartment for anyone to manoeuvre. The situation acquires an element of farce but the Gestapo agents show no hint of a smile. This is when Bruno acts. He brings his knee up hard between the Gestapo agent's legs. Pulls down the window and flings the suitcase out. All in one continuous fluid motion. Someone steps down hard on her foot in all the pushing and shoving that follows. The second agent has his pistol drawn. He barks something to his colleague in German. His colleague is still bent double, wheezing. Bruno is led out of the compartment. A third agent returns to the compartment. He pulls down the other suitcase.

"Did you know that man?" he asks Evie.

"No," she says. The necessity of disassociating herself from Bruno wants to make her feel the shame of the traitor.

"What about you?" he asks the man sitting next to her.

She is alone in a strange town. All around an atmosphere of purpose, of revived spirits as people head home or to restaurants for lunch. But her spirits are not revived. She is still in shock. Her heart still aching for Bruno. The sacrifice he made to save her. And she can do nothing to help him. She keeps replaying the sequence of events that led to Bruno's arrest. It is like an ache in her body that won't go away. *The Gestapo got lucky*, she tells herself. *If they were looking for us they would have arrested me too.* But it's as if there is something she needs to know that her memory will not yield up. So she keeps replaying the moment of Bruno's arrest.

In a narrow street smelling of stale perfume and cigarette smoke the scrabbling of a pigeon on roof tiles overhead is like the noise of the thoughts in her head. She feels the proximity of tears. For a moment she loses all contact with her bogus French identity. Were someone to speak to her she feels she would have no choice but to reply in English, hold up her hands as Evie.

Her instinct is to not keep the appointment in the church of Saint Florent where the contact is supposed to meet her and Bruno to collect the explosives. Even though she knows she ought to warn him of Bruno's arrest. Even though otherwise she is adrift in this unknown town with nowhere to go, nowhere safe to hide.

Go back to Clermont-Ferrand.

But isn't it craven of me not to warn him?

If Bruno or Xan have talked it will be too late to warn him. Just means you'll be arrested too.

The argument goes on in her head as she walks the streets of the strange town, avoiding eye contact, straining to draw a cloak of invisibility around herself. Everyone looks like an informer today. Everyone looks capable of treachery. There are many Germans too. In cars, in lorries, strolling about the streets. The argument goes on in her head. Making her look, no doubt, suspiciously preoccupied.

Everybody looks preoccupied.

As she is crossing a bridge her attention is held by the sight of a hunchbacked fisherman on the bank below. She is transfixed by the tense quivering arc of the fishing line and the agitated smudge of living gold just beneath the cloudy surface of the water. The fisherman might be battling with some leviathan so arduous is his struggle. Finally he tugs the fish on the line over the stones onto the grassy verge and leaves it there to thrash about. For a while there is a tremendous death-defying fury in the fish as it slithers about on the grass. The fisherman, like a Roman gladiator playing to his audience, flashes a triumphant smile up at the small crowd that has now gathered on the bridge to watch him. He unhooks the fish, wraps it in a dirty newspaper and again looks up at the crowd. There is now a breathless hush. Evie finds herself silently urging the man to throw the fish back into the water. She is thinking of Bruno. The fate of the fish and the fate of Bruno have become superstitiously linked in her mind. She knows a moment of relief when the restoration of the fish to its natural element is greeted by a round of applause and the hunchback fisherman takes a bow.

The appointment isn't until three. When she looks at her watch only three minutes have passed since she last looked. So she has to kill more time. Feeling more and more conspicuous in her aimless wandering. She walks over chalked hopscotch marks on the pavement. Never has her childhood felt so far away. She walks up to the park above the Roman amphitheatre. Away from the men in uniforms. Away from prying eyes. It starts to rain. It rains heavily. She takes shelter under a tree. The rain slides down through the canopy of leaves. Drops slide down beneath her collar. The ground by her feet softens into mud. Mud squelches up over her shoes every time she moves.

She is soaked through when she walks back down into the town. Bedraggled. Like a mad woman.

If they have a description of me they probably wouldn't recognise me, the state I'm in.

She decides she will enter the square ten minutes early.

It has stopped raining. The façade of the church of St Florent is at the far end of the square. There are a dozen or so people milling about. The old women draped entirely in black as if every day is a funeral. But there is a man she does not like the look of. He is standing in the middle of the square. Wearing sunglasses. Smoking a cigarette. She registers him without directly looking at him. She will not enter the church. But she will have to cross the square now. Have to cross paths with this man she does not like the look of. She ruffles up her wet hair. Rubs away some moisture. Pretending her wet hair is her only concern.

Don't do that! Don't show any signs of agitation!

The rebuke brings a flush to her face. Just as she is walking past the man she fears. He is wearing a double-breasted grey suit and a new hat. She looks down at some pigeons. She looks down at the mud on her shoes. She does not look at the man. She does not look at the door of the church. She has to discipline herself not to increase her pace. Her heartbeat is urging her to run. Urging her to look back over her shoulder. To see if the man she doesn't like the look of is following her.

She enters a narrow street with some shops. She seeks out every reflecting surface as she walks. Once or twice catches a spectral representation of the street behind her. A ghost street in a ghost town. It's as if she registers every rustle, every rhythm of activity behind her on the back of her neck. She stops to look at the window of a jeweller's. She can see very little of the street in the reflection on the misted glass. A ghostly haunted woman stares back at her.

She passes a brown door with a Jewish star painted on it in white paint that has dripped. She turns and looks behind her down the street. There is no sign of the man in the double-breasted grey suit.

When she arrives back at the station she has to show her papers to two French *miliciens*. The one who studies her face looks like a criminal with his broken nose and close-cropped hair. It is another effort not to reciprocate his disdain. There isn't a train to Clermont-Ferrand for two hours. She goes to the buffet. Eats a sandwich at a stained and greasy table. She is exhausted.

The train bumps and creaks. It passes flowering lavender fields. The only good thing to happen today. She didn't notice them on the outward journey. She falls asleep. The shrill whistle of the train wakes her with a start. But there are no men in rain-coats in the compartment.

At Clermont-Ferrand station the thought of seeing Leopold cheers her up. She imagines him laughing at the sight of her. The mud on her shoes, her matted hair. She will find it funny too, through his eyes. She walks down the platform behind four Wehrmacht soldiers. They arouse no emotion in her. Then it happens. The most surreal moment of her life. All the weights in her body dissolve. Her mouth falls open. Her hands become fists. Her eyes stare. Trying to make what she sees disappear. Reveal itself as the hallucination it surely must be. Pinned to a board is a photographed copy of Leopold's drawing of her. Ugly script and an official stamp beneath the delicate pencil strokes of her chin. It says a reward of 700,000 francs is offered for any information leading to her arrest.

There is a snap control at the exit. She turns on her heels. She takes a few deep breaths. She wills herself to think clearly. She will have to get on another train. Get off at a small station where there is unlikely to be any controls. Yes, she will get on another train. And get off it as soon as possible.

Xan must have talked.

For a moment she feels indignant. Slanders him as a spineless man. Until it dawns on her what he might be going through.

Anyway, how do you know it wasn't Bruno?

It wasn't Bruno.

She thinks she will not be able to bear it if Leopold has been arrested. She can't keep any of her men safe. Her father dead. Jack dead. Bruno captured. And now Leopold…Please not Leopold.

9

Silence interceptions in progress. The lighted sign behind her head in the Ops Room. She thinks of it now because she has a sense of interceptions in progress all around her. In the darkness. In the undergrowth.

Curfew is in place. She feels safer with curfew in place. Curfew lends clarity to everything. Leaves her alone with the enemy. She has to be as stealthy and silent as any hunted night creature.

She traipses through wooded areas, across vineyards, skirts sunflower and lavender fields. A continuous thread of night sounds all around her. She imagines these sounds transmitted back to some enemy HQ. A man with headphones clamped to his ears endeavouring to decode all the rustlings and snaps and overhead flapping.

How many times she pronounces herself lost. The stars in the sky her only map. She lies down on her back. Feels the pulse of the earth between her shoulder blades and at the back of her thighs. The scent of summer in the blades of dry grass. She stares up at the marvel of the night sky. Until she feels herself dissolved up into its immunity of exile. Her eye traces the pattern of the group of seven stars. Jumping from star to star until she feels she is performing the act physically. She measures the distance between the two pointer stars with her hand. Bridging a distance of millions of miles with the length of her finger. She finds Polaris. Polaris, the freedom star. Why is Polaris called the freedom star? She is thinking back to her training. To Mr Willis and his avuncular soft-spoken counselling in the art of star navigation. She can't remember why Polaris is called the freedom star. Only that it is the North Star and that she therefore has to distance herself from it to find her way back to Compagnac.

It begins to feel like the journey of a lifetime. As if she is acquainting herself with the entire map of her being. Every contact, every sound, every glimmer seems to make contact with her naked body. The choreography of the night like the choreography of her own mind as if they are flowing into each other. She feels the night is embracing her with her own existence. Thorns and nettles bite into her bare legs. The chant of cicadas like waves that rise up over her and then let her go. In the wooded areas she is ambushed by webs. Filaments gumming themselves to her lips and eyelashes. She slides down the steep gully of the ravine. Unable to stop herself tumbling at one point. Crying out in alarm and then in laughter. Freefalling down onto the polished stones of the dry riverbed.

She creeps up on the outline of the house. No lights. A thicker mass of shadow in the great swell of darkness. Underneath the wisteria vine might be the shape of a man. The Gestapo dress to become shadows. The smooth black coats, the dark glasses and dark hats. But it is not a man. Just another of the night's shadows.

Leopold is in his room. He has built himself some kind of fort or cave. He sits beneath a sheet behind a bulwark of pillows and cushions. His shoulders stiffen and his head twists back when she peers down into the entrance of his grotto. His mouth clenched and twisted. It will be one of those times when he finds it hard to get his words out. He has surrounded himself with his "special things". She notices the speckled blue piece of an eggshell, the kingfisher feather, the seashell with its delicate smudge of otherworldly pink, his favourite conker on a string, his stamp album, his sketch book. He is holding a small piece of cloth.

"What happened, Leopold?"

"You've got blood on your legs," he says. Like an accusation.

As if she is some kind of celestial being in his mind. Not allowed to bleed.

She is indignant when he tells her they have taken his mother, his uncle and aunt. That they have left a child alone with a sick grandmother. A woman who doesn't even know there is a war in progress.

"Where did you get that?" she asks, noticing the yellow star on the piece of cloth he holds.

"It was Adela's. I tore it from her jacket."

"Why did you do that?"

"She said it made her feel dirty. She wouldn't see me for a week after she was made to wear it. She wouldn't leave her house."

"So you tore it off?"

"Yes."

"You ought to get rid of it. It's dangerous for you to keep that."

"I don't want to get rid of it."

"Because it reminds you of her?" As her heart goes out to him she also thinks of Jack asking for and treasuring her slip.

"I wish you had something less ghoulish to remind you of her," she says. "Let's make some onion soup."

"Okay."

It is three o'clock in the morning. She senses there is a part of him that is enjoying this. The removal of his family. The sweeping clean of old tracks. The exhilaration of breaking from the past.

The dog follows them both down to the kitchen.

"You tried to warn me, didn't you?" she says to it, stroking its matted fur.

His mother's apron is neatly folded over the back of a chair.

"Your drawing of me is pasted up at the train station."

"It wasn't my fault. They took it."

"I didn't mean it was your fault. We have to think now what we're going to do."

"You can stay here."

"They're looking for me. They'll be back."

"We could hide in the cave."

"I've got to give myself up. Then they'll let your mother and your family go."

"They don't let people go. They didn't let Adela go and she's just a little girl."

"It's a chance I'll have to take."

"But you don't think about me."

"That's not true. It's you I'm thinking of most of all."

She cuts her finger while slicing an onion. She knew this was going to happen a moment before it happened. The foreknowledge like a slight surplus weight in her body. She looks at the bubble of blood as if it contains a ciphered message. Still holding the knife with the smear of bright blood on the blade.

"After dinner you can help me dig up treasure."

Leopold screens his curiosity.

"You shouldn't always pretend nothing interests you."

"You pretend."

"That's different."

She carries him out of the house on her shoulders. He knocks his head against a doorframe. Pretends it doesn't hurt even though she knows from the violence of the crack that it must hurt. "Did you know this house has seven doors that lead out into the open? Like the Plough has seven stars." She is holding a trowel and a candle. She crouches down on the grass. So he can climb off her shoulders.

"That's the Plough up there," she says pointing up at the sky. "It helped me find my way back to you in the dark."

She watches him twist his neck, tilt his head up at the sky. Wonders if he will remember this moment sometime in the future. The future that seems much more remote than the past.

She throws him the matches and tells him to light the candle. She paces out seven steps to the south from the fig tree. The flame from the candle throws an elongated and grotesque shadow of her body across the grass.

"This is where I buried it."

"Buried what?"

"My box of secrets. You have a box of secrets. Everyone has a box of secrets."

The intimate smell of newly turned earth. One of the earliest of all memories. The flame shows up wood shavings and seed husks among the grass. And then the scramble of alarmed insects as she gouges into the earth. The insects that eat the flesh of the dead. Inside the rusted tin is the list of contact addresses Xan gave to her when she first arrived. Her revolver. The cyanide pill. It is this she wants. She will sow it into her knickers. Surely they will not inspect the inside of her knickers. But she sees it happening. Herself naked while a faceless man sitting at a desk probes with his hands inside the white fabric. She doesn't notice Leopold has taken the revolver. Is examining it. The gunshot is first a bright flash in the air and then a tunnelling ricocheting noise. There is what sounds like a cymbal crash of alarm as birds take to the air all around. Leopold fires the gun again. His grandmother begins screaming. From behind the closed shutters above. He fires it a third time. Running and laughing.

"Put the gun down, Leopold!"

The echo of the gunshots hasn't yet died down when she hears the sound of a car creeping slowly over gravel.

She replaces the box of secrets in the hole in the ground. Claws earth over it. She is still on her knees when the four men appear. Appear in the light of the candle. Two in the uniform of the *Milice* and two of the shadow men.

Leopold is still holding the gun.

PART FOUR

1940

1

Jack sees the white cliffs and the green, gold and umber pastures of England broken up into misted flattened vignettes. Down below through breaks in the thickening surf of cloud. The sky is darkening. Visibility decreasing by the minute. The sweat is drying out in his hair and on his back after yet another dogfight with German fighters. The third of the day. The diving and the looping and the tight banking. Hanging upside down in his straps. The entire weight of his body falling on his shoulder harness. His head knocking against the hood of the cockpit. Grit in his eyes. Muck in his mouth. Blood thickening and thinning and aching in his veins. Shouting abuse at his foes. Thanking God when he loses them.

Images of the shot up convoy are still before his eyes. The sinking trawler vomiting out black smoke. The tiny heads in the blackened water. With their matchstick arms raised in supplication. The sheet of flame on the water. The sea burning. By the time he and Charlie and Benedict arrived in B Flight the bombers had disappeared.

He lands through the rising mist and drizzle back at the aerodrome. Stan and Ed, in shiny sou'westers today, waiting to greet him.

"Let's hope that's the last sortie for the day, sir."

"Let's hope so." He pats the wing of his Spitfire. It is now one of the oldest surviving aircraft in the squadron. Every morning he expects at the very least to have to bail out later in the day, every evening he returns his kite more or less intact.

"Any luck?" asks the intelligence officer with his clipboard and pencil.

"Still a virgin," he says. He looks past the intelligence officer. Sees Benedict in the armchair inside the hut and immediately feels much better.

"Did you see anyone go down? We're missing Tom and Angus."

Jack recounts what he saw, though what he saw is now mostly a blur except for the sinking trawler and the tiny heads with outstretched arms in the black burning water.

No one has any kills to report. But the three new pilots are flushed and radiant with relief, with a triumphant sense of accomplishment. They have survived their first sortie. Hugo, Harry and George.

Harry says, "Remind me again. How much do we get paid for this?"

"Eight shillings a day."

Hugo says, "Didn't you squirt me at one point?"

Harry answers, "Bugger. I was hoping you hadn't noticed. Didn't do it purpose, old boy."

"Well that's a relief because I thought we were friends. I thought we were the best of friends."

"It's so damn chaotic up there. Wings flashing to left and right, above you, below you, behind you, in front of you. It's like life is speeded up to 500 miles per hour. But then a minute can seem like a whole day."

"You need to remember the ten commandments," says Charlie.

He must be worried about Tom, him and Tom are as close as Benedict and me, but he's bloody good at not showing it.

"Thou shalt not kill. I know that one. But they'd rip off my wings if I obeyed it," says Hugo.

"Not God's ten commandments."

"Whose then?"

"Can't remember his name. Don't fire until you see the whites of his eyes. That's one of 'em."

"What are the others?"

"Benedict?"

"When in the combat zone shut your eyes and sing rousing hymns to yourself at the top of your voice."

"Ignore everything they taught you about formation attacks."

"That one's true."

The shrill of the telephone brings with it an immediate tense silence.

"Hello Tom," says the orderly.

Everyone relaxes. He and Charlie exchange a wide smile. Charlie moves closer to the orderly's desk. Eavesdropping on the conversation. The orderly says, "I see" several times.

"Tom's okay. He bailed out. But he was peppered by the home guard on the way down. Five of 'em standing in a field taking pot shots at him."

"And?" says Charlie.

"Flesh wound in left buttock. Nothing serious."

"Except the clowns were probably aiming for his head."

"Three more cheers for the fucking home guard," says Charlie. "If we lose, lose the skies, we're fucked, aren't we? Doesn't anyone give these fools lessons in who the enemy are? Know thy enemy. Better advice than know thyself. Get to know yourself after you've worked out who the bloody enemy is."

That evening he and Benedict cycle together to the pub. He feigns nonchalance when he walks in but his blood is up until he ascertains that Evie is not there. Everyone else seems to be there. Even Angus is there. A few raw scratches on his face. Earlier Angus was forced to crash-land in a field near Beachy Head.

"Don't think Herr Fuckface Hitler will be invading tomorrow. Weather's too shit."

"Language, Charlie. There are ladies present," says Jimbo.

"Let's drink to the rain. To rain and fog and sleet and snow."

"To thunderstones, and hailstorms and blizzards and gale force winds."

"It's true. Our greatest ally might turn out to be the weather. England's shit summer weather."

"Ladies present."

"Which is God's work. And God's on our side."

"At the moment he is. Lots of cloud covering and the Hun tactics don't work."

"What are their tactics?"

"What's your name again?"

"Kath. I'm offended you don't remember. What's your name anyway?"

"Pilot officer Charles Wilson. Got any lipstick?"

"Why?"

Harry and Hugo have both fallen asleep. Heads slumped back in their chairs.

"I'll do you a diagram. Of Hun tactics."

"Do it without a diagram. I'm not wasting my lipstick."

"No lipstick, no Hun tactics."

"Let George explain. He likes explaining things."

"Do I?" says George without taking the pipe from his mouth. "Today was the first time I've been called into action. Not sure I'm qualified to explain."

"All the more reason for you to understand the tactical brain you're up against."

"Well, on today's evidence, the bombers keep to a very tight formation. Rather impressive actually. The discipline of it. And this maximises the crossfire of their guns when you try to get in amongst them. Meanwhile the fighters hover above using the bombers as bait. So we attack the bombers and the fighters come swooping down on our tails. Which gives them the advantage.

Because height is key. Height puts you in the driving seat. The higher you are the bigger advantage you have…"

"There you go," says Charlie slapping him on the shoulder. "That's another one of the ten commandments. Height is key. Except you've always got to come down at some point if you're going to fight and there are always more of the blighters up there higher than you waiting to pounce."

"I suppose the thing is, the Germans only have fighters to contend with whereas we have both fighters and bombers. Today we were outnumbered about ten to one. Actually I thought the bombers would be easier prey. But those gunners don't mess around."

"You haven't explained to Kath here why the shit weather might turn out to be our greatest ally."

The door of the pub opens again. But it is not Evie who enters.

"Oh, that's simple. If there's thick cloud cover the German fighters won't be able to see their bombers. They'll be isolated from the fight."

"I've just remembered another of the ten commandments. Follow through every decision you make even if it's the wrong decision. If you get caught in two minds you're done for."

"I want your opinion on something," says Kath, leaning forward on the table with her hands clasped beneath her chin. "All of you."

"You'll have to wake these two up then."

"I'm Jewish."

"So what? We're not bloody Nazis."

"I bought two eggs today. At the farm down the road. The woman wrapped them in the pages of an old newspaper. Here it is. *The Evening Standard.*" She smoothes out the creases of the newspaper page on the table. The headline says, Hitler's Gestapo employing Jews for spying on England.

"Highly unlikely," says George.

"More than highly unlikely given what the Nazis think of Jews. I think the editor of *The Evening Standard* ought to be arrested. A friend of my brother's was arrested for saying we don't have a chance in hell of beating the Germans. He's been put in prison for three months. Anyway, I'm Jewish and I think the editor of *The Evening Standard* should be arrested."

"Mind if I sit down here?" says Angus.

"Go ahead," says Jack. He hides his stupefaction. He looks at the knot in Angus' tie. As if it is nothing out of the ordinary that Angus should be civil with him. More than civil. Friendly with an undercurrent of remorseful humility. He hasn't been paying much attention to anything since Benedict went off to play the piano. And now here is Angus sitting down beside him. In his exhausted state he has a sense of half dreaming it.

"Thought my number was up today," says Angus. "Had three of the bastards after me. Wily old devils stuck to me like glue. Just couldn't shake them off. I was waiting for the sledgehammer blow. Then it came. Stick limp. Oil temperature shooting up off the clock. Glycol streaming out all over the windscreen. I dived for the ground, pretending to be in a spin. Levelled out at about a thousand feet. Couldn't get the damn hood up. Then couldn't find anywhere to put the thing down. Every field in southern England has bloody posts erected all over it. Or else it's littered with concrete blocks and old bits of machinery. I know the idea is to make it difficult for the Germans to land troop gliders but what about us poor buggers? You need to make an emergency landing and you can't."

"And if you bail out you get shot at."

"I'd loved to have seen what Tom said to those home guard buffoons." Angus smiles, seeking a smile in return. He then takes a sip of his beer. "Charlie's right about needing to know who your enemy is. I apologise for being so bloody to you, Guy. Can't really explain it. I see now you're a decent chap. You're also a damn good pilot."

"So are you."

"Friends?"

"Friends," he says. He can't look at Angus because he has the feeling he will cry if he does.

The door of the pub opens again. But it is not her. It is Archie. He shouts out, "The sky's still stuffed full of beautiful unbroken grey cumulous clouds. Not a single star visible anywhere."

"Maybe we'll get a day off tomorrow?" says Angus.

"Maybe."

The familiar groan of the iron springs as he shifts position in bed, plumps up his black and white striped pillow. Once again he takes in the details of this room – the crack in the plaster above his head, the photographs and postcards on the wall above Benedict's bed, his father's two drawings above his own bed, the washbasin, the two tin helmets hanging from hooks by the door. All things that will remain after he has gone.

"Couldn't get drunk tonight," says Benedict from his bed below the window. The glow from his bedside lamp holds him in a kind of halo. He picks up his copy of *Mrs Dalloway*. "What were you and Angus plotting?"

"He apologised to me."

"'Bout time."

"He was nice. Really immensely likeable."

"Spooked out?"

"Me?"

"Him."

"A bit spooked out."

"His number is up. I can sense it."

"You think?"

"Don't you?"

"Maybe."

"One o'clock."

"Three hours sleep."

"A couple of pages of *Mrs Dalloway*?"

"Of course. Mrs Dalloway is our guardian angel."

2

"Thought they might take a day off today, sir. Weather as it is."

The heavy dew on the ground. The mist shrouding the trees. Drizzle in the air. Haze all the way up to the low cloud covering. The sun still not up.

Please don't rain tonight.

"What I wouldn't give to go back to bed," he says. He climbs up onto the wing of his Spitfire. Settles himself in her cockpit. She welcomes him with her familiar smell.

"Why do you think the Boche has been sent over this early in the morning?"

He has a date with Evie later. If only he can survive the day.

"Guess that's what I'm about to find out."

Visibility is less than a mile beneath the cloud base at around 700 feet. Every so often he loses sight of Benedict in swirls of stratus. Benedict who is formatted the other side of Charlie. His aircraft doesn't like this weather any more than he does. Bucks and sways in the turbulence. He has to keep two hands on the stick, then wipe his windscreen. But the rain spattering and misting the perspex diminishes what he is able to see. He has a date with Evie later. If only he can survive the day. If only it doesn't rain tonight. Over the R/T he has learned they are in pursuit of only one enemy aircraft. This news brings some relief. If this were it for the day he might be wholeheartedly relieved. But he knows this won't be it for the day. So it also brings indignation. That they have been sent out in this weather at the crack of dawn to intercept a single enemy aircraft. Probably a reconnaissance plane sent to evaluate the weather conditions. *Would be better to let the damn thing return home and tell Goering the weather conditions are shit.*

The weather conditions are not shit though. By eleven o'clock there are drifts of blue among the clouds.

At least we might be able to have our picnic tonight.

When he's back on the ground again it is the Jewish girl Kath who serves him his tea from the NAAFI van.

At eleven thirty he is scrambled again.

"Dover," he tells Stan and Ed.

"The whole squadron," says Stan, nodding towards all the activity on the grass around the dispersal hut. "Must be something big. I have a feeling you'll get something today, sir."

Evie. Hopefully I'll get Evie.

He climbs in a spiral. Sticking close to Charlie. He doesn't enjoy formation flying when there are enemy aircraft in the vicinity. Too much of his attention is demanded by the constant throttle adjustments necessary to hold position. Making him a much more attractive target for an ambush. Charlie doesn't like these tactics either. Says they should copy the German fighters who fly in pairs or are much more spread out. The controller gives further instructions. Fifty plus including many fighters. "You're very close now." He wishes them good luck.

He is hunched forward. His face set tight with concentration. His eyeballs bulging with what he feels must be comic intensity. Like the frightened heroine in a pantomime. They have been ordered up to 18,000 feet by the controller. They have been told to ignore the fighters. To go for the bombers. Easier said than done.

"There they are. Dorniers down below. Snappers up ahead."

There they are. Flank upon flank of black birds of prey bristling with evil intent in herringbone formation. Spread out above and below. Unmolested. They look like the end of the world.

He switches his gun button to fire. Tightens his straps.

Mentally reminds himself what exactly a Dornier DO 17's capabilities are. Three gunners to worry about. Upper rear, lower rear, turret. No armoured plating in the rear of the two engines. He swallows hard.

Now he has to keep his eyes focused on two places at once. Above and below. He looks across at Benedict. It's a wonder how much courage he derives from the simple sight of his friend. Even when his face is half concealed behind the oxygen mask and flaps.

"For Mrs Dalloway," he says into his microphone.

"For Mrs Dalloway," he hears Benedict say through the hiss and static in his earpiece.

"Whoever the hell she might be," says Charlie. "I'm going to imagine that fat slug down there wants to drop his bombs on my gran. Tally-ho! Tally-ho!"

Charlie peels away banking to port. Jack follows. Out of the corner of his eye he sees the ME 109s come swooping down from a couple of thousand feet above.

He has chosen his target, his method of attack. *Upon this battle depends the survival of Christian civilisation.* He will creep down astern of the bomber, slide into its shadow, firing his guns at its port engine. He has chosen his escape route. He doesn't need to think about any of these things. Of known things. It is the unknown, the unexpected he must be beware of. It is the unknown that can stop him from meeting Evie tonight. It strikes him that at any given moment the unknown is a far more pervasive presence than the known, even if it can't be seen. His eyes dart back and forth between the widening fuselage of the Dornier and his gun sights. His thumb twitching on the fire button. White smoke streams out from the port engine of the bomber Charlie is attacking. He now fires a short burst at his target. The hiss of pneumatics, the smell of cordite that gives him a mainline lift. A bolstering of aggression. White tracer flickers over his cockpit hood, trailing streamers of fire. He worries for a split second he is going to ram into the suddenly enormous

German bomber. As he passes beneath, into the haze of vapour trails and tracer smoke, something falls from the German aircraft. It is a man. A blonde man in a sky-blue flying suit. His parachute gets caught on Jack's starboard wing. Tilting it down towards the ground. For a moment he and the German hanging beneath his wing exchange eye contact. He is just a boy of about nineteen, twenty. He has never seen anyone look so terrified in his life. Then the parachute slides away and his Spitfire straightens up and he digs his chin into his shoulder to see what's going on below. What happens to the terrified young German boy.

Why did he bail out? There was no need to bail out. He must have had some kind of panic attack.

As far as his feeling is concerned the boy has somehow become his friend. He wants him to survive. So he is relieved when he sees his parachute open down below. But he is annoyed with the boy too. He has stolen some of his aggression. Infected him with his fear. He peels off sideways and downwards. Then shoots up again to prepare for another attack. Until he realises he has a ME 109 on his tail. Pumping shells at him. *Never climb when a ME 109 is on your tail.* He rolls and goes into the tightest turn he can manage. His head goes limp on his neck. His face turns grey. Or that's how it feels. Blood punches down into his legs. There is a black mist before his eyes. His head rolls on his shoulders. He twists his neck against his shoulder to obstruct the rush of blood from his head. He takes a deep breath. He sees a Spitfire turn on its back and burst into flames. He gets a glimpse of the letters before it becomes a fireball. It's George. George who likes to explain things. He escapes the attentions of the ME 109. He's down at eight hundred feet and the sky above him is a scribble of spiralling vapour trails. He's not going back up there. Not today.

At two-thirty he is sitting in a deckchair outside the dispersal hut. Neither George nor Angus has returned from the last sortie. Harry saw Angus' Spitfire burst into flames. Benedict was right, Angus knew it was coming. And it came. He is upset about

Angus. Angus, his foe. His foe who got under his skin. His foe who became his friend.

"How do you spell Luftwaffe?" asks Hugo. He is writing a letter to his girlfriend.

"V E R M I N," says Charlie.

"I wish I could hate them more."

"You will. Don't worry about that."

All hell breaks loose just after the NAAFI van arrives. Just after he has his tea and cream bun. The telephone orderly leans out of the window shouting. Ringing the bell.

He tosses away his mug of tea. The air raid siren begins its wail. The CO, running with everyone else, a comical run that aspires to the disciplined pounding of a professional sprinter that everyone secretly imitates, shouts to get all the Spits up into the air as quickly as possible. A voice over the hissing loudspeakers announces an expected raid on the airfield. "Take cover. Take cover. Stukas heading in this direction. Take cover. Take cover."

They haven't time to intercept the Stukas before they begin their attack on the airfield. Concussions of white smoke that blacken and mushroom up. Direct hit on a hangar. He remembers seeing the WAAFs folding parachutes on the tables inside earlier. Another direct hit on the ammunition dump. But he and his squadron are ready for the Stukas when they come out of their whining dive.

He thinks of Evie down there, of Stan and Ed, of Benedict's green silk dressing gown, of *Mrs Dalloway*. He can't see clearly what the bombs are hitting now. There is no word from the controller. He knows Evie is on duty in the control room.

He swoops down behind Charlie. Down at these black Nazi machines that rise up lighter now that they have dropped their bombs. Dropped their bombs on his home. The Stukas are slow cumbersome things when coming out of a dive. Easy prey. He wishes all German aircraft offered such an easy target. He is soon able to line one up in his sights. It glitters with a demonic malevolence. Swastika on its tail. The gun in the rear of its cockpit flashes. It flashes again. A stream of white smoke flashes past him. He waits. He presses his thumb down on the fire button. It is unresponsive. He has forgotten to switch it onto fire.

You bloody idiot. You bloody fucking idiot.

He switches to Fire. Presses his thumb down on the button. This time his Spitfire shudders faintly, so sensitively responsive to his every touch that she seems like another facet of his will. The most powerful and agile facet of his will. The sudden smell of cordite feeds exhilaration into his blood. He presses his thumb down on the fire button again.

Surely something hit the bastard that time.

He sweeps beneath the belly of the black beast. Its shadow vacuuming up all the light from the cockpit for a split disarming second. Fields and roads and a river and a windmill slide by under his wings. There are voices over the R/T, excited voices, but not the voice he wants to hear, not the controller's voice. He will attack from below this time. He will bring the thing down this time. He veers round in a tight turn. Charging at the Nazi war machine head on from below.

"Watch out everyone. Snappers coming down from above."

He screws his neck from side to side. His RAF issue shirt chafing his skin.

Must get a silk scarf.

"Benedict, you've got one on your tail."

3

The airfield has had its face burned off. In some parts is now a wasteland of craters. The stink of burning still persists. There are more craters in the garden outside the mess. The windows are missing glass. The grass is strewn with powdered dust and glass and pieces of paper. Uprooted flowers scattered about like broken promises. All but one of the timber-based hangers has been hit. Two are gutted. The damaged aircraft in the throes of being repaired destroyed. The station headquarters and sick quarters damaged.

Jack is still annoyed at himself for not shooting down the Stuka. The perpetrator of this carnage. For forgetting to switch his gun button to Fire. Still annoyed at himself until he notices bloodstains on the concrete outside one of the hangers. And then sees the arm. The arm reaching out from beneath the large unhinged metal door that lies flat on the ground.

"Poor thing has copped it," says an armourer he recognises. "I was this close to copping it myself."

He walks over to the arm with a sick feeling.

The operations room is still standing. Barely damaged.

He walks up close to the outstretched arm. The outstretched arm that has no body. The hand is curled up like a claw. But it is not Evie's hand.

"Her wristwatch is still working, still counting out time. Gives you the creeps a bit, don't it, sir?"

He looks down at the wristwatch. Looks down at the moving second hand.

He tells Benedict about the outstretched arm, the moving second hand back in their room that, unlike some of the other rooms, is undamaged.

"It was Kath. The Jewish girl who served us our sandwiches. In the NAAFI van."

Benedict acknowledges the sad fact with a weary sigh.

"Are you still abandoning me tonight?" Benedict asks. His face is a doodle of red scratches. His left eye bloodshot. A few splinters of his shattered windscreen have marked his flesh. He has had a narrow escape today. His Spit shot to pieces.

"'Fraid so. You've got to see the medic anyway."

"I hate medics. I hate hospitals."

But Benedict also got his first kill. One of the Stukas that bombed the airfield.

He feels a bit more alone now. He who still hasn't got a kill to his name. As if Benedict has moved on, left him behind.

He wheels his bicycle past an unoccupied gun emplacement. There is activity all around as men with shovels fill in the holes made by the bombs. The sun is low in a pale blue sky. Evie arrives at the guardhouse, in her close fitting WAAF uniform, with her bicycle. He waits while she signs herself out. Then together they cycle past the MP at the station barrier.

He has a rucksack slung over his shoulder.

"What's in the bag," she calls out as they cycle down a country lane, side by side.

"Only my hopes and dreams," he calls back. "Nothing important."

They make themselves a nest on the riverbank. She takes off her shoes. He keeps looking at her stockinged feet. The sunset colours of the sky are reflected in the water.

"We were plotting today's raid all the way from the coast," she says. "The Observer Corps telephoning in the coordinates. And then there was the moment when we all realised we were to be the target. It felt like characters in a film were suddenly stepping down from the screen into the auditorium. We all put on our tin hats and ran for it. The controller told us not to worry. That those Stukas were all mouth and no trousers. Pretty soon they had him eating his words. I remembered the drill. Face down. Hands over ears. Mouth half open. Teeth parted. My bedroom has no windows and my underwear and bed clothes are covered in splinters of glass."

He pictures her bedclothes. Pictures her underwear. Pictures himself picking out the splinters of glass. From her bedclothes. From her underwear.

"At least up in the sky we have some control over what happens."

"In your beloved Spits. A pilot once told me his Spitfire was like his ideal woman. In fact it was Angus. Poor Angus. He said he only needed to give her the slightest nudge and she would do exactly what he wanted her to do. Is that what your ideal woman is? You give her a nudge and she grants your wish."

"Give her the wrong nudge and she might burn your face off."

He watches her toes curl up inside the stockings. Strain against the material as if seeking their own nakedness.

"You men are strange creatures. Do women have an ideal man? I don't think so. I don't. It implies you have a kind of secret scorecard on the go while you're talking to a woman. Eyes six out of ten. Hair seven out of ten. How many points would you give my nose?"

He opens the bottle of wine. "Maximum points," he says. "Definitely maximum points for your nose."

And your hair and the line between your top and bottom lip and the shape of your face and your legs and the back of your neck and your hands.

Later, after they have eaten, bread and cheese and strawberries, they talk about the war again and he tells her about forgetting to switch his gun to ready.

"Had this Stuka nicely lined up in my sights. Perhaps the one that sprayed glass all over your bed. I pressed the button.

Nothing happened. It was so bloody idiotic of me. Could have cost me my life in other circumstances. Benedict got his first kill today. I still haven't hit a sausage."

"Men and their scorecards again."

"Yes. I don't like this business of individual scoring. But probably only because I'm still on zero. I'm one of about three virgins now."

It's as if some unacknowledged part of himself wants her to know he is a virgin. As an excuse for any and all the blunders he might make.

"And it bothers you?"

"No one wants to die a virgin. Initially I was terrified of being terrified. And that the other chaps would see it. That was the first obstacle to overcome. To go into combat as if it's just another part of one's day. It's clever the way we all hide our fear from each other. It's like a silent pact. There was one chap who always vomited before he reached his aircraft. You could tell he was deeply ashamed of showing his fear. He, of course, soon got the chop. The fear is natural but you mustn't show it."

"It's how we're brought up, isn't it? To not show our true feelings. I used to think I was two different people. There was the visible me and the invisible me. When people talked to me their talk seemed to go wide of the mark. Often it never touched me."

"Do you know I think you've just solved the problem? I know why I'm not hitting anything."

He enjoys the mystified look she gives him.

"Charlie gave me lots of advice to begin with. One of the things he advised me to do was never to be predictable, never to fly in straight lines, never to do perfect textbook manoeuvres. Be a bit ragged. He advised me to fly with a bit of rudder trim on – so the aircraft skids away from where she is pointed. Deflection shots from any enemy attack then tend to go wide. Trouble is I've been forgetting to adjust it when shooting, which means my shots go wide."

He turns to look at her. Reflections from the water ghost dance on her face. There is a mournful drone in the sky.

"German bombers," he says and then he yawns.

When he wakes up, startled, she is gone. Except her uniform, her stockings and shoes and wristwatch are by his side on the grass.

How long have I been asleep?

You bloody idiot. How could you fall asleep?

He looks at his watch. Nine-forty. He has been asleep for almost an hour. He can't believe he has fallen asleep. It's as if he has slept through the most important moment of his life.

She must have gone for a swim.

He looks out across the water. The silver disc of the moon sliding back and forth in the gentle current. No sign of her. He takes a fold of her skirt between finger and thumb. Picks up one of her stockings. Caresses his face with it. Inhales its musky scent. This scent is what makes life worth living.

"You've woken up then."

He drops the stocking. For a moment he can't see her. It's as if the night, the moon, the stars and the rustling water are talking to him. Then he makes out a ripple of silver on the water and the dark outline of her head.

"I'm so sorry. Hardly had any sleep this past week. Always up at four."

The mist of sheen on the water parts gently as she swims towards him. Her arms reach into the sliding glaze of the moonlight and she scatters it all about her for a moment.

"It was a kind of marvel how you suddenly weren't there with me anymore. As if a spell had been cast."

"Isn't it cold? In the water."

"It was at first. Now it's heavenly. Probably stupid of me because I'll be cold when I come out. And I haven't got a towel. But I couldn't just leave you there asleep and I began to feel a bit stupid just sitting on my own. Probably the bombs today played a part too."

"What do you mean?"

"I don't know. Stopped me from taking tomorrow for granted for the first time in my life. A week ago I wouldn't have gone swimming. But what's the point of living at all if all the time we're putting off the things we feel like doing until tomorrow? In the water I decided that from now on I'm going to live life on my skin more. And live it now."

She stands up in the water. She is wearing a slip. Her nipples urgent against the thin cloth. Water glistening on her bare legs. He takes off his tunic. Walks to meet her with it held up like a towel. She stands still, lets him rub her shoulders and hair. He kneels down in the grass and towels her legs and feet. Amazed how pliable she makes herself to his will. He is on tenterhooks, for fear she will tell him to stop. He slides his hands under her slip, over her knees, following the curve of her thighs. He presses his mouth to the inside of her thigh. The heat and musk. The scent that makes life worth living.

When they kiss the imprint of her wet body becomes a growing dark smudge on his trousers and shirt.

"I'm almost dry," she says. He smiles back. "I'll be in trouble if I don't get back," she says.

She doesn't make him turn around when she lifts off her slip. The simple grace of the gesture. She stands there before him naked.

"Can I have that?"

"My slip?"

"Yes. For luck."

"Promise you won't show it off? Like a trophy."

He nods. "This is like the extreme opposite of war. Of what I was doing earlier."

"If it wasn't for the war this wouldn't have happened…"

"I know. Praise be to Adolf Hitler."

4

The moment by the river is over forever. It will never happen again. Except as a memory. A memory he will play over and over again but that is already slipping away from him, losing texture, losing taste, losing definition. Of all the injustices of life this is the worst – that a moment so swept through with insight and thanksgiving and high tide excitement should be so brief in the overall haul of a lifetime and happen only once.

He slept with her slip on his pillow. It was there when Benedict read the next four pages of *Mrs Dalloway* before falling asleep. He told Benedict about it despite his promise because never has he been so proud of an achievement and because he doesn't want to create distance between himself and his friend by keeping any more secrets from him.

"So I woke up and she was gone. Vanished into thin air. Except her clothes were heaped beside me on the grass. She went for a swim. Stripped down to her slip. This slip."

"Crikey. So Miss Evie Devereux is a mermaid," he said. "But what are you doing with her undergarments?"

"I still can't get over how beautiful she was. Emerging from the water in the moonlight."

Now, at four in the morning, while he eats breakfast with the rest of his squadron, her slip is crumpled under his vest. Touching his skin.

It is touching his skin when Stan and Ed wish him luck and he climbs into his Spitfire. Starts her up and taxis into the wind. Full throttle now. Her thrusting energy, her trembling impatience to leap up into the air even more connected to his own capacity for excitement and wonder than usual.

Up at seven thousand feet Benedict gives him an ironic sheepish wave. It tells him everything is fine between them again.

He's a bit jealous of Evie and I was a bit jealous that he got a kill before I did and some of our affection and intimacy was missing when he read Mrs Dalloway *last night. For the first time we had something to begrudge the other for. For the first time we both felt a little betrayed by each other.*

Now his Spitfire's wings are his wings and he is soaring up into the higher reaches of sky under his own steam. Never has his mind felt so lucid. His body so wholeheartedly thankful for its existence. An alpine landscape of rolling cumulus at about ten thousand feet. The sky a dazzling blue above. The fields and villages of England drift in and out of view below. That green and pleasant land. And beyond the sea, that looks no bigger than a lake he might swim across if he chose, he can see the coast of France. Occupied France. The visual wonder of the world outside his cockpit is like an extension of his mood. It is difficult to believe that soon black shadows will appear and darken everything with menace.

He looks at the altimeter. *Turn on oxygen.* The constriction of his oxygen mask spoils his good mood a little. Makes him feel more captive. The snugness of the cockpit with its bracing smell of leather, oil and grease emits the faintest breath of claustrophobia. He has to listen to the sound of his own breathing. Goggles up on his helmet.

He follows Charlie. Flying at full speed. Climbing higher and higher. Follows Charlie eastwards. For the advantage of the sun.

"Tiger leader. This is Sapper. One hundred plus approaching Dungeness at angels twelve. Vector 140. Over."

They first appear as an ugly black etching on the pale blue transparency of the sky. The antithesis of Evie standing naked by the water. He and the squadron are not quite up-sun. Not quite high enough to surprise the enemy.

Nick orders them into a diagonal line.

"Okay Tiger Squadron. Tally-ho," says Nick, sounding almost bored.

Evie in the ops room will have heard this signal to attack. He wonders what she is feeling. If she is nervous on his behalf. This is the accolade he wants, this is his DFC. He banks and dives down after Charlie towards the black armada. Streaking down at full throttle. Losing height rapidly. Blood thumping and rushing through every artery. He glances across at Benedict. Thankful that this won't be a head-on attack. The Nazi bombers begin to acquire detail. To begin with he has no clear idea which of the countless aircraft at various heights will be his target. Then, without him consciously choosing it, one singles itself out as his prey.

Strange how the target always picks itself.

He goes after the Heinkel 111 on the outside of a formation of three. Remembers to turn his guns to ready. Remembers to adjust his rudder trim. At four hundred yards he fires off a quick burst. More for the encouragement of its bluster, the rousing hiss of the pneumatics and the bracing smell of cordite than with any hope of scoring a hit. The recoil shudders up through the seat of his pants. Imparts a purring sensation along his thighs that is almost sexual. Now he is in amongst the swarm of enemy air-craft. All flying at various heights. The attack though has shaken them out of their tight formations.

The coordination between his feet on the rudders and his hands on the stick as unthinking as walking, as breathing. He can see the hateful swastika on the 111's tail. The rear gunner opens fire. A darting red string of tracer bullets curves wide of his cockpit. Just as he is about to press the fire button the German pilot throws his stick forward and goes into a steep dive. Making for the cloud. He loses sight of him for a moment. But follows him down. His eyes now straining to take in all 360 degrees of the sky around him. He is aware of streaks of glitter above and behind. ME 109s flashing down in pursuit. The 111 is back in his reflector sight.

Aim for the starboard engine.

His thumb tense on the button. Someone screams in his ears. Awful hysterical screaming. He loses his concentration for a moment. Swept in imagination into the cockpit of the screaming pilot. Probably on fire. Who? Impossible to tell. The noises he is making are inhuman. They contain no trace of language. *Please not Benedict.* They have reached page 120 of *Mrs Dalloway*. Doesn't bear thinking about that someone else should sleep in Benedict's bed.

Concentrate, you bloody fool.

At two hundred yards he fires again. He waits. Willing some damage to appear on the enemy aircraft. He gives a shout of joy as he sees its undercarriage drop down. Vapour begins streaming out from beneath it starboard wing. He realises then that the rear gunner is shooting at him. Bullets rip into his wings. Create a jolt of shock. He ducks his head lower behind the windscreen. He can see flickers of flame now from the starboard engine of the Heinkel. He fires off another burst before overshooting and sliding underneath the 111's left wing. His windscreen is filmed in oily vapour. He glances back at the damage he has done to the iron-crossed twin-engine bomber.

He visualises his next move then is performing it unthinkingly. He pulls up. Turns over 180 degrees. Streaks up at the 111 head-on. He reckons he has no more than five seconds before he will have to yank back the stick and roll to the left to avoid collision. His thumb presses down on the button. A longer burst this time. Bits of the German cockpit fly off. More oily smoke that mists over his own windscreen. He peers into the enemy cockpit as he swings by. Not wanting to give his enemy a face but overtaken by curiosity. There is more shouting in his headphones. The 111 begins to slide earthwards. Belching out black smoke. There is a moment of elation. As if he has cleanly hit a whopping six at cricket. He has stopped one bomber from flattening a piece of England with its deadly cargo. Then he realises there are four men inside. Fighting for their lives. Four young boys. A gust of flame streaks from the 111. It slews, the nose drops and it turns over onto its back. Then it begins dropping down out of the sky. He thinks he has probably killed the pilot. He has killed another human being. Benedict told him last night that he felt depressed. "I almost feel like going to church. It's just not a nice feeling to know you have killed another human being. Four human beings in fact."

"Those bastards started it. They're dropping bombs on innocent civilians."

"I wonder if there's any such thing as an innocent civilian."

His thoughts cut short. ME 109 on his tail. He becomes aware of it in the nick of time. The bastard wants revenge. He rolls onto his back to gain acceleration. Hanging from his straps. Then he puts her into a steep diving turn. He turns and then turns again. A barrelling heaviness in his legs. His ears hurting. G forces sucking vision from his eyes. Sweat gumming his underclothes to his body. He who never sweats. Evie's slip. He had forgotten all about Evie's slip. It is soaking wet again. As it was last night.

Stop running from the fucker. Attack him.

Someone is singing the National Anthem over the R/T. Even though the voice is woefully out of tune it gets his blood up. It is part of the issue of his being, this song. He takes a look over his shoulder. The Jerry is about forty yards away. Stuck to him. Some puffs of smoke appear and the fuselage rattles.

The bastard has hit me.

He performs the tightest and coarsest turn of which his aircraft is capable. She utters barely a protest. The ME 109 overshoots and a few seconds later he has it in his sights for a split second.

Didn't expect that, did you?

He is ecstatic again. He has hit it. A small piece of debris detaches itself and spins past his cockpit. Another six. He has that feeling now that he will go on to make a century.

Shoes on the other foot now, mate.

He follows it in a series of downward spirals. The ME 109

turns on its back and something falls out of the cockpit. The pilot. Jack swivels his head round at a 180 degree angle. Sees the chute mushroom open and there he is, his adversary, a dark haired German in a pale blue uniform, floating down towards the fields and farms of England.

He pulls open the hood. Lifts his head up to the fresh air.

Stan and Ed have given up asking him if he has had any success. He senses they are a bit embarrassed on his behalf. He always feels he has let them down. Today, finally, he will be able to reward them both for all their hard work.

5

The German fighter pilot he shot down broke his leg after getting caught up in the branches of a tree and then falling twelve feet onto a concrete road.

When he and Benedict stroll into his hospital room the young German boy in bed with his plaster cast left leg suspended on pulleys looks alarmed. Even more so when Benedict clicks his heels and performs the Heil Hitler salute.

"Just joking," he says, holding out his hand. "Officer Pilot Benedict Harold Frederick St Aubyn."

The German boy in stripy pyjamas with the black hair and green eyes seems reluctant to shake Benedict's hand, as if fearing a trap.

"Do you speak English?"

"Not so good," he says. He avoids steady eye contact but instead steals shy scared childlike glances up at Jack and Benedict.

It's like trying to win the confidence of a wounded and frightened animal.

"I'm afraid it was me who shot you down."

"No understand."

Jack mimics a dog fight with his hands. Makes gunfire noises. One hand chases the other hand through the air over the German boy's bed. "This hand you, this hand me," he says.

"He thinks we're both raving mad."

He mimics a falling aircraft, a man floating down to earth beneath a parachute.

"You?" says the German boy.

"No, you," Jack says. "Anyway, I've brought you some presents." He gives the boy two cream buns and the tin of Players cigarettes.

The boy looks at the gifts and then up at him with bewilderment. He tries to blink tears out of his eyes. But tears slide down his cheek.

"Thank you," he says. He keeps saying thank you and the tears keep sliding down his cheek.

He and Benedict go to the local pub afterwards. Here too people keep saying thank you. People insist on buying them drinks. Insist on shaking their hand and patting their shoulders. Saying thank you over and over again.

"It's like being royalty," says Jack.

"At least, I suppose, they have a reason for being thankful. What did our Jerry have to be thankful for?"

"Kindness. He didn't expect kindness."

"You think?"

"I know."

Another man comes over to their table with two tankards of beer. "Here you go, lads. On me. As a thank you. I fought in the last war and I know what it's like. But I just want you to know that it's bloody marvellous what you chaps are doing. You're saving our bacon, that's what you're doing. You're saving England's bacon."

"Thank you very much."

On the wireless the newscaster announces that today fifty-four enemy aircraft were shot down for the loss of only fifteen of ours, of which twelve pilots bailed out safely.

There is a cheer and another round of drinks arrives at the table.

Benedict drives them back to the base. In a dead pilot's car that his father donated to the squadron. Through the blackout. With the regulation hooded headlights. But it is not completely dark. There is a red glow up on the skyline to the west.

"Wonder if the birds think it's sunrise."

"Do birds think?"

"Neither you nor I can prove they don't."

"They talk to poor Septimus in *Mrs Dalloway*. They quote Shakespeare and the Greek philosophers. Where is that they're bombing anyway?"

"Dover?"

"Bastards."

"Let's try to make that MP laugh," says Benedict.

"Which MP?"

"The one at the barrier. The sentry."

"He won't laugh. Not if it's the one I'm thinking of."

"That's the one I'm thinking of too."

"How we going to make him laugh?"

Benedict stops the car. "Take your clothes off."

"All of them?"

"All of them."

"He'll put us up on a charge."

"Can't. We're fighter command pilots. More valuable than the King's Jewels."

They both take off their clothes outside the car, beneath the stars. It's like a song they're singing, he thinks but isn't quite sure what he means. Then they get back into the car naked and he has second thoughts because he's no longer quite as drunk as he thought he was.

"I've never driven a car naked before. Rather like it," says Benedict.

Benedict pulls the car up at the barrier of the base.

"It's him. Poker face."

"Yes."

The pencil moustached MP steps out from his bunker of sandbags. "Good evening. Can I see your pass please?"

Benedict has it ready. He hands it out the window to the MP. The man shines his torch on it. Then shines his torch into the car.

"As I was saying, to my mind, *Mrs Dalloway* is about the duality of identity. Or even the idea that we all have multiple selves, both public and private."

"And the disparity between clock time and interior time."

"Everything in order, corporal?"

"Told you he wouldn't laugh."

They walk naked through the mess. Uniforms and shoes bundled in their arms. Its displaced chairs and newspapers. Its taste of stale tobacco and spilt beer.

"There was the faintest tremor of a smile."

"After he had contemplated and dismissed the idea of putting us up on a charge."

"Before this war is over I'm going to make him laugh."

"Home, sweet home," he says looking at Evie's slip on his pillow. "I love this room. Our room. Yesterday was the best day of my life, today has been the second best day of my life."

Benedict is buttoning up his pyjamas. "I wish I was so easily pleased. I'm beginning to feel like I belong to a different species. Normal life just doesn't seem very normal anymore. I wondered tonight, while we were in that pub, if I'll ever be able to go back to all that."

"Go back to what?"

"Taking tomorrow's dinner for granted."

"We can sleep until eight. What bliss."

"What bliss indeed. Ready?" he says pulling out *Mrs Dalloway* from under his pilot's flying logbook on the bedside table.

"Ready."

6

Later he is going to the cinema with Evie. He only has to survive five hours. But he has left Evie's slip in his room. He was so tired when his batman woke him that he forgot about it. He has made up his mind to tell Evie his name is Jack, not Guy. Every time she calls him Guy his mind darkens, his heart sinks.

The formation of German bombers in two groups of straight lines. He counts fifteen in each line. The fighters wheeling and zigzagging above the ordered geometry of the bombers. All of them vivid against the sun.

"Okay, chaps. You know the drill. Leave the fighters alone. Hit the bombers. Tally-ho!"

From astern, he is streaking down towards the vapour trails of the bombers, the evil looking Stukas. Benedict is beside him. For a moment he thinks they have both chosen the same target. He manoeuvres to get on the tail of the Stuka he has chosen as his prey. The German swerves off violently to the left. Performs a skittish and nervous half circle. It is easy to turn inside him. In about five seconds he will have a perfect deflection shot. His pulse moves to his thumb on the button. His face hot behind the oxygen mask. But as he is about to experience another moment of triumph it is as if someone gives him a hefty shove between the shoulder blades. The stick slips from his hand. He stamps down on the left rudder at the same time as glancing up at his mirror.

Where the hell did he come from?

Malevolent puffs of smoke that turn into zipping red fire

balls come streaking towards his cockpit. There is a tug on the left wing. The aircraft rocks and shudders. There is a crunching pain in his left foot. The aircraft rattles again. Grit and dust flies up into his face. The smell of cordite. The engine begins to vibrate. An ailing noise. She is less responsive to his demands. Her physics have changed. In his mirror he sees the ME 109 circling to take another shot at him.

This might be the moment he has always dreaded. Is he even capable of it? The leap of blind faith out into the sky at ten thousand feet. He has heard too many stories of parachutes not opening not to feel terrified. He wills and begs his Spit to recover her former agility and grace.

Come on, old girl. Please don't make me have to jump.

He glances at the instruments. Needles are tottering. Oil temperature off the clock. Oil pressure almost nil. The cockpit is filling with burning oil fumes. Making it difficult to breathe. He will have to jump. When he sees the small flames from the oil tank flickering up at his boots in the corner of the cockpit he knows he has no option. He has difficulty undoing the harness that straps him to his seat while at the same time compelled to throw his aircraft around the sky to elude the pursuing and bloodthirsty 109.

For fuck sake, bugger off you bastard. You've hit me; what more do you want?

"Red two here. I'm baling out." He says this for Evie. So she will know when he is not there at the guardhouse waiting for her tonight that he has not purposefully stood her up.

He thinks of Evie as he reaches up to tug at the toggle of the hood. Tries to picture her in the most vivid detail. As she was when she emerged from the river in her slip. In the moonlight. He can't get the bloody hood open. He tugs at it with both hands. With all his strength. There is blood in his boot. Sticky and viscous. The pain has subsided but his foot feels numb. He has no feel for the rudder beneath it.

Will you fucking open!

The aircraft goes into a violent spinning dive. He has to keep telling himself not to panic. He manages to pull her out after she has spun him into a state of dizziness. The dwindling clarity in his mind. The clamp of greyness and then the black mist. There is no strength in his arms. They flop down from the hood and his head rolls on his neck.

Get a grip of yourself.

He wrenches at the hood and, hallelujah chorus, this time it slides open. The blast of fresh air revives him.

Now off with the oxygen, turn her over on her back and out you drop. A penny from heaven.

His heart is racing. His skin stiffens with resistance to this unnatural act.

Do it! Unless you want to be burned alive.

He is hauled out of the aircraft, as if lifted up by his hair, the moment it begins to tilt. His breath thumped out of his body by the cold blast of air. He somersaults. The panic in his body to regain a foothold. The wind lashing at his eyes and ears, punching down into his lungs.

Calm down. Think of Evie.

He passes through some wisps of cloud. The speed with which he leaves them behind gives him a sense of how quickly he is falling. Down below he sees his Spitfire nosediving towards its demise.

There goes my baby.

He feels groggy, as if about to go under an anaesthetic.

Pull the damn string, you fool.

He fumbles for the ring.

Okay, this is the moment of truth.

His relief when the parachute cracks open above is swiftly curtailed by the fistthump to his groin as the straps yank him up under the crotch. He wants to vomit. In mid-air. Flailing about like a puppet.

And then he becomes aware of the circling presence above of the German fighter.

Bloody vulture. He isn't going to machine gun me, is he?

The German wiggles his wings at him and shoots off.

There is a sense of joyful detachment. As if he has died and nothing can hurt him now. He feels almost drowsy with happiness. At the heart of a religious silence. Then he looks down. The geometry of thin dark green lines enclosing paler green and gold and amber rectangles and squares.

Thank heavens I'm not over the sea.

There is the occasional curving line. But mostly the marks on the earth are straight. The spaces boxed. There is a pristine cleanliness to everything. An encompassing silence. Geometry, cleanliness, silence. It's as if some secret of the nature of life is being disclosed to him.

He notices the toe of his boot has been ripped open. He can see between the two flaps of leather his bare toes. Crusted in dried blood.

He then has the sense that he is falling too fast. He twists his head up to see his shoulder straps are tangled and the chute is not fully open. He gyrates, performs gymnastics in mid-air. Swearing aloud at the tangled straps.

The wind twists him round. One minute he is facing the sea. The next there is a small town of whitewashed houses below. He does not want to land in a town. He imagines it. Crashes onto a roof and slides down onto hard concrete. Dead. He begins experimenting with the rigging lines. Pulling this one. Pulling that one. Begins to get the hang of directing himself. He passes over the town. Upturned faces down in the streets. He feels like some kind of circus attraction.

He lifts his feet as they brush the uppermost branches of a few oak trees. He intrigues a few sheep. Lands in a field.

Verdict?

I bloody enjoyed it.

There are specks of blood on his ripped trousers. The red is pretty against the slate blue cloth. It causes him pain to put his weight down on his left foot. He hobbles while gathering up his parachute.

A burly farmer with flushed cheeks and a twelve-bore shot-gun under his arm is strolling towards him.

"Oi," the man calls out.

"Oi what?"

"That's all right then. If you're English."

7

Benedict, Charlie, Tom and Hugo are sitting around his bed. His family. His pride in them is immense. He wants all the nurses to see his friends. To experience the chemistry of glamour and excitement they create together.

"Missing half of a toe. Otherwise nothing but a few cannon shell splinters in my left leg. I'll be back at the 'drome this time tomorrow."

"Bastards bombed it again today," says Charlie.

"And?"

"WAAFs are being moved to a nunnery. You can imagine the jokes."

"What nunnery?"

"Ursuline convent. That red brick building a couple of miles towards the sea. You've seen it."

"Any causalities?"

"'Fraid so. Direct hit on the shelter trench near the hangers. Seven dead."

"Who?"

"Don't worry. Your muse is safe," says Benedict.

"Muse? What muse?"

"Her," says Benedict, nodding towards the door.

His heart leaps up in his chest. Evie has walked into the ward. In her uniform. She is wearing bright wet strawberry lipstick. Carries a bunch of violet flowers. He sees her register the heightened attention of his friends. He can tell she is suddenly shy, suddenly has second thoughts about what she is doing.

Intimidated by intruding into this scrum of male camaraderie. There is an ache in him to put her at her ease.

"Time for us to head to the pub, I reckon," says Benedict.

"I forgot your slip today," he tells her when they are alone. "That's why this happened."

"You don't wear my slip?"

"You think that's funny?"

"Yes."

"I don't wear it."

He is walking with her in the grounds. Hobbling rather than walking. Across the lawn towards a baroque fountain.

"I like you in pyjamas," she says.

He doesn't have the courage to tell her his name is Jack, not Guy. He is too scared of disappointing her.

ing to break. He imagines her earlier preparations for
Imagines her in the act of stepping into her knickers.
down from the waist to pull them up over her legs.
g into the satin or lace or whatever they are made of.
heedingly she would perform the act. Probably barely
what she was doing. How wondrous a spectacle for
meaningless to her.

t are you thinking?"

h of guilt raises his temperature.

the most precious gifts people give to us they often give
even knowing that they are giving a gift."

t makes you say that?"

n't know. One thought leads to another. How many
have you had today that you wouldn't like me to read?"
ens." Her smile in the darkness reaches him as another
of wellbeing coursing through his body.

t just desire she inspires in him. He senses in her the
ty of exciting enduring friendship. Like a female equiva-
enedict. And it's this promise she offers of a liberating
oldening intimacy he most covets. She is someone with
share secrets. And this is why he knows he will have to
his name isn't Guy.

8

A foxtrot with Evie. In a crowded and smoky ballroom. In a
room of mirrors. Where reflections take spectral form and then
blur behind the smoke. In an atmosphere of raised raucous
voices and sexual excitement. A crackling swirling current of
desire. The desire of bodies for the approval and kindness of
another body. The basic instinct for human warmth. Before
more bombs arrive. Before the invasion arrives. He returns to
the music. Allows its rhythms to pulse through his limbs. Then
he apologises for hobbling instead of shuffling. Evie tells him he
is doing fine.

"What about me? How do I measure up to your Spitfire? The
sense of oneness?"

He watches her remove a strand of hair from between her
lips. "What a pompous oaf I can be," he says.

"I liked you describing how it feels in the cockpit."

"Stupid, isn't it? But I do mourn her demise. I've got a new
one but it feels a bit like replacing a beloved old dog. And then
there's the damn superstition. My old Spit was part of my good
luck."

In truth he could not currently be more thankful for the
demise of his Spitfire, the wound to his foot. It has earned him
two days leave.

Evie is the most beautiful woman he has ever had in his arms.
A continuous current of excitement flows through his hands. A
flow of coded messages. When her thigh touches his thigh the
intimate flurry of heat makes him more vivid to himself.

A foxtrot with Evie. Surrounded by men without women sitting at tables. Watching her. Watching all the women while smoking cigarettes and pipes. Benedict and Charlie are both dancing with girls too. Charlie gives him a cheeky encouraging look every time he passes him on the dancefloor. And Tom, drunk, snake-eyed, is swinging around some saucy red-haired factory worker girl he has met. The three new pilots to the squadron, rushed through training school, are sitting together at a table. Max, Tim and Knoxy. No one will befriend them until they have survived four or five sorties. Because what's the point of ushering gratuitous sadness into your life? A foxtrot with Evie. Tomorrow, all the tomorrows, banished for a while. Knowledge that he may never foxtrot with Evie again.

Savour every moment. Prolong every moment.

His foot wound makes him hobble rather than shuffle. When the dance is finished she tugs at his shirt where it is tucked into the waistband of his trousers. He is incredulous at how happy this simple teasing gesture makes him. How wanted and singled out and thankful it makes him. He wants to tell her how happy she makes him but all words sound inadequate when he imagines giving them a voice.

It was Evie who suggested they share a room for the night. While sitting by the fountain in the hospital grounds. After they had kissed again. He feeling more vulnerable in his pyjamas. More exposed to both wonder and pain. And the kiss seeming to enclose them within the spouting and splash of the water in the fountain. There was no trace of embarrassment in her voice when she suggested they share a room for the night. "Let's find a room soon," she said. "Yes," he said.

Mrs Savage charged him ten shillings for the room for the night. He counted out the coins. The coins that are buying him the most thrilling moment of his life. He was thankful to Mrs Savage for not making him and Evie feel seedy. They have her goodwill. He is a brave fighter pilot. Evie is no less to be admired for enduring those bombs. They deserve a little love. He has

the key to Mrs Savage's bed and break
schoolboy nervous every time he sto
for him. More nervous than he was
He had training for that challenge. H
tonight's challenge.

After the dance they cycle togetł
house.

Savour every moment. Prolong ever
"Your chain needs oiling," he say:
thrilling in life than to make her smile

He suggests they smoke a cigarett
out on his back beside her. The smell o
earth in his nostrils. An intoxicating al
stars and the moon. The night sky. A
dwells in the sky.

"If this war goes on I might apply
code officer," she says. Her voice soun
stars. There is more fate in it.

"LACW Devereux?" he says but he
she is willing to leave him.

"I'm not sure I can go on much longe
of pilots being burnt to death. There wa

"Hugo," he says. "He came to see me
brought me two oranges."

"The very good looking boy?"

"Yes." Now he is jealous of a man wh
in his cockpit.

"It's horrible, the waste, isn't it?"

"Horrible how unheeding one is forc
to remember Hugo this afternoon, his
voice, and then had to stop myself. We'ı
our thoughts anymore."

We're not allowed our tears.

They are stretched out side by side i
the night sky. Distant algorithms of lig

light waiting to break. He imagines her earlier preparations for tonight. Imagines her in the act of stepping into her knickers. Bending down from the waist to pull them up over her legs. Wriggling into the satin or lace or whatever they are made of. How unheedingly she would perform the act. Probably barely aware of what she was doing. How wondrous a spectacle for him; how meaningless to her.

"What are you thinking?"

A flush of guilt raises his temperature.

"That the most precious gifts people give to us they often give without even knowing that they are giving a gift."

"What makes you say that?"

"I don't know. One thought leads to another. How many thoughts have you had today that you wouldn't like me to read?"

"Dozens." Her smile in the darkness reaches him as another current of wellbeing coursing through his body.

It isn't just desire she inspires in him. He senses in her the possibility of exciting enduring friendship. Like a female equivalent of Benedict. And it's this promise she offers of a liberating and emboldening intimacy he most covets. She is someone with whom to share secrets. And this is why he knows he will have to tell her his name isn't Guy.

the key to Mrs Savage's bed and breakfast in his pocket. He gets schoolboy nervous every time he stops to think what's in store for him. More nervous than he was before his first solo flight. He had training for that challenge. He has had no training for tonight's challenge.

After the dance they cycle together towards Mrs Savage's house.

Savour every moment. Prolong every moment.

"Your chain needs oiling," he says. There is nothing more thrilling in life than to make her smile.

He suggests they smoke a cigarette in a field. He stretches out on his back beside her. The smell of her and the smell of the earth in his nostrils. An intoxicating alchemy. He looks up at the stars and the moon. The night sky. A part of him now always dwells in the sky.

"If this war goes on I might apply to become a cipher and code officer," she says. Her voice sounds different beneath the stars. There is more fate in it.

"LACW Devereux?" he says but he is alarmed and hurt that she is willing to leave him.

"I'm not sure I can go on much longer listening to the screams of pilots being burnt to death. There was another one today."

"Hugo," he says. "He came to see me in hospital last night. He brought me two oranges."

"The very good looking boy?"

"Yes." Now he is jealous of a man who has just burnt to death in his cockpit.

"It's horrible, the waste, isn't it?"

"Horrible how unheeding one is forced to become. I started to remember Hugo this afternoon, his smile, the sound of his voice, and then had to stop myself. We're not allowed to finish our thoughts anymore."

We're not allowed our tears.

They are stretched out side by side in a field. Gazing up at the night sky. Distant algorithms of light. The sense of more

A foxtrot with Evie. Surrounded by men without women sitting at tables. Watching her. Watching all the women while smoking cigarettes and pipes. Benedict and Charlie are both dancing with girls too. Charlie gives him a cheeky encouraging look every time he passes him on the dancefloor. And Tom, drunk, snake-eyed, is swinging around some saucy red-haired factory worker girl he has met. The three new pilots to the squadron, rushed through training school, are sitting together at a table. Max, Tim and Knoxy. No one will befriend them until they have survived four or five sorties. Because what's the point of ushering gratuitous sadness into your life? A foxtrot with Evie. Tomorrow, all the tomorrows, banished for a while. Knowledge that he may never foxtrot with Evie again.

Savour every moment. Prolong every moment.

His foot wound makes him hobble rather than shuffle. When the dance is finished she tugs at his shirt where it is tucked into the waistband of his trousers. He is incredulous at how happy this simple teasing gesture makes him. How wanted and singled out and thankful it makes him. He wants to tell her how happy she makes him but all words sound inadequate when he imagines giving them a voice.

It was Evie who suggested they share a room for the night. While sitting by the fountain in the hospital grounds. After they had kissed again. He feeling more vulnerable in his pyjamas. More exposed to both wonder and pain. And the kiss seeming to enclose them within the spouting and splash of the water in the fountain. There was no trace of embarrassment in her voice when she suggested they share a room for the night. "Let's find a room soon," she said. "Yes," he said.

Mrs Savage charged him ten shillings for the room for the night. He counted out the coins. The coins that are buying him the most thrilling moment of his life. He was thankful to Mrs Savage for not making him and Evie feel seedy. They have her goodwill. He is a brave fighter pilot. Evie is no less to be admired for enduring those bombs. They deserve a little love. He has

8

A foxtrot with Evie. In a crowded and smoky ballroom. In a room of mirrors. Where reflections take spectral form and then blur behind the smoke. In an atmosphere of raised raucous voices and sexual excitement. A crackling swirling current of desire. The desire of bodies for the approval and kindness of another body. The basic instinct for human warmth. Before more bombs arrive. Before the invasion arrives. He returns to the music. Allows its rhythms to pulse through his limbs. Then he apologises for hobbling instead of shuffling. Evie tells him he is doing fine.

"What about me? How do I measure up to your Spitfire? The sense of oneness?"

He watches her remove a strand of hair from between her lips. "What a pompous oaf I can be," he says.

"I liked you describing how it feels in the cockpit."

"Stupid, isn't it? But I do mourn her demise. I've got a new one but it feels a bit like replacing a beloved old dog. And then there's the damn superstition. My old Spit was part of my good luck."

In truth he could not currently be more thankful for the demise of his Spitfire, the wound to his foot. It has earned him two days leave.

Evie is the most beautiful woman he has ever had in his arms. A continuous current of excitement flows through his hands. A flow of coded messages. When her thigh touches his thigh the intimate flurry of heat makes him more vivid to himself.

9

The first sortie in his new Spitfire was uneventful. Vectored over Maidstone there was no sign of any enemy aircraft. The sky, at odds with his radiant mood, murky with heavy rain clouds. Visibility poor. Everything clear in his mind, heart and soul. A whole new album of images of Evie to marvel at. His powers of concentration, he feels, have never been sharper. Eventually the squadron was sent back to base. Only strange thing was that his goggles were missing from his locker. He had to go to stores for a new pair. He asks himself what this might mean. Convinces himself that his old pair of goggles had nothing to do with his quota of good fortune. Were just a pair of goggles, like any other. He has Evie's slip tucked inside the waistband of his trousers. His amulet. The only amulet he needs.

"Your bloody joie de vivre is beginning to get on my nerves," says Benedict. But he smiles. He doesn't mean it.

The cloistering rain increases the tension inside the hut. The telephone on the desk silent but sinister, like a delayed action bomb that might go off from one moment to the next. He stands by the window. Drops sliding down the misted glass. Outside ground crew in oil skin coats are rearming and refuelling the squadron's Spitfires. Shadowy figures with belts of ammunition, spanners, cloths, oxygen tanks, clambering up and down onto the wings of the aircraft.

He says hello to the three new pilots. Tim, Max and Knoxy. He is feeling generous, a swirling current of thanksgiving in his blood. Max is reading *Henry V*.

"Don't get the wrong idea," Max says, inserting a chestnut tree leaf between the pages as a bookmark. "I'm not in it for the stirring speeches. I thought I might be the squadron's Falstaff."

"So you're brushing up."

"So I'm brushing up."

"The three most common mistakes a novice pilot makes in combat. Your take?" asks Tim. Tim is small and wiry with dishevelled hair and wild staring eyes.

He has their full attention, as if he is an oracle. In six months his standing has risen from fledgling youth to adult mentor.

"Flying as though you've got your instructor behind you and you're trying to impress him. A perfect line is a predictable line. Especially to the idealistic German mind. It's what they expect."

"It's what I expect," says Max. "I always expect perfection. So rarely get it. Sorry. You were saying?"

"Cockiness. You're at your most vulnerable when you're congratulating yourself. If you shoot down a Hun or you're about to shoot down a Hun one of his mates will probably be on your tail in a jiffy. For revenge."

"Right."

"And up there curiosity does kill the cat. A burning aircraft or a pilot baling out is a compelling spectacle. It's hard not to stare. But if your gaze stays riveted to one spot for more than a few seconds you're likely to get bounced. Watch the whole of the sky the whole time. Your neck should ache like hell when you go to bed tonight."

"If we go to bed tonight," says Max.

"Better believe you'll go to bed tonight," says Charlie. "Because if you don't believe it your bed will be empty tonight. And Pilot Officer Knox here will have to look at the imprint of your body on the sheet from last night and your slippers on the floor and the photograph of your mum and dad by the bed."

"I don't have a photograph of my mum and dad by the bed," says Max.

"Argumentative chap, aren't you?" says Charlie.

"Because I don't believe in mystical hogwash?"

"You might want to save all this hot air of yours for the Germans," says Charlie, clearly irked. Jack has never seen Charlie irked by one of his own squadron before.

"I've got German cousins," says Max.

"Meaning what? You're going to turn your guns on us?"

Tom finds this funny but the usually unflappable Charlie is clearly riled.

The shrill of the telephone makes Jack jump. It always makes him jump. He hates the damn thing.

"Scramble red and white sections Dungeness angels one five."

A mug falls to the floor, a chair scrapes and topples, there is a scrum at the door, and then he is running over the grass. It suits his mood to be running over the grass. Stan and Ed are waiting for him. Ed with his rag and polish. Stan straps him in.

"Good luck, sir."

The sky is clear above the cloud base at seven thousand feet. The people of England can't see the sun but he can. The Nazi armada is even more impressive today. Flying along leisurely at staggered heights. Filling the sky for miles around. A trail of white streamers behind. The bombers below, the fighters above. The squadron forms up into line astern. Each of the Spitfires peels away down into the fray. He does battle with a Heinkel. The streams of tracer blazing back and forth make a gilt mesh in the air. He hits one of the bomber's engines before breaking away as the black machine fills his gunsight. He then loses sight of it as he takes evasive action when he spots a ME 109 pouncing down on his tail. Another ME 109 passes below. Turns left and goes into a climb. The pneumatics of his guns hiss again. A Spitfire below is trailing black smoke. He imagines the pilot fumbling in the smoke-infested cockpit to disconnect his radio lead and oxygen tube. He catches sight of the aircraft's letters. It is Charlie. Charlie who went up into the air tense because of the argumentative boy with his German cousins. A parachute appears. His good mood returns. Charlie is safe.

A minute later he is alone in the sky. The fields and roads of England begin to appear between the whitening and thinning cloud layers.

The intelligence officer greets him at the door of the hut. His solemn expression frightens him.

Please not Benedict.

He looks past the intelligence officer into the hut. Sees the three new pilots in a group and various other isolated figures in chairs.

"Charlie," says the intelligence officer.

"What about Charlie? I saw him bail out. Definitely bailed out and his chute was fine."

"Bastards shot him to bits as he was coming down."

He looks over at Max. He is pale. His eyes downcast. Impossible to feel any anger towards him. He settles himself on the arm of the chair Benedict is slumped in. They all wait for Tom.

Tom is the last one back. When he enters the hut he is grinning. He has a story he is itching to tell. It glitters in his eyes. An amusing story he wants to tell Charlie. His eyes roam from one corner of the dispersal hut to the other. The glitter fades, the grin is gone. No one says anything. There is no need to.

The fourth sortie of the day. Hopefully the last. After two slices of buttered toast and a mug of cocoa made with condensed milk. The taste of the powdery cocoa still a vivid memory in his mouth at fifteen thousand feet.

Can't believe Charlie won't be in the mess later.

He forgets about the moving vulnerability of the pilot he shot down. His disbelieving gratitude at the kindness shown him. He feels a loathing for the Germans now. For their primadonna Nazi goosestepping, their hate spawning guttural language, the vainglorious melodrama of their emblems and banners. He will fire his guns in anger today.

The three-tiered formation of enemy aircraft is intercepted over Hastings. Twenty-five bombers down below, twenty 110s and thirty 109s above. A squadron of Hurricanes arrives from the south-west.

Nick reports the sighting to the controller.

"Okay chaps. You know the drill. Let the Hurricanes get in amongst the bombers; we'll take care of the fighters. Line astern. Tally-ho! Tally-ho!"

He dives down steeply to the right. He has an image of Charlie in his head every time he gives a quick burst of his guns. A ME 109 dives down to his right, spirals and then spins. Another opens fire but out of range. He sees a bomber become a fireball below to his left.

That's one less of the bastards.

Another 109 whips past, just above his cockpit.

Didn't even see that blighter.

He has a prolonged dogfight with a 109. Constantly twisting through 360 degrees. He yells abuse at the German pilot. The sound of his voice sounds strange. More frightened than he is aware of being. He is dizzy and drained with all the acrobatics, with the horizon constantly turning upside down. Finally he loses sight of the German in the clouds that have returned. He checks his fuel gauge.

Time to return home.

When he comes down through the cloud he is surprised to find himself over the sea. The white cliffs and the barrage balloons over Dover are not where he expected them to be.

Completely lost my bearings.

He leans to one side and gazes down out of the cockpit. About a mile away there is a smudge of yellow on the grey sea. He soon sees it is a dinghy. He drops down low to investigate. Three German airmen in a yellow dinghy. He still has some ammunition left. He thinks of Charlie.

Shoot the bastards.

He swoops down low enough to make his presence felt in their hair. He can feel their fear as if it is transmitted up to him along radio waves. But he can't shoot them. It isn't in his nature.

And so he makes another discovery about himself. He feels sorry for the three young German airmen. Miles from home, bobbing about helplessly in this vast expanse of enemy waters. He radios in to Air Sea rescue. Recounts the situation and gives a fix. As he flies away he wiggles his wings at the German airmen. He sees in his mirror one of the Germans wave back at him.

In the mess that night everyone gets very drunk. To honour Charlie's memory. Everyone except Max, who plays the piano, and Benedict, who has a headache and has gone to bed. At nine o'clock there is a hush as they wait for the radio announcer to broadcast today's score. Sixty-four enemy aircraft shot down as against only twelve RAF fighters. An almighty cheer goes up. Even though Charlie is one of the twelve. There is a piggyback pillow fight. He has Tom on his shoulders. Tom knocks Tim off Knoxy's shoulders and Tim is taken to sick quarters with a suspected broken wrist.

"Very good impression of a drunk person trying to enter a darkened room without making too much noise," says Benedict, a dark moving shape on his bed.

"Sorry."

"Couldn't sleep anyway. How's Tom?"

"He broke Tim's wrist. You all right?"

"Can't say I'm looking forward to tomorrow."

"No," he says slipping his braces off his shoulders. "At this rate one of us will be made the new CO soon."

"Better you than me. I wouldn't be able to give any order and at the same time take myself seriously."

"What makes you think I'm any different?"

"I can't imagine you with parents."

"That's what Evie said. That she couldn't imagine my childhood."

"She probably can't imagine any childhood without footmen and ladies in waiting," says Benedict.

"We both have dead fathers. She said the whole world seems fatherless at the moment."

"Why don't you read tonight?"

"I don't think we should change the pattern."

"Bad luck?"

"Bad luck."

"All right. Turn the light on."

"Remind me what's just happened."

Benedict screws up his eyes against the harsh electric light for a moment. He yawns. Then he reaches out for his copy of *Mrs Dalloway*.

"Clarissa is being a snob about that dreadful Miss Kilman and her cheap mackintosh."

10

He waits outside the operations room. Waits for Evie to appear. Heart in his mouth. Erection coming and going in his trousers. Like a shameful secret he imagines she would be offended by if she saw. But he doesn't know for sure. The mystery of a woman's mind. Impossible to ever know what they're thinking. What she's thinking. The rattle and hum of his aircraft is still in his ears. Its choreography of acrobatics still a pulse in his body. He hasn't seen Evie since they woke up together in Mrs Savage's guesthouse, three days ago. Since he sat on the edge of the bed watching her put her stockings on. Since they sat at the dining room table eating toast and marmalade. The taste of the homemade marmalade returns to his tongue as he recalls the morning. Since he told her his name is Jack, not Guy. He keeps thinking this might be the biggest mistake he has ever made.

So he is more nervous than excited. He exchanges some pleasantries with the guard on duty. They are from the same social background. The private knows this. It is evident in the ironic way he calls him sir. More of a snob than any aristocrat. He sits down on an upended tar barrel by the sandbags. Smoking another cigarette.

When Evie emerges he jumps up off the barrel with a big smile on his face but she walks straight past him. As if he wasn't there. Laughing with one of the male R/T operators. It is perhaps the most bewildering thing that has ever happened to him. He stops himself from running after her. The guard has a smirk on his face.

Fuck you, private.

Two days later he waits for Evie to appear at the cocktail party in the mess. Benedict introduces him to his mother and father and sister.

"Your people not here then, Guy?"

Most of the pilots have invited family. He, of course, could not invite his grandmother and grandfather. He saw his grandmother counting out pennies for the gas meter, sucking on an unlit cigarette with curlers in her hair. His grandfather without a collar to his shirt, marking down X's on the football coupons at the chipped and stained kitchen table. He feels ashamed of himself for snubbing his own family. Unclean, as though there is the stink of smoke and ashes on his clothes. The smoke and ashes of his childhood.

"My mother and father are both dead, I'm afraid."

Benedict's father's face shows alarm.

"Long time ago. I barely knew them."

"Ah," says Benedict's father, clearly relieved. "A little less pressure at the crease then. My pater demanded boundaries from the first ball of every over. Never gave me the chance to find my own rhythm. The sins of the father and all that, eh? Probably have more freedom to develop your own game without an eagle-eyed father pointing out your every mistake."

"I want to thank you, Guy, for being such a good friend to Ben. He talks about you all the time, doesn't he, Clive?" says the mother.

"Nothing like a reliable partner when you're out there on the crease," says Clive.

"We've only got a paltry four runs between us," says Benedict.

"You have to think of how many bombs those four would have dropped, how many innocent civilians they would have killed. There are people out there who owe you two their lives. I still can't get over how young you all are. Even your squadron commander. What's his name again?"

Tom brings over his parents. Lord and Lady Vane-Temple. The two mothers begin chatting about mutual acquaintances.

Outside the Spitfires of Cygnet Squadron can be heard revving up and throttling their engines. The Spitfires of the base's other squadron are already in the air.

"Just leaves us now."

"Fabulously decadent, isn't it, being scrambled in the middle of a cocktail party?" says Benedict. "Shame the Nazi hierarchy can't see how absolutely bulldog determined we are not to alter our way of life."

"I just wish I could meet the pilot who shot up Charlie," says Tom. "If I had his letters…"

"If you had his letters, what? You'd stooge up to every 109 to check if he was your assassin and then stooge off with apologies for the mistake when you realised he wasn't your man?"

"Better solution is to pretend every Nazi pilot is him."

"Go a bit easy, Tom. It's only us three now from the old team. Nick reckons we're due some rest."

Benedict's parents return. Wanting to be introduced to the station commander. Jack goes out into the garden. Max is standing alone by the hydrangeas. Skulking.

"Falstaff has no parents here either?"

Max is one of those people who echo back at you everything you say and make it sound trite.

"Shame a few Junkers don't come so we can provide some better entertainment for our guests. I was just picturing them all out here on the lawn with their champagne and sherry admiring the beauty of the contrails of a dogfight."

"You don't approve of cocktail parties?"

"Sometimes today I was looking at these women's hands and trying to imagine them touching a penis. Why is such a natural act so impossible to imagine? I couldn't work out if the shortcoming is mine or some failing in these women to inspire imagination. Do you blame me for that pilot's death too?"

"Charlie? No." He can still hear Charlie's laugh. See his loose-limbed way of walking.

"When's his funeral?"

"Tomorrow. No one in the squadron is allowed to go of course. They'll probably send a couple of pen pushers who didn't even know him."

"I can be pig headed. Especially when I'm scared."

"Charlie was shot down about five times. He was the bravest of the lot of us. He took greater risks often. The difference this time was that some mean-hearted bastard opened fire on him while he was swinging down under his umbrella. How is that your fault?"

"Actually I would have invited my girlfriend today except Tom hisses at me every time he sees me and I didn't want to have to explain to her why."

They are called to readiness over the loudspeakers. He turns on his heels, about to dash to the transport waiting for them outside.

"Guy."

He turns to face Max. "Yes?"

"Thanks."

Max is the last one outside. Max refuses to run like everyone else. He has to jump aboard while the truck is moving.

He apologises but still wants to single himself out.

"I'm jealous of your dad," he says to Benedict.

"I'm glad."

"Evie didn't show up."

He does not have her slip stuffed into the waistband of his trousers today. He has left it under his pillow in his room.

"Probably on duty."

"Not what I heard."

"I've completely gone off girls."

"Oh?"

"All those women in their high hats and delicate gloves. Who are they kidding?"

"Themselves probably."

"The combination of champagne and my mother's company have conspired, I fear, to unman me. Not in the mood for this today."

"Me neither."

They are vectored towards Dungeness. He feels wretched. Alone in his cockpit the full implications of Evie's absence from the party hits him. There is no mobility in his limbs. He feels sculpted into an eternal gesture of defeat.

I'll never find anyone else as beautiful as her. She's dumped me, hasn't she? After one bloody night.

Okay, snap out of all this doom and gloom. Unless you want to die.

That's exactly what I want. To die. At least that way she'll have to feel something for me again.

That's pathetic. I hope you're ashamed of yourself.

Been ashamed of myself all bloody afternoon.

The German armada of bombers appears as he rises up through a layer of cloud. About forty Heinkels. The sun blinds him to what lays up above. But he knows the 109s are up there. Knows too that he won't see them swoop down until their roundels are large enough in his sights to look like evil pairs of eyes. The squadron could not be in a more unfavourable situation. They don't have enough height and they are blinded by the sun. They will have to wade into the bombers head on.

He eases the throttle to reduce closing speed. He ducks as he ploughs into the formation of Heinkels. Whizzing fiery comets of tracer embroidering the transparency of sky all around. Cockpits and underbellies and tails flash by. Close enough at times for him to see an outline of the German pilots and gunners. There is no time to observe any possible hits. Too busy avoiding a collision with the panicking bombers that veer off to left and right. Too attentive to the anticipated imminent attack of the German fighters.

When he comes out at the far end of the bomber stream, stick hard forward, stomach lurching, head knocking the cockpit roof, the 109s appear. But miraculously not one of them fastens on him. Three have ganged up on another Spitfire. He sees it is Max. Wonders for a moment if the last conversation Max is ever to have on this earth will be the one with him by the hydrangeas.

He looks around. He can get out of this. He convinces himself he has done his bit for the day. Up and up he goes. As if he is going to curl round and swing down in a dive. But there are no prying eyes upon him. The madcap etchings of the spiralling smoke trails further and further below. He has the sky to himself. It begins to turn cold in the cockpit. A deathly cold that settles in the bones.

The heaviness in his limbs returns. The feeling of there being no future for him. He entertains the idea of detaching his oxygen. Switching off his life support system. Anticipates the grogginess and then the rising tide of impenetrable darkness behind his eyes. Then he wouldn't be there anymore.

Suppose you come round just as she's going to hit the ground? And suppose she crashes into some family home?

He can't do it. As much as anything it is the thought of leaving Benedict alone that stops him. But he will not return to the fray. He's had enough for one day.

This is what your father was shot for doing.

Like father like son.

Strange that his father should return to haunt him today. Today when he feels most oppressed by his history, his family tree, and, as a result, bereft of any kind of future.

11

Another raid on the station in their absence. The worst yet. All the power lines are down. Entire walls disappeared. Disclosing new vistas. He can't remember what building used to be where now there is a mound of smoking debris. The operations room, unoperational, has been moved to a furniture store in the local town. When he puts his Spitfire down, weaving between the white flags marking the craters, he sees the charred naked body of a woman missing both her legs hanging by the crook of her arm from a tree. Her hair now and again lifting in the breeze. People grouped beneath with a ladder. He forgets to register the absence of Stan and Ed when he climbs out of his cockpit.

There is a crater full of oily water in which a shoe floats. He stands with his hand raised to his mouth. The officers' mess has received a direct hit. He and Benedict, still in their yellow Mae Wests, search amongst the powdered debris for *Mrs Dalloway*. Instead they find a shred of Benedict's green silk dressing gown. Its lime green lustre the brightest thing in this new blackened world. Their room does not exist anymore. The solid seeming walls and ceiling that provided privacy and continuity pulverised into dust. He regrets now not taking Evie's slip with him. It's the only thing he had of hers. The only evidence she wasn't just a dream, a fantasy. He doesn't remember his father's two drawings until later. Lost forever now.

He is told Stan and Ed were both killed in the raid. Along with thirteen other ground crew. That he will be allocated a new fitter and rigger. The WAAF guardroom is destroyed too. As

209

if one by one the war is intent on erasing all his memories of Evie. He wonders if Mrs Savage's guesthouse is still standing. The squadron is transferred to an advanced airfield closer to the coast. Still further away from Evie. He and Benedict share a tent. There are no amenities. No women. Certainly no library. Not even a bath.

"Never has so much been owed by so many to so few," says Benedict. "And we get a flipping tent."

"First time I've ever slept in a tent."

"Me too, come to think of it."

"It's only for a while."

"Do we believe that?"

"Tell me it doesn't matter that we didn't finish *Mrs Dalloway*."

"It doesn't matter that we didn't finish *Mrs Dalloway*."

Max is dead. Two more young boys have joined the squadron fresh from training school. He feels a hundred years old when he talks to them. They make him feel the war is going to be lost. Despite the wildly chauvinistic scoring of the newspapers. 140-16: RAF's Biggest Victory. The invasion though is expected every new morning.

Benedict has a nightmare in the middle of the night. Wakes up yelling. It's the third time this has happened this week. It is unnerving to hear Benedict yell. Yelling plays no part in the Benedict he knows. Benedict becomes a stranger. He talks him back to the Benedict he knows. In the darkness of the tent and its sour smell of mildew and damp canvas.

When he is woken the next morning his body is stiff in every joint. He crawls out of the tent onto the dewy grass, into the luminous grey air. The tea is luke warm. The porridge too lumpy. He splashes some cold water on his face. Has no toothbrush or tooth powder. No one does. Joe, his batman, promises he will get some later.

"And try to get a copy of *Mrs Dalloway*, will you, Joe?"

"Sir?"

"It's a book. A novel."

"Yes sir. I'll do my best."

They are scrambled at eight am. So near to the coast it is impossible to achieve much height before they intercept the German formations. The clouds like mountain ranges of snow. While they attempt to sow panic among the disciplined ranks of the bombers the German fighters swoop down out of the sun to ambush them. Always the same. Always the ambush. Seems to him the Germans use the bombers primarily as bait. He wonders what the German bomber crews think about this. Rarely, he realises, does he give any thought to what the Germans might be thinking. They are a subspecies to him now. Nazis. Unworthy of any kind of consideration. He is shouting at one of them now. The pilot of the 109 on his tail. His latest adversary in this game of cat and mouse.

He shakes off the yellow-nosed predator. Returns to the fray where the ME 110s are performing their textbook circling manoeuvre, like some insane circus trick.

"Been hit. Engine on fire. Can't get the damn hood to open."

It's Benedict. He sounds calm. As if suffering a minor inconvenience. Like not having a toothbrush.

"Going to try to put her down in a field."

"Okay, Ben. Good luck," he says, his voice sounding equally unconcerned.

There is no word of Benedict when he is scrambled for his second sortie of the day. He finds it hard to believe the two new pilots have returned safely but that Benedict got shot down. Joe hands him two toothbrushes, tooth powder, and, beaming with triumph, a copy of *Mrs Dalloway*. He feels bad afterwards that he didn't reward Joe with a smile or a kind word, but the new copy of *Mrs Dalloway* with its different alien cover made him realise how feeble are our attempts to keep change at bay.

His new fitter and rigger wish him luck. He can't remember their names. It depresses him how readily individuals can be replaced.

As if no one is indispensable. But that isn't true. Benedict and Evie are indispensable for me.

He checks the petrol gauge is showing full. Sees his hand is trembling. Tries to hide it from the rigger who straps him in.

He gets his third kill. Over the radar station at Dover. More by luck than design. Seems the Germans too are now resorting to young inexperienced pilots. Idiot gave him the perfect shot. Turned across his sights. He sees bits jump loose from the German machine. He ducks as something swings past his cockpit. The 109 heels over. Wreathed in darkening smoke. Its nose dips, it flops, impotent and resigned, it begins to spin and plummet down towards the earth four miles below. He keeps an eye open for the appearance of a parachute. But no parachute appears.

Benedict is in hospital. He has been badly burned. He is told he cannot visit him for a while.

If I'm still alive in a while.

He will be alone in the tent tonight. But first he, Tom, Harry and Knoxy are going to drive to London. He and Tom toss a coin for who does the honours. He wins. He is in the driving seat. Driving along the dark streets. Through the blackout. Headlights hooded. Three times he gets hopelessly lost. Most of the signposts have been removed. You have to take a wild guess where every road leads. Or that's how it seems. Through the open windows the drone of the invisible bombers up in the night sky can be heard every time he stops the car. It takes three and a half hours to reach London. To arrive in the West End. Outside the nightclub in Leicester Square a group of young girls shine flashlights at them and ask them for autographs. The girls talk in loud and shrill voices. Then the air raid siren begins howling. Searchlights make prongs in the sky. It looks like the scissoring beams of light are holding the clouds in suspension above the city. As if they will fall from the sky if the lights are extinguished.

Evie is inside the nightclub. One of about three hundred dancers and revellers. She is startled to see him. She quickly pretends she hasn't seen him. In the mirrorball whirl of coloured lights.

The violence of her emotion gives him new heart. She almost immediately disguises it. Tidies it away behind a mask of good cheer and flippancy. But he saw it. Like a glimpse of a secret part of her, as if a breeze had momentarily whipped up her skirt.

Tom and Knoxy get very drunk very quickly. Evie chats with Tom on the dance floor. But refuses to catch his eye. He suspects Tom is telling her about Benedict. Because of the distraught drooping of her features. He is troubled by the idea that Benedict's misfortune might work to his advantage. Might awaken in her some sympathy for him. He sits with Harry. Trying not to look at Evie. She is with the R/T operator from the operations room. He hates this R/T operator from the operations room. Hates him more than any German.

After his third beer, without any explanation to Harry beside him, he marches over to her. Ignores the R/T operator she is dancing with. Coloured discs floating across the dancefloor.

"Can we talk?"

She leads him out onto the balcony. He misses her usual lightness of step. There is a drag in her body as if she is wading through debris.

Outside the prongs of the searchlights swivel about over the glazed ghostly skyline. As if in search of something lost. Like the sick yearning in his own body.

"It's not how it looks," she says, a burden dragged through her voice.

She is looking at the dance of the two tunnelling beams of smoky light. A barrage balloon is caught in the light for the moment. A sight that has no precedent.

"It looks like something magical is about to happen," he says. "But it doesn't feel like that. Have you replaced me with that R/T operator?"

"David. He's nothing to do with it."

He still has the adrenaline of his earlier combats in his body. Some of the aggression too unfortunately.

"Nothing to do with what?"

"It's not my fault there's a war, Guy. Or do I call you Jack now?"

"Is it because I lied to you?"

"Lied about who you are? It didn't help."

"Only because I had lied to everyone else. Only because of my father. The stigma of my father. I haven't lied to you about anything else. Only my name."

"It isn't only because you lied to me."

What she gives him of herself is as if measured out carefully in a teaspoon. She makes him feel like a pit she is afraid of falling into.

"I miss you, Evie. I know I did something wrong…"

"It's just not the right time. Perhaps in a different time…"

"How can there ever be a different time?"

"I don't know."

The light catches hold of their shadows. Stretches them out, two thin shapes joined at the hip, far into the night.

"I miss hearing about your day. I miss not telling you about mine. It's like a dripping tap inside me that I can't turn off."

"You have to stop missing me…"

She talks to me as though I'm a child.

"There isn't a nice way to go about this. It has to be over between us. That's all."

"Is it my background? Your family wouldn't approve."

She swivels round to return to the dance. He catches her. Tries to kiss her but she wriggles free. It is the only time he has touched her when his fingers didn't feel the presence of his entire being on their tips. When he returns inside she is resting her head on the R/T operator's shoulder.

Tom is fast asleep in the front of the drum kit. He and Harry have to carry Tom to the car. Tom snarls at him, hurls abuse at him. Then Tom vomits over his shoulder. The smell of the vomit gets worse in the car. He has to stop the car and vomit himself. Knoxy vomits too. They stand side by side by the roadside, vomiting over the wildflowers. It is three thirty when he stops the car at their new station. They have less than two hours before they will be woken.

"You fucking idiot," he says to Tom.

Tom smiles with his eyes closed.

He barely recognises himself alone in the tent.

12

"Probably have to set my sights a bit lower now with regards to my love life."

It is only when he speaks that the patient in bed, swathed in bandages, his face a puckered raw effigy of a human face, like a child's drawing of a face on an egg, his legs and arms suspended on wires, recognisably comes to life as his friend Benedict. The best friend he has ever had. There is no longer the volatile arc of his eyebrows, the subtle choreography of his lips, the little geographical notches around his eyes and mouth, the distinctive way his hair sits on his head to give expression and dance to Benedict's inner life. All his personality is now in his voice. The voice comes as a shock. It is unaltered. The only thing about him that is unaltered. He even smells different. Of salty nose-tickling unguents and antiseptic lotions. Reminding him of childhood accidents. But if he closed his eyes and listened to the voice Benedict would have his face returned to him.

"How ghastly do I look? I haven't plucked up the courage to go anywhere near glass yet."

"You're still much better looking than Tom," he says.

The line of his lipless mouth lifts at the corners. Benedict comes brimming up into his eyes that have no lids or brows.

Insincerity. Deception. These are the ploys Benedict will inspire now.

"I was blind for a whole day. Can't say I liked that."

He breathes hard against the tears welling up behind his eyes. Selfish tears that would be the most damning gesture he could perform for Benedict at this moment.

"Where do they find the nurses here? They're all, without exception, stunningly beautiful."

"I suspect it's some kind of consolation prize for us barbecued husks on behalf of the Air Ministry."

This is the face that woke up yelling in the middle of the night. He keeps thinking this as he sits at Benedict's bedside. He remembers the burned man the last time he visited Benedict in hospital. How uncannily similar Benedict looks. The shape of his skull different but the razing of his features to a stark prototype of a human face almost identical. It appears now like an awful prophecy. As if there are oracles flitting about us at every moment.

"We're being withdrawn somewhere up north for a rest. Apparently."

"Bombing London now."

"Yes. Fucking Germans."

"My poor father. He always religiously has a nap between five and six."

"Oh, here's something for you."

"*Mrs Dalloway.*"

The tears well up again.

He is given twenty-four hours leave.

"You're on the verge of getting the twitch, Guy," says Nick. "You're no use to us dead. Try to get some rest. In a week we're to be taken away from the frontline for a while. Unless the Hun bastards start attacking the Yorkshire Dales."

He discovers he doesn't want twenty-four hours leave. When he gets off the train at Norwood Junction home has never seemed less like home. A group of people at the ticket desk applaud him. They all want to shake his hand, pat his shoulder. A little boy with scabbed knees looks up at him wide-eyed, as if he is a naked thing from another planet.

"You're back then?" says his gran. As if he nipped out to the local shop to buy some cigarettes. She walks towards him in an old pair of carpet slippers. "I suppose you'll be wanting a cup of tea. No sugar mind you. Not for weeks now. Where have you been anyway?"

"I'm in the RAF, Nan."

"I know that, you silly goose."

He puts his arm around her. Holds her in a mock headlock. "But do you know what the RAF is?"

"Get away with you. Sonny Jim."

He has often wondered if his grandmother pays any heed to the world outside her home. It certainly holds little interest for her, except for gossip about the neighbours.

"The RAF. What is it? I'm not letting you go until you tell me."

"The army, ain't it?"

"Teasing your grandmother again?"

"Hello Grandad."

His grandfather's face is both flushed and sunburned. He walks every day to Crystal Palace and back. About six miles. Just for the exercise.

"Good to see you still in one piece, my boy." His handshake almost breaks his knuckles. Grandad, with his braces hanging loose, feigns a left jab. Bobs and weaves. "You ought to write your grandmother more. You know what women are like."

"I don't think I do. What are women like, Gran?"

"Get away with you," she says.

"Your old school copped it. An eight hundred pounder went straight through the roof."

"Good. No, I didn't mean that. Anyone hurt?"

"Mr Giles, the janitor."

"Mr Giles? I don't remember any Mr Giles."

"Whether you remember him or not he's danced his last waltz."

"What about you two? Still going dancing?"

"Of course. Three times a week. You don't think Hitler's

going to stop your grandmother dancing. The police were here looking for you."

"And?"

"They want to speak to you. They said you need to report to them. That you're avoiding conscription. What's going on, my lad?"

"They must have made a mistake. What do you think this uniform is, fancy dress?"

"You told me you were doing hush hush work. Now all of a sudden you're in the RAF. If you're spinning me a yarn, young Jack…"

"No yarn. Just tell them you don't know where I am. Can't explain more than that."

In his room, the broken soldiers, the mouldy tennis ball, the jigsaw puzzle with the missing pieces, the clothes he has grown out of, the threadbare rug over the wooden floorboards, the battered betrayed props of the games and adventures of his boyhood. Though there is no longer any communion it is all a part of who he is, perhaps the part Evie saw and recoiled from. He sits down on the bed. It groans out his own exhaustion, his sense of depletion. When he begins crying he has some control over his tears. They are like a consolation he offers himself. But soon he feels himself slide down with them into an abyss where there are no consolations, where it is as though he too has lost his face.

It is the sound of a Spitfire that brings his sobbing to a halt. Through the open window, behind the excited shouting of children, he hears the familiar hum of a Merlin engine. He rushes out onto the street to watch. The sky a ciphered script of vapour trails. The street is full of people cheering. He didn't realise people did this. Ran out of their homes to cheer. From now on perhaps he will picture people down below cheering him on. He sees the Spitfire pilot is inexperienced. Frightened too. His only chance is to become aggressive. Attack. But he is intent only on preserving himself.

Now's your chance. Turn inside the bastard!

But the Spitfire pilot doesn't attempt to turn inside the ME 109. He goes into a steep climb. And within seconds is trailing back smoke and plummeting down. The cheering of the people around him increases. Only he recognises the stricken fighter is a Spitfire.

13

"Start engine," he shouts out, while running over the grass. Running through the rain.

Running beneath the low black storm clouds.

His new fitter and rigger strap him in. He asks them their names. It is not their fault they are not Stan and Ed.

His battledress is already soaked through as he sits in the open cockpit. Sending shivers of wintry coldness through his body.

He starts her up. His new rigger and fitter pushing at the wings at a trotting pace. He taxis her into the wind that gusts a torrent of rain at the windscreen making him feel he is already under attack. He looks over at Knoxy and Harry. Can barely see them through the rain-spattered perspex. His two wingmen for this operation. Three enemy aircraft plotted over Pas de Calais.

"So what?" he said to Roger the intelligence officer. "Three measly Huns. They're making us go up in this for three measly Huns."

"Should I interpret this as insubordination, Guy?"

"Sapper. Red leader here. We are airborne. Steering 170 and climbing to angels seven."

His aircraft shakes and shudders in the turbulence. She doesn't want to be up here anymore than he does. Kindred spirits again. He keeps having to wipe the windscreen. Not that it makes much difference. He is as if cocooned. Even the roar of the engine is muffled. This intimacy he feels with himself is oppressive. He loses sight of Harry and Knoxy. Expects to see them reappear into the lighter shade of grey between the merging layers of leaden cloud. But they don't reappear. And impenetrable murk encompasses him. It is like being blindfolded.

And then there was one. Me.

"Red leader to Sapper. Visibility is virtually nil. Any more information about these bandits? Over."

Nothing.

"Sapper, do you read me?"

Obviously not.

"Red leader to Red Two. Do you read me?"

The crackle and hiss in his ears is like a burst of scornful laughter.

He weaves about a bit. Searching for a sign of his two companions. His hand tense on the stick. The stick that is heavier today in these appalling weather conditions. His eyes foiled in their attempts to burrow through the mist and rainwriting on the windscreen. He might be alone in the entire universe. That is his feeling.

His altimeter shows seven thousand feet. He decides to drop down slowly through the murk. Feels a desperate craving to escape this claustrophobia of cloud, a longing for light, for some visible detail beyond the confines of his cockpit. He presumes he is about half way over the Channel. Foolhardy to carry on.

I'll take one last look around and then I'll head home.

He carries on muttering to himself. Against the hissing and scratching noises in his headphones. Visibility does not improve. He sweeps in and out of black holes. He feels the cloud is stealing his air. The aircraft shudders and bucks but otherwise he has little sense of movement. There is a seed of panic at the back of his mind. Germinating. He feels trapped in a confined space. Absurd because he has the whole sky to himself. He tries to calm himself with rational rejoinders. Doesn't work. Something in his body is scrambling desperately for an exit. He opens the cockpit hood. The rain comes streaming in. He lifts up his face to it.

Right, now pull yourself together, Jack.

Altimeter reads two thousand feet. Cautiously he drops down a little lower. Throttle lever in one hand, stick in the other. The leaden cloud layers take on a lighter shade of grey and then converge again into billowing black faces. He peers out of the side of his cockpit for some sign of life. For some kind of fix. The sea must be down there somewhere. Then it happens. The black leviathan appears from nowhere. Like a great malevolent beast rising up from the depths of the sea. Looms gigantic in his sights. Shrieks in his ears. His aircraft rocks as if she too is terrified. The German bomber passes so close overhead he screws shut his eyes, ducks down his head and feels its colossal momentum whip at the tendons in his neck. He opens his eyes in time to see the huge swastika flash by within ten feet of his head. His thumb squeezes down on the fire button. At the same time a quicksilver thread darts by his cockpit. Usually there is a rush of adrenaline when a Nazi machine is hauled into his sights. But today it is different. He feels an almost supernatural connection with the German bomber and its crew. Alone together in this apocalypse of driving rain and crush of black cloud.

A splash of black oil splatters onto his windshield. The bomber is already a ghost of itself. A nightmare apparition. Just as it is erased by another billowing of black cloud he is jolted up in his seat. His left foot kicked off the rudder. The stick slips from his hand. For a moment there is nothing he can do to prevent her from going into a steep dive.

The bastard has hit me.

He manages to level her out after a couple of spins. The aircraft becomes like a horse he is trying to reassure by leaning forward in the saddle and breathing words of reassurance into its neck. The huge swastika is as if branded on his pupils. He still sees it. Even when he looks down at the smoking gash in his instruments panel. His heart is still pounding. At the intimate violation of the encounter. Sweat soaking through to the roots of his hair. His whole being primed for its sudden reappearance. This ghost machine.

"Evie, this is Red Leader. Do you read me?"

What are you doing? You've got to bail out.

Smoke is gusted up into his face. Smoke with a stink of burning oil. He is trying to pretend everything will return to normal. He leans out of the side of the cockpit. The windscreen is opaque with muck.

I can put her down.

Put her down where? You're over the sea.

Which is why I don't fucking want to bail out. Who the hell is going to find me there in this weather?

He looks at his watch. He has been up in the air almost an hour. He realises he has no idea whatsoever where he is. He has been flying through some twilight zone. Petrol and glycol are leaking out of the engine. Hosed up into his face by the slipstream. His eyes begin burning. He has to close them. Inadvertently he rubs the petrol into his eyes and can no longer see.

Look, bail out. For fuck sake bail out before she goes up in flames.

He disconnects the radio lead. Unfastens his safety harness. Checks he is wearing his Mae West.

Of course you're wearing your Mae West.

He rises up a fraction in his seat to pull open the hood. Forgetting it is already open. A terrific force takes hold of him and pops him out of the cockpit like a champagne cork. For a moment he doesn't understand what is happening to him. Unable to open his stinging eyes he thinks he is still in the cockpit and his aircraft has gone into a freefalling spin.

Hold out your arms.

He does as he's told. Rotates a few times and then straightens up. Dizzy with all this spinning. He tries to squeeze open his eyes. To see the space he is hurtling down through. He gropes about for the ring of the ripcord. Gives it a violent tug.

Red Leader to Evie. Do you read me?

The chute hoists him up with a winding thump to his groin. When the nauseous feeling in his stomach ebbs away he is able to give himself up to the exalted quietude of this new dimension he finds himself in. He sees Evie naked again. Naked by the window. Her back turned to him.

There is a sense of timelessness, swinging down through the endless layers of cloud. He looks down between his feet. Expecting to see the leaden grey swell of the sea reach up for him at any moment. The expected panic does not arrive.

I'm going to die but I feel calm.

He catches a glimpse of a gleam of light below. Then he is sailing down through the last tufts of cloud. There is countryside below. A map of fields and trees. He can hardly believe his eyes. It is like a beautiful piece of music swimming through his body. He twists his head and spies a farmhouse. Keeps it in sight as it grows larger and acquires detail beneath him.

That does not look like an English farmhouse, Jack.

14

The parachute blossoms again in the wind and drags him over a small stretch of unploughed muddy earth. Just like English muddy earth. But he knows he is not in England.

Navigation isn't your strong point, is it, Wentworth?

No sir.

Must be France. He has never been to France. Evie's mother is French. Evie spoke to him in French when she woke him up in the guesthouse bed. Woke him up before the sun had risen. Mischief in the tilt of her head. She had pushed the sheet back. His naked body exposed down to his thighs. Her voice intent and absorbed like a needle she was guiding in and out of fabric.

"What are you saying?"

She said something else in French. But she called him Guy.

"Evie," he said. "My name isn't really Guy Wentworth."

This is when she stopped speaking in French.

I knew if I ever told the truth....

The raindrops sliding down his face taste of petrol.

Everything is still. The rain still coming down. No sign of life anywhere. Not even a cow or sheep. There is a drab film of unreality over everything. As if one blink of his eyes will lodge him back in the cockpit of his aircraft. He picks some wet grass and rubs at the stinging in his eyes. He takes his cigarettes from his pocket. A sodden pulp. He thinks of all the cigarettes he has wasted in his life. What he wouldn't give for one of them now.

He is on a stage with no lines. No idea what is expected of him. No cues. No language even. The only thing he can think of doing is to hide the parachute. So he does that. Gathers up the bundle of wet white silk, struggles to make it as compact as possible and stuffs it in a ditch. Covers it with soggy leaves crawling with insects.

What else?

Create a false trail, they said.

You mean, what I've been trying to do my whole life?

It seems somehow inconceivable that anyone out there should know of or care about his existence. But his aircraft must have crashed somewhere. Caused a good deal of excitement. Probably there are people searching through the wreckage at this very moment. This rupture of separation from his kite draws forth an ache of physical tenderness for the dead aircraft. So much of his self-esteem resided in that machine. He pulls out his RAF identification papers. Feels a wave of sympathy for the innocent youthful face in the photograph. He realises he is now officially missing in action. Which means dead. He wonders if Evie will find out. He takes some bitter pleasure in the thought of her experiencing him as dead.

He starts to walk. Drenched through. Doused in aviation fluids. Wearing a RAF flying suit. Fur-lined boots. What chance does he have of evading capture? He can't though quite tune in the realisation that this countryside is under the jurisdiction of the Germans. The enemy. The sinister Nazi soldiers he has seen in the newsreels at the cinema.

"Hello France," he says aloud. To gee himself up. To make light of the situation. "*Parlez-vous anglais?*" he says and his chuckle of laughter at his own buffoonery frightens him a bit.

He pictures what will be happening at base now. There is still a residue of disbelief in his body that he will not be back at base later. Keyed in to its rituals. Infected by its energy. The energy of tense and harried men celebrating another moment's respite. The only tension in this countryside is his own.

Things go on without us. Evie will still laugh. Benedict will finish Mrs Dalloway.

Now and again it occurs to him that he needs some kind of plan. But every time he thinks himself beyond the moment he becomes despondent. Better just to hold on to the illusion that he is enjoying a walk in the French countryside. Which in other circumstances might be a source of wonder and peace.

It has stopped raining. The puddles are drying out. But his clothes are still damp and cold against his skin. He walks along the side of a road. Prepared at every moment to dive down into the cover of a ditch. More light fades from the sky. He is thirsty. He is hungry. His body cries out for warmth.

A dog barks at him from behind a hedgerow. He catches a glimpse of it. Underfed mangy thing but with strong jaws. Showing its teeth and its gums.

"Thank heavens there's a hedgerow separating you and me, old man," he says to it. But he crosses over to the other side of the road. Just in case. Fifty yards further on the dog is no longer behind the hedge. It is waiting for him at the side of the road.

Don't show it any fear.

Easy for you to say that.

It is growling at him. Poised on its hind legs to spring. He looks around for a tree he can climb if it attacks. He walks on. Determined not to be intimidated by a dog. It appears the dog is frightened of crossing the road.

"You bloody coward," he says to it. It stops barking.

He walks past a farmhouse. Arrives at a fork in the road. A signpost. Labourse, it says. His predicament extends further into hallucinogenic realms. As if he is a piece being moved about in a board game. Labourse is where his father was shot. In all probability where he is buried. In an unmarked grave. The man he went to see told him so. The man who shot his father. Who can't forgive himself, even more than twenty years later, for shooting his father.

"They got him drunk with rum so he wouldn't know what was happening. There was a dirtiness about the whole thing. A shame everyone felt. He kept saying he wanted to see his wife and son before he died. Pleading he was. Blindfolded and trussed up like a pig being taken to market. He had a piece of white card hung round his neck. Resting by his heart. That was what we were supposed to aim at. The white square of card over his heart. I don't think he was any more a coward than any of us. He just wanted to see his wife and son. You."

He didn't warm to this man. Felt he was being manipulated by him. Used like a dishrag for the man to wipe away his guilt on. The only thing that bothers him about the man is how he came to have two of his father's drawings. He never asked him. Never acquainted himself with such a key part of the story.

He has probably walked ten miles. But he is going nowhere. He begins to look for somewhere he can sleep. He cuts across fields. Stumbling and tripping on the ploughlines. There is little light in the sky. Then he sees the shadow of a figure in the middle of the field. Too late to hide. The figure faces him unflinchingly.

"*Bonjour*," he calls out.

No answer.

He moves forward.

"I don't speak French, I'm afraid. But I apologise if I'm trespassing on your land."

No answer. The figure remains deadly still. He takes another few steps toward it. Holds up his hands in surrender. "Do you have anything to eat you can spare." He makes a gesture of eating with his bare hands.

What's the damn matter with this idiot?

"I'm very hungry."

It's then he realises he is talking to a scarecrow. Every moment of beauty and excitement he immediately wants to share with Evie. But this is a story he wants to share with Benedict. "And there I was, standing in the middle of a dark field in France, talking to a scarecrow." He sees Benedict's face as it used to be crease up with laughter.

He decides to steal the scarecrow's clothes. Try them on for size. Better to look like a scarecrow than a RAF pilot in Nazi occupied France. He imagines dressing the scarecrow up in his own uniform. The picture he forms in his mind amuses him. An effigy of himself staked in the middle of this field in France. In this place, or near this place where his father was killed.

He has stripped down to his underwear when he is torn out of the darkness by the funnels of two headlights. Frozen to the spot in this sudden spray of circus light. He shields his eyes. Peers out at the source of the spotlight that has rooted him to the spot. It is an armoured German vehicle. It stops, still with its headlights tunnelling a trail over the field. Two soldiers from the newsreels get out and call out to him in German. Rifles at the ready.

Told you it was a stupid idea. Swapping clothes with a scarecrow.

PART FIVE

1944

1

"You are not Monique Maupin. We know you are not Monique Maupin. Monique Maupin is a fiction. Monique Maupin does not exist."

"Can I have some water?"

The man leans just a fraction forward at his desk. She senses this movement rather than sees it. Because her eyes are tightly screwed shut.

There is a guttural scream from the room next door. Never has she heard so much horror, so much terror in a noise. She almost loses her balance, as if it is a physical force that knocks against her.

"You can have some water when you tell me what contacts you made in France and where the wireless operator is. Where Marcel is."

"I don't know."

He has the contents of her bag on his desk. She can no longer see them because a blinding light is trained up into her eyes. She can no longer see her interrogator either. He has disintegrated into the pulsing specks of white light that fill her eyes even when they are closed. She remembers him though. A wiry little man with deeply hooded eyes and a mean fidgety mouth.

She has been standing by his desk so long her legs are trembling with fatigue.

"You are a British agent. You have been working as a courier for Francois Pilain, code name Xan. He has been very cooperative. He told us about the postbox in the Brassier du Cygne. We have arrested the waitress. He told us about the postbox at the radio repair shop in Clermont. We have arrested the owner. He told us where to find you. We have arrested you. It is pointless for you to continue with this charade of pretending to be someone you are not. I do not have very much time to waste on you."

Always the bored monotone of his voice.

To begin with it was a good-looking athletic officer in a grey green uniform with frosted blue eyes who questioned her. Led her up a flight of stairs with a desolate echo and through three interconnected offices to this room in a building in Paris with its two desks and closed shutters. Questioned her in German which the typist, a prim French woman wearing dainty gloves, translated. There were two other men, wearing caps with the SS skull and crossbones. These two men circled her, shouting German invective in her ears.

She was photographed.

"Are you Jewish?"

"No."

"How do I know you're not Jewish?"

"Can I have some water?"

"Tell me where Marcel is, I let the boy and his family go."

"Leopold and his family are innocent."

"Then tell me where Marcel is."

"I don't know."

"You are not Monique Maupin. We know you are not Monique Maupin. Monique Maupin is a fiction. Monique Maupin does not exist."

It is not true. Never has Monique been less of a fiction. She can't now escape Monique. It is Monique's memories she is guarding. Monique's integrity she is protecting. Monique has never felt more real to her. Never felt more dear to her. If anything it is Evie Devereux who is becoming a fiction. Who is ceasing to exist. As if Evie Devereux is in a deep sleep. And will not be woken. As if Evie Devereux no longer belongs to the world.

A door opens. A door leading to an adjoining office. She forces open her eyes. Blinking away the burning tears. She has to immediately close them again. But she catches a vivid image of Bruno. Stripped down to white shorts. Hanging by his wrists from a ceiling beam.

"Open your eyes!" It's the first time the rodent man has shouted.

"I can't."

"That was another of your accomplices. What was his mission? Where did he plan to put the explosives he was caught with?"

"I don't know."

"You look like an intelligent woman. It is a disappointment to discover you are really very stupid. Do you think we can't find out everything you know? Sooner or later."

She can't erase the picture of Bruno from her mind. His body a matrix of lacerations and burns. His hair thick with blood. She keeps seeing more details.

The typist returns with a tray. Soft-footed, stiff, punctilious. She sees her through a blur of tears. She has to stand in the middle of the room while her interrogator eats some lunch. She has now gone how many hours without food or water? The light of the lamp is still burning into her eyes. Now and again, between mouthfuls of bread and sausage, between sips of coffee, he asks her the same questions.

Xan is brought in to the room by the two men with the SS skull and crossbones caps. There are no marks on his face or hands. He has no difficulty in walking. But he is belittled and broken. A wizened husk of himself. All his old vanity and condescension and impatience gone from his puffy eyes.

"I was never told her real name," Xan says. "But yes, this is my courier. Anais."

"You are not Monique Maupin. We know you are not Monique Maupin. Monique Maupin is a fiction. Monique Maupin does not exist. You are a British spy. What's your real name?"

It's like some mad parlour game. What does it matter what her real name is?

2

She wakes up to the sound of voices. Disembodied voices. Cheerful singsong voices exchanging wellwishings. She is curled up on a thin straw mattress underneath which are three planks of wood on a rusted frame. Her lips are gummed tight with thirst. There is a strand of hair caught in her mouth. Not her own hair. Strange how one knows. How one can recognise something alien in the texture of a hair that is not one's own. She pulls it out. Repulsed as it unsticks from her palate and brushes against her lips.

She is curled up beneath a scratchy horsehair blanket crusted with stains. It smells of dried vomit. When she pushes it away the damp sepulchral odour of the cell is like a weight in her chest.

She listens out for the voice of Bruno. She tries to fit faces to the voices. Wonders about the relationship between voice and identity. How much of who we are is disclosed by the timbre of our voice. She finds she is attracted to one or two voices more than the others. There is the voice of a woman she likes. Someone whose friend she senses she could become. The voices are all wishing one particular prisoner luck. A man called Auguste. She understands it is the last day of his trial today. It surprises her that the Nazis hold trials. She wonders if this will be her fate. If she will be judged in front of a jury of scornful hardened faces.

A game is instigated where you recite loud and clear any poem you remember or whistle any song or piece of music. She is too shy to participate but she takes some heart from the poems and songs. She thinks of introducing herself to the voices, of joining in, but is no longer sure by what name she should go. She wakes up as a ghost of Evie, a bewildered childish Evie who has lost everything that once belonged to her. But concern for Leopold and Bruno quickly return her to Monique.

Then someone begins whistling *Clair de Lune.* She is moved by the beautiful simplicity of the melody. It lifts her out of herself for a moment. Out of the cell. Out of her predicament. Connects her to moments when life was a heartening presence felt on her skin. The disembodied voices all fall silent. She hears heavy footsteps. The sound of keys rattling. So vivid she can smell the rust on the ring holding these keys. Her heart quickens. But the footsteps pass by her door. Her door with its peephole behind a metal flap that makes a clicking noise when it is lifted, when she is being spied upon.

The cell is five paces in length. She counts them out. The range of feeling available to her is no less shrunken, no less prone to dereliction. She paces back and forth several times beneath the fan light high in the whitewashed wall that is blotched with stains, gouged with inscriptions. Someone above her is doing the same identical thing. He coughs frequently and mutters to himself. She can hear all the intimate details of his incarceration.

In her cell she has a washbasin. When the water collects in the brown stained enamel basin she looks down at her reflection. Her face drowning in a swirl of dirty water. She has an ugly enamel jug by the slop pail.

A woman opens the door to her cell while she is kneeling on the floor. Reading the inscriptions on the wall. The woman is wearing the black shirt and insignia of the Nazi party. She has blonde pigtails that swing either side of her elfin ears. The woman starts shouting, telling her she is required to stand up whenever in the presence of a German. The woman barks at her. Telling her she is to be allowed no privileges. No exercise, no toiletries, no books. She wonders what has happened to this woman to make her so possessive of her anger. When she finishes shouting the woman throws a small brush on the floor. Tells her she must sweep clean her cell.

The pigtailed Nazi woman returns who knows how many hours later. This time she is already standing. Interrupted in the act of pacing back and forth. She is told she is wanted for interrogation. She is handcuffed. Marched past the two parallel lines of grey cell doors in the narrow corridor. She is taken back to the Gestapo offices. Driven in a car through tree-lined streets. The big chestnut trees seem like a kind of miracle to her. She tries to catch the eye of a pedestrian. To establish a connection with the world she no longer feels she belongs to.

"You are not Anais Maupin. We know you are not Anais Maupin. Anais Maupin is a fiction. Anais Maupin does not exist."

She waits for them to hurt her. To inflict physical pain. But they do not hurt her. The good-looking officer with the frosted blue eyes offers her a cup of coffee. Speaks of other circumstances in which they might be guests at the same dinner table. As if he's tired of the war. As if he's full of daydreams. The man with the fidgety mouth and the pasty indoor complexion isn't tired of the war. He tilts the lamp up into her eyes. Makes her stand for hours while he asks the same questions.

When she is returned to her cell she carries out her plan. She knocks out a message in morse on the wall. As she has heard someone else do. She asks about Leopold. "Does anyone know if a young boy is being held here? His name is Leopold."

She kneels down with her ear pressed to the stained wall. The anxiety of anticipation makes her feels like she is dangling from some high ledge. The pulse urgent in her wrists. The moment of suspension before letting go. Before dropping down to the ground. Her hunger for friendly contact reminds her of her childhood dogs. How much she would love to wrap her arms around one of those animals now. When the muffled series of tappings arrive her excitement is out of all proportion. As if she has made contact with the other side. With the dead. She has the crazy idea she might now communicate with her father and with Jack.

"I will find out. What is your name?"

She is thinking what she might say to her father, what she might say to Jack. She is Evie again. With her men. The men she has let down.

Get a grip of yourself.

She taps back ANAIS.

"Hello Anais. I am Jacques."

3

"Anais, I have lost weight."

"Hello Bruno. I have lost weight too."

She is in her cell, he is in his cell, separated by half a dozen other cells. She doesn't quite recognise the sound of her voice. So thin and parched sounding, echoing out from her larynx into the underworld labyrinth of sinister corridors and locked iron doors.

"Yes, but you don't need to lose weight. You are already perfect, Anais. Whereas I, I have lost weight to make myself irresistible to you when we get out of this place."

There is laughter.

"Of course you will have to ignore my missing teeth and my broken nose."

"You must be missing your garlic sausages."

"No. I am only missing you. And my teeth."

"I'm here, Bruno."

"But I miss your abuse. You've become much too kind hearted, Anais. It worries me."

"I am kind hearted, Bruno. It was only teasing."

"I know that, Anais. I liked your teasing. Your teasing was ambrosia to me."

"Have you seen Leopold?"

"No, I have not seen our young patriot but I am reliably informed he is being well looked after by Mimi and Juliette."

"Leopold is here with us," says another voice. A husky female voice with a breathless catch in it. "He can hear you but he refuses to speak. He is shy I think. Are you shy, Leopold?"

"Hello Leopold," she says.

To picture Leopold in a cell is horrible. She dwells in the shame he must feel every time he is forced to do his waste with the two women present. The two prostitutes he shares a cell with. No one knows anything about his mother.

The opening refrain of *Clair de Lune* is whistled. The warning that a guard is arriving. The terror awakened by footsteps. Everyone falls silent. Everyone shrinks back into his or her own cloistered anxiety. Recites the same silent prayer. That it will not be he or she who is to be taken off for interrogation.

It is her they have come for again. Voices follow as she is marched along the chemical blue haze of the corridor. Voices urging her to be strong, to deny everything. She could draw a map, matching the voices to the cells. Each voice has a vivid imaginary face for her now. The pigtailed Nazi woman shouts at the voices to shut up. A soldier puts a chain around her wrists outside the guardroom. Then she is led out into the thin winter sunlight that hurts her eyes.

She is asked the same questions. She gives the same answers. Again no physical harm comes to her.

Back in her cell she ladles up another spoonful of the bitter brine to her lips. Between mouthfuls she speaks to Suzanne next door. Suzanne has become her closest friend in the world. Even though she has no face. Suzanne's crime was to employ an old Jewish man as a music teacher for her daughter.

When she has finished her soup she inspects her damaged hair. She runs the lifeless knotted strands through her fingers. She remembers Jack complimenting her on the beauty of her hands. Now they are red and swollen with fissures in the dry skin beneath her long blackened nails.

Always the hope she'll wake up tomorrow with a little more fight in her.

And wilt thou leave me thus? Say nay! Say nay!

The cold has become more hateful than even the Gestapo interrogator. It steals under her clothes. She sits with the blanket over her head. Warming herself as best she can with her own breathing. Beneath the blanket she tries to think of only happy moments. Beneath the blanket she is alone and invisible, burrowed back into the secret game between herself and life that began in childhood and remains the essence of who she is.

One day she holds back her spoon. Not because she has any need of it but for the triumph of tricking the Germans. She uses it to chisel out words on the wall.

The Nazi woman forces her to undress. Makes her balance on one leg while she examines the sole of her lifted foot. Her teeth chatter. The tips of her fingers bloodless, the colour of corpse skin. Never has her skin felt so unclean, so alien. The Nazi woman asks if she is Jewish. Her fingers probing in her hair. She doesn't give an explanation. Is she trying to find the things she feels crawling about in her clothes, in her hair?

It is a young French boy now who passes her the food through the hatch. The watery potato peel soup. The slab of black bread. Who fills her stoneware jug with water. Who takes her slop pail. The passing out of which no longer causes her embarrassment. He whispers news of the war. The Germans are being driven back in Russia. The Allied forces are advancing towards Rome. Russia and Rome and meanwhile the cold burrows deeper and deeper down into the core of her being. "They say they will be landing in France any day now," the boy says.

The Gestapo interrogator asks her about the landings in France. He loses his temper. He tells her he could have her shot. But still they don't hurt her.

One day Bruno doesn't answer when she calls out to him.

"He was taken in the middle of the night and hasn't returned," the voice she knows as Odette says.

She could draw a map, matching the voices to cells.

Then one day, perhaps a week after the disappearance of Bruno, she sees the real faces of some of the voices. None are as she imagined. There is Suzanne. Older and more plain looking than she pictured. And Odette who has dried blood on her dress and cold sores on her lip. She has idealised all these women. She has painted the courage and spirited beauty of their voices onto their faces. She exchanges shy smiles with them. Catches Leopold's eye at the far end of the corridor. She is still perplexed as to why they have brought Leopold to Paris. Surely they have not interrogated him too. She is relieved to see there are no marks on his face. No one is allowed to talk. They are all standing outside their open cell doors. They are to be transferred to a camp in Germany. Just the women and children. There is one other child.

She is taken outside. Made to climb into the back of a vintage Parisian bus. Two armed German soldiers sit at the front and two on the open balcony at the rear. Poker faced beneath their scrimmed helmets. Despite the teasing of one or two of the girls. The girls of the night, in their dirty thin dresses and wooden platform shoes.

They are marched through the station at Pantin. It is exciting to be back out in the world again. The little leaps of imagination that spring from eye contact with strangers. Strangers whose ease of manner and air of entitlement make them exotic creatures to her. She watches the choreography of moments breaking up into other moments. And even though she is conscious of herself as a vagabond, a captive, a scarecrow woman, she feels for a brief moment what it is to be free.

The presence of Swedish Red Cross personnel at the station reassures her, the presence of moral overseers, as if decency hasn't been completely driven from the world.

The train stops and starts. It is a passenger train except she is behind wire meshing in a goods carriage. Leopold is not with her. She talks with Suzanne and the other women who all have faces now.

They are ordered off the train. The tracks have been bombed. She is relieved to discover she is still in France. There are two children on the platform who point and make disparaging masks of their faces. It pains her to be mocked by children.

They are marched down a country road. Sixty or so prisoners marshalled by six guards. Open fields puddling into darkness on either side. She manages to slip forward in the line, sidles in beside Leopold. She feels the embrace she wants to give him rustle a moment's warmth and wellbeing down to the roots of her being. Instead, so as not to attract the attention of the guards, she takes his hand. Surprised at how much eloquence of communion there is in the contact. She squeezes his hand. Feeling his presence fold into her, like a bee settling inside a circle of petals on a hoard of pollen.

"And wilt thou leave me thus? Say nay! Say nay!" she whispers.

"What language is that?"

"It's English. It's a poem. A poem my father taught me."

"Why did you say it in English?"

"Because it was written in English. And I have to keep reminding myself who I am."

"How do you do that?"

"I put a blanket over my head."

She sees the smile alight on his face, a simple reflex action of all the complicated chemistry in his young body, mirroring the smile on her own face.

They are marched across a high road bridge. Adjacent to the railway bridge that has been bombed. The chill wind bites through her summer clothes. She looks down at the moon on the water far below. No bigger than her thumbprint.

"Can you swim?" she says. Her heart is pounding so hard she has to press her palm to it.

"No," he says, surly.

"Don't worry," she says. "It was an absurd idea anyway. I keep having these absurd ideas. That's what I mean about having to remind myself who I am."

"That's why you put a blanket over your head?"

She squeezes his small hand again. "That's why I put a blanket over my head."

PART SIX

1944

1

The ingenuity involved is a marvel. Like going back in time to when civilisation engineered itself out of the caves. The forging and stylising of one thing into a new thing with a different and more refined purpose. The process of metamorphosis. The ability some men have to change the fundamental identity of a thing. Its purpose. So the spring from inside a gramophone becomes a saw. A piece of shoe leather becomes a valve. Kitbags become the bellows of an air pump. Tin cans became air ducts, tools, lamps and wheels. Mutton fat becomes the fuel that feeds the flame of the lamps. A pyjama cord became a wick. The men who come up with these inspirations are the kind of men who built civilisation. Who can strip things down to their base components and find a more profitable use for them. Unfortunately he is not one of these man. He has played no part in the creation of the complex environment thirty feet below the ground. Where there is electricity, an air pump, an air conditioning system, a railway network of trolleys, holding stations, store rooms.

But he does have a gift for mimicry. For forgery. And thus is a member of the forgery team. His talent for drawing is reawakened. He has earned the accolade of draughtsman. His father's gift. The first time he has been thankful to his father. The first time his father has offered him a way forward. He sits at a desk painstakingly reproducing in black ink the lines of the eagle and the swastika. The precision of the lettering in Gothic script required an unprecedented strain on his eyes. He turns out the necessary passes. The light grey and brown documents. On coffee or tea stained paper. The *Ausweise*. The *Kennkarte*. The *Bescheinigung*. The ugly words of Nazi rulemaking. He has a tiny paintbrush made of his own hair. He sits at a desk carving out the eagle and the swastika in the rubber heel of a flying boot. He sees the eagle and the swastika when he closes his eyes at night. Sees it float across the hut in the smoky white swing of the searchlight. He is proud of his work. It is something else he wants to show to Evie.

He likes this business of tricking the enemy. It suits his nature better than all forms of open combat. He is made to feel devious every time he catches the eye of a German guard. He is inwardly aglow with the knowledge of being the keeper of illicit secrets. It's like being a young boy again. The pains he took to conceal every new piece of knowledge he acquired from all adults. Probably it is this game of subterfuge and ciphers within life in the camp that makes many of the prisoners seem and act a bit childish. The rough and tumble games, the banter of abuse and mockery and sexual innuendo that in many men passes as a disclosure of affection. The only way they can express the consolation of camaraderie.

He has new friends. Each of them makes him miss Benedict in some different way. Each of them parodies in both touching and irritating ways the intimacy he shared with Benedict. None of his new friends makes him feel as vivid and attractive to himself as Benedict did. Evie once told him that the first thing that attracted her to him was the closeness she perceived between him and Benedict. She said to begin with she didn't quite know if it was him or Benedict she felt drawn to. It was the effect of the two of them together. He goes over his conversations with Evie time and time again in his head. Trying to locate in them evidence that he made a lasting impression on her. That his ghost will haunt her. He remembers the sudden shine of light that came into her eyes when she interrupted him, when her need to share a story or an idea was an irrepressible rush of blood in her body. That he has not been able to replace Benedict is therefore a good sign. It means there are ghosts that will not cease in their haunting of us despite the influx of new companions.

Neither Johnny nor Matty nor Piper will haunt him. Or any of his new friends. One of his old companions at OTU is in the camp. Shot down in his Lancaster bomber over Hamburg. A chap he stole some biography from to colour and sculpt Guy's counterfeit background. But he has outgrown Guy Wentworth now. The insecurities that prompted the creation of Guy Wentworth have lost their power to humiliate him. Anyway he has another bogus identity now. He is Frederic Tarriet. French labourer. The papers he mostly forged himself.

He has learned French. Learned it well in the three years of his captivity. Because you have to feel a year has counted for something. That you have added something tangible to your list of accomplishments. In one of his daydreams he speaks French to Evie. In his daydream she widens her eyes at this new accomplishment of his. Every new accomplishment he takes to her for her approval. He has learned some German too. Little else to do here except try to learn some of what other men know.

Sometimes he worries he is losing his looks. The coarse soap that leaves an itchy crackle in his hair. The gristled masculine austerity of this life in the camp. Sanding away some sheen of sensitivity and freshness on the surface of his skin. He has tried to convince himself he did enough to make a lasting impression on Evie. Because she is what he means when he thinks about freedom.

He has only been down in the tunnel once. The thought of going down there again brings him out in a cold sweat. The elemental starkness of it. The primeval texture and fumes of it that awaken the primeval in his own being. His grip on who he is, the essential shape and heft of his identity was wrestled from him in the tunnel. He had to fight to preserve his outlines. The sense of a colossal weight pressing down on all sides, squeezing the air out of his lungs, the light out of his memories. The tunnel wants him nameless. A thing yet unborn. Someone joked it was like the birth cavity. But he could find no humour in the tunnel. He had to take many deep breaths to calm his heart. But every deep breath seemed to exhaust the air supply to his lungs and his heart pounded all the more franticly. Desperate for a vision of sky.

"Could be our last ever night in these bunks."

Johnny is in the bunk below.

"The Goons were suspicious today."

Des is in the bunk below Johnny.

"Who can blame them? We were like an excited troupe of chorus girls about to go on stage all day."

"Funny thing is a part of me will miss it here."

"Which part is that then?"

"Odd isn't it. A change of circumstances and we're one foot nearer the grave. I suppose that's what it is. Do you reckon any of us will actually make it home?"

He doesn't join in the discussion. He lies with his hands interlaced behind his head. The scent of the high pines comes in with the chill air through gaps in the woodwork of the hut. Swimming around with the brewing masculine stink of old socks and perspiration and stomach disorders. He thinks about Evie. Because she is what he means when he thinks about freedom.

2

"If you can lie about something as pivotal as who you are…"

It is his turn. His turn to descend down into the birth canal.

"Good luck, Jack."

"Who's Jack?" he asks. "I don't see any Jacks in the vicinity."

It surprises him he is capable of making light of the situation. If only in speech. He slides down into the shaft. His body immediately registering with a chill prickle of anxiety the drop in temperature. He slides down the laddering of the shaft with the aplomb of a professional soldier. Another act of mimicry. In his civilian clothes. The flat cap made out of an old blanket. The scratchy trousers made from sacking. Boot polish on his face. The dyed and re-tailored battledress tunic with his forged documents in the wallet in the inside pocket. His first act as this new man. Frederic Tarriet. There are two letters in his pocket addressed to Frederic. From his girlfriend in Paris. His fictitious girlfriend. Jeanne Cellard.

Be lucky, Frederic Tarriet. Be brave. Be resourceful.

Down in the shaft with its slanting wooden beams he is told there is a slight problem.

"The tunnel exit isn't quite where it's supposed to be. Miscalculation somewhere along the line. Unfortunately it doesn't exit in the woods."

"If it doesn't exit in the woods…"

"It exits in full view of the guards beyond the fence. The good news however is that there's a system."

"There's a system."

"Coded rope tugging. You'll get the hang of it. Piece of cake really. So I've been told."

He finds he doesn't care. Doesn't care that the tunnel exits in full view of the guards beyond the fence. He doesn't care because he has so little belief he will ever emerge from the tunnel.

He lays belly down on the trolley. He settles himself into the board with little shifts of his hips. His penis the part of his body he is most aware of. Pressed against his belly in a warm tingle of nerves. He makes the knocking noise with the trowel on the wheel. The signal he's ready. And then the wheels of the trolley creak into motion and he enters the narrow low mouth of the tunnel itself. This artificial vein thirty feet below the surface of the earth. It's like a child's game. A game that would make a child cry out with a bleeding together of excitement and fear. He remembers the toboggan his grandfather made for him. Can feel the grain of the wood again on his hands. It's okay when he's in motion. There's even an undercurrent of carefree abandon. The novelty of being belly down on a cart moving through a succession of lights in a realm that pulsates with secrecy.

He reaches the first station. The first chamber. Leicester Square it's called. Leicester Square was the last place he saw Evie. A chap called Jarvis he barely knows mans this station. Smudged streaks of boot polish or dirt on his face. Ghoulish in the aquarium light. There is height enough here to scramble up onto his knees. The ghost train disappears back into the tunnel.

"Bad show about the tunnel being too short. Sooner or later I'm waiting for the sound of whistles. Every fibre of my being is primed for the shriek of whistles. It's about to happen at every moment. Can't you hear it?"

He doesn't like it here. And the peevish fatalism of this man Jarvis is not helping. It's the stillness that makes his heart thump up into his veins. When he can feel the weight of the earth gathering in a swell around him. Down here he understands why temples were built, why civilisations sought solace in holy texts and illuminated arcane symbols and trinkets of sanctified jewellery. He settles onto the second trolley. Jarvis wishes him luck. Then, headfirst, he is rolling deeper into the underground labyrinth. Every now and again a glint of tin flashes up at him – the pipeline of welded cans through which his air is being pumped inspires little confidence. The thinness of the air registers itself as heaviness in the flow of his blood. Something he experienced at very high altitudes in his Spitfire.

But this is like the absolute antithesis of flying.

The air raid siren, when it makes its saw-toothed wail, seems to come from inside him at first. Whoever is up ahead pulling the cord of his trolley stops pulling. Then all the lights go out. The siren continues its wail. But in another dimension. Muffled and sinister. There are mutterings. They reach him as scratchy rodent noises. As pulses of distress in the dark.

In the thickening swell of darkness there's no question. Evie has forgotten all about him. He has been deluding himself. Everything he has ever thought with desire in it is a delusion. A forgery.

What if the chap working the air pump stops working the air pump?

It is deep swills of darkness, not air, he takes down deep into his diaphragm. Darkness that is billowing inside him. It has a grainy texture, this darkness he is taking into his lungs. Like soot. Like ashes. It steals from him his sense of the shape of his body. He has a sense of his eyes bulging, like a shored fish.

The chap won't stop working the air pump.

He might. In the darkness. In the confusion. Perhaps guards are checking the hut. Any bloody thing could be happening up there.

If he lifts his head a fraction it makes contact with the wooden boards above. If he spreads out his elbows they touch the wooden boards on either side of him. Every time he touches the press of the walls he feels a shudder of terror, as if he has touched something with an ancient curse on it. Panic is a hair's breadth away. Panic welling up from oceanic depths. He is wedged inside this underworld shelf with the first feelers of panic crawling over his skin.

"If you can lie about something as pivotal as who you are…"

"It doesn't change who I am with you, Evie. It's just a name."

"What are we if not our names?"

"My father was shot as a coward. I was terrified I might be a coward too. I thought if I became someone else, if I didn't have his name…"

"So I'm to call you Jack now?"

"If you want."

"Jack suits you better than Guy."

"I've come to realise that. I think."

"I'm not very brave, Guy, Jack. You ought to know that."

The lights stutter back on with the shock of hallucination. For a moment, blinking away the sorcery of darkness behind his eyes, he thinks he has been caught. He thinks the game is up. Then he is jerked forward on the trolley. Almost losing his balance at this renewal of animation in the world. Almost losing his hat. There is greater urgency in the momentum of the ghost train. The judder of the wheels shakes him about like a dice inside a clenched fist.

Then he can stand up again. In his civilian clothes. In his flat cap. In the scratchy trousers made of sacking. The forged documents of Frederic Tarriet in his inside pocket. Close to his heart. He hits his head on one the slanting beams.

"I was about to warn you about that."

This is Roger. The crease of strain around his mouth conveys the tension he now feels he has left behind. He steadies his right foot on the first of the ridges in the wooden panelling. Poised to spring up. Gripping the rope along which the message will arrive. His neck strained upwards for a glimpse of sky, for the glitter of a star. *Per Ardua ad Astra.* A wash of white light sweeps past overhead. The rope tautens in his fist. Goes slack. Tautens again.

"Here I go," he says.

"Good luck, Jack."

Up he goes. He sees his head emerge from the gash in the

ground from the perspective of someone up there. He becomes to himself a burlesque. A character in a satyr play. A character with mischief as his mission. Then his head really is emerging from the gash in the ground. The chill cleanliness of the air is a benediction. The searchlight sweeps off to his left. He heaves all his weight up into his shoulders. His face in the grass and dirt. The peppery tang of moss and herb in his nostrils. Like another boyhood adventure. He knows only relief now. Not fear. He can spit out the menace of a couple of German guards with guns. He has escaped from the obliterating suck of the blackness underground. He is returned to all his memories. His idiosyncrasies. To the map of who he is. He runs crouched down inside himself towards the trees. Making himself as small and insignificant as possible. A shadow slinking across the face of the earth.

3

The road slopes down into a sleepy small town. She spies a cat, black with white markings, padding in the shadow of a vine-draped wall. She keeps thinking there must be a way to avoid getting back on that train. She keeps thinking soon it will be too late. And she will live to regret not taking advantage of the chance she now has. Freedom is all around. Behind every corner. On the other side of every door. Everywhere except in this line she is forced to walk in with Leopold by her side. But there are six guards walking alongside the sixty or so prisoners strung out in pairs. Six guards with rifles. It infuriates her that only a piece of machinery gives these unexceptional uniformed young men a wholly unearned bloated power over her and Leopold. She feels the heavy undertow of reluctance in Leopold's gait. The child conforming with inward rebellion to the dictates of the adult world. Peevish rather than frightened. She feels an impulse to look at the cat again. But when she looks back it has vanished.

They enter the town's main square. The closed brown shutters of the buildings of weather beaten stone. A Nazi banner outside the most imperious building where there is a solitary sentry. Like the last man standing in a town of ghosts. The station must be near now. A girl skips out of line, over the cobbles, to go to the fountain. There is a bluster of shouting from the guards. A moment of disorder. She increases the pressure on Leopold's hand. There is a brown door to her left. About four paces away. About ten heartbeats away. It looks larger than life. Filling her entire field of vision. Gleaming with consequence. The flaking paint, the grain of the wood, the scuff marks and splinters where the wood has been chipped. She has an instinct it is faintly ajar.

She wills it to be open with the most impassioned prayer she has ever bodied forth. She pulls Leopold violently out of the line. Offering no explanation. She hears the incensed bark of the German voice. The chiselled metallic click of a rifle. She doesn't hesitate. She pulls Leopold by the hand. Barely in control of her own determination. Only half aware she is hearing the bark and the metallic click in imagination only.

She pushes at the brown door.

"And that's how you escaped?"

"And that's how we escaped. We were in a dark hallway, full of bicycles."

"You expect me to believe that?"

She lifts her arm across her face. Presses her lips to the skin near her shoulder. Tasting herself. Jean Paul, in the bed beside her, is smoking a crumpled cigarette. With his usual air of flaunting himself, of revelling in the triumph of being himself.

"Of all the doors in the world this is the one I'll probably always remember."

"The door of doors."

"Strange thing is, I recognised it as soon as I saw it."

"Pierre thinks this story is implausible and that you're a spy."

"Leopold thinks you're something worse than a spy."

"What's worse than a spy?"

"You'll have to ask him."

"He doesn't like me."

"You don't like him."

"No. I don't much. I can't help it. It's the way he looks at me. We're jealous of each other. You wouldn't understand. It's a thing between men."

"He's a child."

"You need to get rid of him. He's a liability."

"I'd get rid of you before I got rid of him."

"That's why I'm jealous."

"Be jealous then."

"What's wrong with him anyway? What's it called? What he's got."

"Muscular dystrophy."

"Makes him slur his words."

"Only when he's upset."

"In that case, when isn't he upset?"

"When you're not around."

"He needs to become more manly."

"Sometimes I'm not sure I like you."

"But here you are in my bed."

She would like to believe it is Anais, not Evie, who has taken Jean Paul as a lover. But the attraction she feels for him is a pulse in her blood, a current moving over her skin. It has no purchase on her mind that she can easily rationalise. She would not be able to explain it in a letter. It's a connection forged by smell and chemistry and the magnetic pull in the air when they are in the same room. An unacknowledged hollow in her being into which he fits.

The first time she saw him he was fencing an invisible opponent. The dainty juggling of his feet on the wooden boards. The narrow-eyed venom of his thrusts and parries. A swashbuckling pirate with his thin moustache and shirttails and braces hanging loose outside his breeches. He has a scar under his left eye, a thin puckering of skin that makes the eye above look hooded. Makes him look like a villain. He is a man who needs both an opponent and an audience to become vivid to himself. A trait that in other circumstances would repel her. Later she listened and watched while he played the piano. The workings of his shoulder blades tailoring the folds in his white shirt. The piano was an opponent too. She couldn't help marvelling at the passionate ease with which he brought it under submission.

She and Leopold have been taken to Nancy. Jean Paul says

there is an English wireless operator here. That he will arrange a meeting. Even though he disapproves of women getting involved in politics.

He is secretive about his role in the war.

"Just in case you *are* a spy."

She pushes back the blanket and sheet. The warmth of his and her secretions now a chill spot on her inner thigh, a gummy crackle in her pubic hair.

She notices he seems more fascinated by his own nakedness than hers.

She hasn't told him she is English. She hasn't brought up the subject of Evie Devereux. She is playing a game of charades with him. As Guy or Jack played a game of charades with her.

4

The three men interrogating him are civil. They drive him in an old truck that runs on charcoal to a kind of storeroom in a backstreet alley. Rusting and broken bits of machinery scattered about. Obsolete things that have served their purpose. He has noticed one of the men, a man with a loosened tie and a crumpled jacket, the man he least likes, has a revolver tucked inside his belt. He is not the spokesman though. The spokesman has neatly parted hair and his fingers are blackened with newsprint.

"You understand we have to make sure you are who you say you are?"

He nods.

"It's hard to believe you made it half way across Germany without being detected. Perhaps more than hard."

"I walked from dusk to dawn."

"And you say a woman helped you. A German woman who hated the Nazis but who was working for them."

"She worked for the Wehrmacht. On encryption machines at the Transport Command in Hamburg. At least that's what she told me. And I have no reason to disbelieve her."

"We have checked and it's true there was a breakout from the camp you mentioned. Can you tell me the name of your squadron, where it's based and who the commanding officer is?"

"I'm afraid I can't divulge that information. Anyway, I've been a POW for so long any information I have about the squadron is probably now ancient history."

The man with newsprint on his fingers asks him about clubs

in London. He has never heard of any of these clubs. He is reminded of standing before the committee when he applied to join the RAF. Of his Wings examination. Of his first solo flight. Of losing his virginity to Evie. All the moments when he was on trial. All the moments when he had to overcome his own scepticism. His own self-doubt. The man with newsprint on his fingers asks him about statues outside or near London's architectural landmarks. He doesn't do very well in this part of the test either.

"How about RAF slang?"

"Fire away."

"Aircrew."

"Grease monkeys."

"Ambulance."

"Blood wagon."

He's waiting for the next one when the man with the loosened tie and crumpled jacket brings his knee up hard between his legs.

"Fucking hell," he moans, doubling up.

"Forgive me but we had to make sure. I think we now have the proof that you are who you say you are."

All three men are grinning. He understands now that they have been looking forward to this moment. A school playground moment. Nothing caused as much excitement in the school playground as a fight. As the sight of inflicted pain. The interrogation has all been a sham. He was brought here so the man with the loosened tie and crumpled jacket could perform this one act.

He is taken to a house. "You'll have to stay here for a couple of weeks," says the man with newsprint on his fingers. "Marie will bring you your food. You mustn't leave this room. Or even look out of the window. In the meantime we'll work on getting you to Switzerland."

"Thank you," he says.

He is soon bored. Yet more of his life frittered away on waiting. He is twenty-four years old now. He has to severely ration his cigarettes. Mentally he paces back and forth in the stretches of time before he allows himself another cigarette. Every period of forced abstinence a desert. Much as it was in the camp. He sits on the bed, looking over towards the forbidden window. In this town with a woman's name. Nancy, the name of the girl he made pull down her pink knickers in the tool shed when he was nine years old.

The woman Marie arrives with a tray. Onion soup in a chipped bowl. A piece of bread. She calls him Frederic. It makes him uncomfortable to answer to another false name. Thins out the reality of what is happening to him to no more than a painted surface. Marie has a large birthmark on the left side of her face. Shaped like the map of a country. He would like to convey to her that it doesn't matter. But he knows it does. It has shaped her entire life. It is why she is unmarried, childless. She has a nice figure. Inside her ugly clothes.

She will be shot if she is caught sheltering an escaped British POW. Another rule of the game.

"So you can look out of the window without being seen," she says, nodding at the mirror he has arranged near the window.

"Yes. Might help pass the time. When I've had enough of Victor Hugo for a while."

"It must be boring. Being cooped up like this."

"Yes. It is a bit. But I'm incredibly grateful."

The mirror reflects a segment of the narrow street below. One table outside a café. Café des Amis. Six doorways. The kerb and a sliver of the road. Like a stage set. This is his horizon now. After the infinity of the skies. *Per Ardua ad Astra.* The cockpit smell of leather, oil and grease returns to him. The spectacle below of a sunsheened surf of cloud. It comes and goes in an elegiac flash. Sometimes now he feels the best years of his life are already behind him.

For a while the glass is empty. A blaze of sunglitter. He reads his book. The Victor Hugo novel in French. He understands about two words of every five. His tenses are weak, past and future. Most of what he says in French he is careful to posit in the present tense. He is a prisoner of the present tense. But so far no one has taken much interest in his past. Then, when he looks up, there is a cat in the glass. He had forgotten all about cats. So long since he saw one. The cat pauses by a wall. Begins to clean itself with its paws. He watches mesmerised. Then it suddenly scurries off and an SS officer and a man holding a bunch of flowers sidle onto the mirror's glass. The heart racing drama of it. The tint of unreality shaded into the scene by the glass. The SS uniform somehow heightened in its prepossessing clarity. Probably because he is able to stare at it without restriction or distraction. It is hard for his body to understand there is no danger that he will be suddenly exposed in this act of voyeurism. His heart continues to race. He watches as they lean into each other. Alert and secretive. Talking in whispers. Then the man with the flowers takes a step back. As if outraged or surprised. He pretends the bunch of flowers is a sword. His legs perform a prancing scissorlike movement. He thrusts the flowers at the SS officer. The SS officer has a smile on his face. The man with the flowers has his back turned in the mirror's reflection. Silver highlights in his sleek black hair.

5

"Flowers?" she says.

Jean Paul holds out his offering with a gesture of vaudeville gallantry. The usual healthy flush on his face despite the food rationing. "Why not? Just because there's a war on…"

"Doesn't mean a man can't give a woman flowers."

"You want to finish my sentences for me now."

"Thank you. For the flowers."

She kisses him on the cheek. Then she holds out the cluster of blue, violet and lilac flowers for Leopold to see and smell. Leopold stands awkwardly, as if holding a heavy bag in one hand. He ignores the flowers.

"Hello Leopold. Why not try a smile? Just this once. To mark the occasion."

"Leave Leopold alone."

"Seriously though."

"I'm taking Leopold to the zoo," she says.

"Not much of a zoo. No lions. No tigers. No snakes. What kind of zoo is it that doesn't have a single animal that can kill you?"

"I don't know. You tell me. What kind of zoo is it?"

"There you are and there's a lion prowling back and forth six feet away." He embarks on a swaggering, loose-limbed walk across the room.

"Is this supposed to be a lion you're imitating?"

Even Leopold can't help smiling.

"Do you see lion, Leo?"

"This beast that can run as fast as a train. That could dismember you in two minutes. And it holds your eye while it pads back and forth." He is still doing his swaggering loose-limbed walk. Looking at her now from under his brows, with narrowed eyes.

"I still don't see a lion. Leo, do you see a lion?"

Leopold shakes his head. Some light has returned to Leopold's eyes, some of the beauty of expression has returned to his face.

"And you stand there feeling very small. You stand there marvelling. Because this is definitely something worth seeing. This is something you will continue to see long after it's no longer there in front of your eyes. As impressive as any damn cathedral or pyramid."

"But there are no lions at the zoo in Nancy."

"Exactly my point. The best you'll get is maybe an ostrich." He stretches up his neck, puckers his mouth.

"We want to see the monkeys," she says.

"Are there monkeys? I think you might find there are only ostriches. Ostriches without sand to bury their heads in."

"I've been told there are monkeys."

He does an impersonation of a monkey for Leopold. Beating his chest with his fists and making monkey sounds.

"By the way, we've got an appointment at six. After you're done with the monkeys."

"Appointment?"

"The British wireless operator. He took some persuading. Like the British in general he's cagey and over cautious. But he finally relented. After getting the nod from London. London apparently is happy Anais is safe. London was fearing the worst."

"We're not going through this again, are we?"

"Did you know Anais was her field name?" he says to Leopold. "How many names do you have anyway?"

"Seven. The last time I counted."

"One for each day of the week. No wonder you're so changeable."

"Am I?"

"Some days I look at you and I think, who is she? At least Leopold here is consistent. At least I know where I stand with Leopold."

The searching look he gives her does not run very deep. He is not trying to root her out despite any protest he might make to the contrary.

Everything is a game to him.

"Don't pretend you want to live in an ideal world," she says.

"Don't I?"

"No. You don't expect much from the world."

"Or from you. Because if I did…"

She looks at him with widened eyes and a smile.

"We both know what would happen. Well Anais or Monique or Aurelie. Six o'clock at the café des Amis. On the corner of Rue Debussy and Rue Villiers. You might want to find it on your map."

"I'll have to bring Leopold."

"Excellent. I'll buy him an orangeade. I'll buy you an orange-ade, Leopold. What do you say to that?"

6

He puts aside the Victor Hugo novel. There are pages missing. Ruptures in the narrative that leave him feeling suddenly lost and disheartened. That make him think of the missing pages in his own life. All the stories his parents might have told him had they not died.

He is not allowed another cigarette until after dinner. He thinks he might have a bath before dinner. He looks up at the tilted mirror. It shows six doorways and an empty table outside the Café des Amis.

He goes down into the kitchen. Tells Marie he would like a bath. She is rolling pastry at the kitchen table. The sleeves of her grey cardigan rolled up. Its white snowflake pattern hidden behind her apron. A sheen of sweat on her brow. White flecks of flour in her hair. He tries to think what country her birthmark resembles in outline. Belgium perhaps. She catches him looking at the mark on her face and he blushes. He fills the largest copper pan with water. Puts it on the stove. More waiting. He talks with Marie about trivial things. Except they don't seem trivial in a foreign language. His every sentence is an achievement he can take pride in. He enjoys talking in French. His hands are more animated. Chiselling out meaning in the air.

Then he carries the pail of hot water up the stairs and empties it in the tub and repeats the procedure again.

The water in the tub only reaches the undersides of his legs. A forlorn affair, this bath. He looks down at his genitals. A recognisable part of who he is. He would recognise his own genitals in a crowd. He smiles at the absurdity of this image. He remembers one of his lines when he played Orlando in a production of *As You Like It* at the camp. He says it to himself quietly. "You touched my vein at first; the thorny point of bare distress hath taken from me the show of smooth civility."

The memory of the rehearsals and the production itself has some glamour in it. One of the few dashes of lively colour in the monochrome repetition of life in the camp. The atmosphere blended of play and disciplined toil. He remembers the thrill of understanding the meaning of his lines. A knowledge of the blood before it became an idea he could express in words. He returns to the attic room wearing only a towel. More Orlando than himself. Whistling, as if back in the Forest of Arden. He leaves wet footprints on the bare wooden boards behind him. His flesh puckering up into goosebumps. He unknots the towel. Dries his hair with it. Out of the corner of his eye he sees a boy in the glass. A new story in the mirror. He pauses in the act of drying his hair. The boy's head is twisted up at an odd angle. A kind of grimace on his face. There is something wrong with him. Some ailment that means he has to keep twisting his head back. For a moment he has the uneasy feeling he is meeting the boy's eye. That a connection is being made in the glass. Marie earlier wondered if it might be possible to see the reflection in the mirror from down in the street. He feels an affinity with this boy. A tender concern for his welfare. It's his air of being outcast, separated from the central narrative of his life. Then the man from earlier walks into the frame. The man with the flowers. Except he has no flowers now. The man who is friendly with the SS. He can tell the boy shares no intimate bond with this man. The language his body speaks is diffident and sulky.

Poor little chap.

A woman now joins the scene. His heart begins pounding before his mind makes the connection. She looks like a scruffy older version of Evie. Uncanny. Then she looks up towards the window. As if registering some intensity of interest in the air above her.

He runs out of the room. Half way down the stairs he remembers he is naked.

"Damn," he says. "But it can't be her. It can't be Evie. In France."

Marie has appeared by the bottom step.

"What on earth is the matter?"

She ignores his nudity. Her expression is one of stark alarm. As if they are in mortal danger. Or she sees his nudity only as a curious background detail.

"I have to go outside. Hang on."

He is back in his room. The mirror is empty now. He throws on his clothes. Still doing up buttons as he runs down the stairs.

"You mustn't go outside. It's dangerous."

He understands what she means. Even in his state of high agitation. It is dangerous for her too.

"Just to the corner. Only to the corner."

But when he arrives at the corner there is no sign of Evie.

"I think I might be going mad," he tells Marie. "I thought I saw my old English girlfriend outside. And she was with a man I saw fraternising with an SS officer earlier."

"All this happened in that mirror of yours?"

He nods, pinching the back of his neck.

7

"Who was that man?"

Leopold means the British wireless operator. He and Evie are walking alongside a high stucco wall on which are pasted defaced Nazi propaganda posters. There are ugly posters on every telegraph pole too.

"Better you don't know," she says.

Leopold's body can't help dramatizing every inflicted hurt. They erupt on the surface in little jerks and spasms of his muscles or a more contorted twist of the neck, a dropping of the jaw, a stiffening of the shoulders, a bobble of white saliva gummed to the tip of his tongue. His body is like a compass. Registering every change of his emotional life.

"I don't like keeping secrets from you, you know. Let's make a pact. When the war ends I'll tell you all my secrets." She takes a bite of the pear they are sharing and then hands it to him. His coat, she notices, is crookedly buttoned.

"The war won't end just because you want it to."

"The more people who want it to end the sooner it will end though."

"Lots of people like being slaves to the Nazis. They like being told what to do. They're like sheep. They only wake up if someone shouts at them."

"Do you want to get us arrested again?"

"Where do you think my mother is? Where do you think Adela is?"

"Probably in a camp somewhere. You'll see them again when

the war is over. In the meantime I'm afraid you're stuck with me. Isn't it about time you had a haircut?"

"Do you keep secrets from him?"

"Jean Paul? Lots," she says with a big smile. "He doesn't even know my secret name."

"Evie," he says.

"Ssssh. That's something between me and you."

"Hush hush," he mocks.

"We're going on a journey soon."

"With him?"

"No. Yes. For a while. He is going to drive us some of the way."

"A journey where?"

"I can't tell you."

She registers his protest without looking.

"All right. We're going to the Pyrenees."

"What's that?"

"Mountains. Mountains that border France with Spain. We're going to help someone escape from the Germans."

"Who?"

"Someone I don't know. An English pilot. But you mustn't breathe a word."

"I wish *he* wasn't going."

"Why do you dislike him so much?"

"You've already asked me that."

"I'm asking you again. Without him, what would we do?"

"We'd be just you and me."

"Without any money. Without a roof over our heads."

"You could earn some money."

"But why don't you like him?"

"He never means what he says."

She stops in mid-stride. In the narrow street between sandstone and greystone houses with iron balconies. Latticework of scrolls and florets and twisting bare vines. A draped figure poised between two columns on the façade of the building at the end of the road. Two winged creatures higher up on the lintel.

"Why do you say that?"

"He pretends he likes me but he doesn't. He buys me an ice cream so you will think he's kind."

"I don't think he wants me to think of him as kind."

"He wants you to like him."

"Everyone wants us to like them."

"The Nazis don't."

"No. You're right. The Nazis don't. But at least that shows he's not a Nazi."

8

"No more looking at the world in the mirror," says Marie, once again wearing her grey cardigan with its white snowflake pattern.

"They've arrived?"

"Just pulled up outside."

Jack nods.

"I've made you some sandwiches. Here."

He shifts slightly sideways to her. Fearing if he looks her directly in the face he will cry. Ridiculous that his overriding concern is not to be seen with tears in his eyes but there it is. Tears perhaps not only for the kindness she has shown him but for all the partings he has known in his life. All the forked paths that have led him away from the people he grows fond of.

"Thank you so much, Marie." He kisses her on both cheeks. On the birthmark that reminds him of the geographical outline of a country. Belgium perhaps.

Out on the street again he feels light headed, raw, exposed. With that gust and lightness in the mind that doesn't let you anchor any clear thought. That causes you to think things without knowing why you're thinking them. The van is parked at the end of the road. A clapped out grey affair. The number plate attached with string. Opposite the Café des Amis. The driver is smoking a cigarette on the pavement. He's like someone watching himself smoke a cigarette. It's the man he saw fraternising with the Nazi in the mirror. He is wearing a blue pinstripe suit. Jack stops in his tracks. Contemplates running off in the opposite direction. He's on the very brink of springing forward, of breaking into a run when the man sees him. Absurd as it is, a kind of social etiquette takes over. A deeply ingrained reluctance to appear rude. So he carries on walking. He sees the man is talking to someone inside in the truck.

"Not exactly a Spitfire," says the man, slapping his palm against the side of the truck. "Runs on charcoal and doesn't like hills. So you may find you have to get out and push."

He doesn't understand half of what the man is saying. His French isn't good enough. The man leans back, away from Jack, when he shakes his hand. He edges past him. Wanting to see who he was talking to. Wanting to know just how much danger he is now in. The sight of Evie is like having his hand knocked off the stick of his Spitfire when bullets rip into its fuselage. All the needles of his instruments precipitated into a sudden wild dance. The moment of unreality, of suspended disbelief, goes on happening. The shredding and jostling of the fundamental structure of what is usually taken for granted, the basic frames of experience. He barely seems to own his thoughts or even his own body.

But even through the skipping heartbeat and dust storm of disbelief he registers the entreaty in her eyes. Her frightened and popping eyes tell him to say nothing.

"No one told me this was going to be a reunion," says the man who has introduced himself as Jean Paul. He is very good looking, this man Jean Paul, in a smooth slippery kind of way. The kind of man who makes a game of exciting mistrust in a woman. "I mean, something tells me you two already met."

"No. We haven't already met," says Evie.

Her voice, his favourite voice in the world, seems to slide down his spine like probing fingertips. The last time he heard her speak French they were in bed together. He wonders if she has ever returned to that moment in memory.

"You might want to take a look at yourself in a mirror," says Jean Paul. "As if you had seen a ghost only tells half the story."

"He, you, remind me of my brother. It upset me for a moment. I'm sorry."

"Brother? Did you ever mention a brother?"

She holds out her hand. "Aurelie," she says. "Or Anais."

"Frederic," he says. Almost able now to allow a little mischief into his eyes. "And what about you, youngster? What's your name?"

"My real name is Leopold but I'm pretending to be Xavier Ricoux."

He sees Evie smile for the first time. Her smile is like something that belongs to him. As familiar and moving as the rediscovery of any cherished keepsake.

"That's the spirit kid. You tell everyone who you really are. We get stopped by the Gestapo you say, my real name is Leopold but I'm pretending to be Xavier Ricoux. You might even get a smile out of a Gestapo goon saying that. Just so there's no misunderstandings here, you ought to know that Xavier Ricoux here is the brains of this operation. He's also our senior officer. Okay Mr Frederic. You're in the back."

He is jostled and thrown about in the back of the truck. It's like that man Jean Paul's anger. Tossing him from one side of the truck to the other. It's like the slipstream of his own suspended disbelief too. His attempt to anchor the idea that only a metal partition separates him from Evie.

How important and omnipotent she had once been, a presence in every breath of air he took into his body, and then how distant and estranged she had come to seem. And now here she is again. Here she is again with another man. Because he is sure they are lovers. Her and this Jean Paul. This Jean Paul with his Nazi friends.

9

"You two have history. Intimate history, I'd say. And the chances of you meeting up on a street corner in Nancy were about one million zillion to one. So your eyes went bigger than the sum total dimensions of your head."

She smiles. She is still in shock but she smiles because at the moment it's the easiest thing to do. Jean Paul's hand brushes against her thigh as he does something with the gear stick.

"He reminds you of your brother. Why don't I believe you?"

"Why don't you try keeping your eye on the road? And stop driving as if there's a woman about to give birth in the truck."

"You're English, aren't you? You're an English spy. I knew your real name wasn't Aurelie. I could never say it without feeling I had a strand of hair caught in my mouth. So what is your real name?"

"Evie," she says. Feeling she is betraying Leopold. Inflicting another hurt that he will retain in his body. Disclosing the information that was their private secret. A seal of trust and kinship.

"Evie," he says. "Why is it I suddenly feel like a piece of the wrong jigsaw puzzle?"

"That's what we all are. If you stop to think about it."

Jean Paul slams his foot down on the brakes. The truck rattles and jolts to an abrupt halt on the country road. "Okay, let's stop to think about this."

She hears a crash behind her. Behind the metal partition.

"You're thinking of him, aren't you? What must he be thinking? Have we been pulled over by the Germans? That's what he's probably asking himself at this minute."

"I'm thinking you need to get a grip of yourself."

"What do you reckon, kid? How about you and me form an alliance now?"

Jean Paul starts up the truck again. Wrenches it violently into gear. It jolts forward. There are more crashing noises from behind the metal partition.

Jean Paul drives recklessly. He swerves round a horse-drawn cart stacked with firewood. He begins whistling. The Marseillaise. Shrill and flat.

She sees there is a roadblock up ahead. Before the road arrives at a bridge. Two makeshift wooden barricades with twists of barbed wire. Two German soldiers with rifles slung over their shoulders. A motor and sidecar parked at the side of the road.

Jean Paul stops whistling the Marseillaise for a moment. Then starts to whistle it louder, more shrill, more flat. He shows no sign of having seen the roadblock.

"We've all got papers," she says.

He turns to her, still whistling. A smirk in his eyes. He puts his foot down on the accelerator. She takes Leopold's hands. She watches curiosity become alarm on the face of one of the soldiers. She wants to slap Jean Paul. The impact with the barrier throws her forward and sideways in the seat. There are more crashing noises from behind the metal partition. She pushes Leopold's head down under her shoulder. Waiting for the gunshots. Waiting for the chase.

10

Jack picks himself up off the floor. Scrambles over to the rear window. Thirty yards away he sees a leather-coated German soldier in owlish goggles on a motorbike. His sidekick in the sidecar is taking aim with his rifle. Taking aim directly at Jack's face. He throws himself back down on the floor. The crack is muffled. Like an echo. There is a metallic pinging noise just beneath him. The truck swerves off violently to the left. And he is rolled over on the ribbed metal floor. Thinking a tyre has been punctured. The truck bucks and its whole frame shudders. Worse than his Spitfire in turbulence. He clambers up onto his knees again. Looks out of the grease-filmed window. The German motorcycle has stopped and gets smaller and smaller at the end of a steep rocky road winding up through trees. He positions himself by the window. Several times he is knocked off balance. He watches the unfurling of the road behind. Keeping an eye open for the German motorcycle. It reminds him of being in his Spitfire. Except now he has no guns.

They overtake a horse and cart laden with milk pails. After two hours or so the truck stops.

"You're still alive then?" says Jean Paul, letting him out of the back of the truck.

He doesn't want to talk to this man or even look at him. He looks over the man's shoulder. The marvel of Evie in a dress. A blue print dress patterned with violet and lilac flowers. Against the storybook backdrop of a stout walled French farmhouse. The setting sun glazing a gold wash over an expanse of meadow and plough land. Then the man talks again. Spoiling everything. Spoiling the marvel of Evie standing there in the luminous landscape to which her presence bequeaths a bewildering intimacy.

He can't believe how shy he feels around her. How difficult it is for him to take the sight of her for granted. As if it's only some act of intense and precarious concentration on his part that holds her to the spot. It's like the Victor Hugo story with the missing pages. The disorientation all of a sudden of landing in a moment that has no recent history, no immediate links, because a great chunk of the story is written on pages that are missing.

There is a woman sitting on the doorstep of the grey farmhouse. Peeling potatoes. A tower of neatly stacked firewood on either side of her. The individual stones in the façade of the farmhouse highlighted by the low slanting light. A wooden ladder lying on the gravel. Then three men come out into the courtyard. One of them introduces himself as English. He is wearing blue overalls and a beret and a red neck scarf.

"Damn good show escaping from a Jerry prison camp," he says. His shirt is stiff with dirt and grease.

Then he is left alone with the strange afflicted child, with Leopold, while the others wander off in a self-important huddle.

"I expect your vocabulary is more extensive than mine," he says, joining Leopold by the side of an old hay cutter. "Every mistake me making, you correcting me. Deal?" he says, deliberately making mistakes.

"You've got a funny voice."

"Voice or accent?"

"Both."

"So who's this Jean Paul?"

"Just a man."

"Nice man?"

"What do you mean?"

"Do you like him?"

"No."

He grins. It is a childish feeling, he knows, this triumphant blast of one-upmanship, but he wants to lift the boy up onto his shoulders and run down a hill with him. Singing this new pact of theirs at the top of his voice.

"I don't like him either. I don't trust him. So that's already one thing we've got in common. I wonder what else."

"We're both here."

"Yes. I wonder where here is. Any idea?"

"No. She says we're taking you to Spain. There's no war in Spain."

"No. They've had their war. I wonder what happens afterwards. After war."

"We see again the people we've stopped seeing."

"I hope so. I hope you're right, Leopold."

"I still can't believe you're here," she says, walking towards him, scattering the hens on the flagstones. "Every time I see you again I have to pinch myself."

But there is none of the wonder she alludes to in her tone of voice. Her voice is guarded, matter of fact. He remembers rolling over in bed and pressing his mouth to her neck and how she woke up and sighed and stretched out the entire length of her body beneath the sheet that smelt of her. There is no way back to that moment. It's like a tide has washed it away, deposited it on a remote ocean bed where it will forever remain, lost to sight.

She's embarrassed because she's with another man now.

"I don't recognise myself. Speaking in English," she says. "It's been so long. I even dream in French now. I even curse in French."

"Did you think I was dead?"

"I was told you were missing."

"Who told you that?"

"A friend of Benedict's."

"How I miss Benedict."

She covers her face with her hands. "Oh god, you probably don't know, do you?"

"Know what?"

"Benedict is dead. He killed himself."

Like Septimus in Mrs Dalloway.

He turns away at the same moment he sees Jean Paul walk over towards them. Humiliating to be caught with tears in his eyes by this man. The rival. The traitor.

"I thought it was good news you were supposed to be bringing," says his rival.

"I haven't told him yet."

"You haven't told him yet. What could possibly be more important?"

"The invasion is taking place soon. That's the good news. The messages have arrived."

The tenderness he sees in her eyes is a gift. He gives her back a look that says thank you. He wipes his eyes, or rather his left eye, because the tears came from there, not his right eye. *Odd that.*

"Messages?"

"The BBC transmits coded messages every night. Leopold and I like to listen to them together. Don't we? You can listen to them with us tonight. But because of this news there's been a change of plan. I have to go to Marseille. To help organise the *Maquis* there. We're taking you to Dijon. Tomorrow. There you'll meet a man who will accompany you to Toulouse on the train."

This news makes him miserable. He tries not to show it. Especially to Jean Paul. He is doing his best to act his part with Jean Paul. A part unspokenly scripted for him by Evie. The disowning of all their shared history.

Difficult to believe Evie has been returned to him and yet he is miserable. More miserable than he was as a prisoner in the camp.

After dinner he announces he is going to take a walk. Hoping Evie will join him. So he can tell her what he knows. What he knows about her new lover. The rival. The traitor. But she doesn't join him. It's the first time he feels betrayed by her. The first time he feels the old understanding between them is no longer active.

The first time he feels he might have lost whatever it was that attracted her to him. He writes her a note. About Jean Paul. It feels a bit churlish. Raising doubts about her new man, as if it is just the rancour of a forsaken lover.

When he returns to the house there is an argument about the sleeping arrangements. She wants to share a room with Leopold. He finds he is a bit annoyed by this coyness on her part, this duplicity.

If they're sleeping together what's the point in pretending they're not?

"I'm more than happy to share a room with Leopold," he says. "If Leopold will have me."

Leopold is grumpy. Only Jean Paul has got the arrangement he wanted. The rival. The traitor.

He slips Evie the note on the stairs. She looks at him with a hint of alarm, a flush of embarrassment.

11

"Twenty-six."

Jean Paul is naked. He is down on the floor of this echoing room with its pink flowered wallpaper doing press ups. He does press ups and talks at the same time as though she ought to be impressed.

She gets into the iron bed with its frayed yellowing sheets and scratchy prison blankets. Only with reluctance has she taken off her dress. She will not take off her slip. She tore up Jack's note and scattered the pieces out of the bathroom window. She imagined Leopold finding them and piecing them back together. It's the kind of thing he enjoys.

She sits up in the iron bed. Beneath the wooden Crucifix and the tiny etching of a grim faced saint in a dark wooden frame. Studying Jean Paul closely. The shifting of his sinews against the taut copper hued skin. The movements of the muscles beneath the skin.

Can I say for certain he's not working for the Gestapo?

"You've acted appallingly all day," she says.

"Out of character? Sorry."

"No you're not."

He finishes his press ups. Thirty. A nice tidy number. He stands with his head tilted back. Breathing heavily. "Can you smell spring in the air? I can smell spring. Maybe this damned winter is finally over."

"You didn't answer my question. You could have got us all killed today. Driving through that roadblock. There was no need."

He sits down at the dresser. Talking to her reflection in the greasy mirror. "No need for most of things we do. I felt like doing it so I did it. I'm still alive. You're still alive. Your English pilot is still alive. At least this was the case last time I checked."

She keeps seeing the loose button on Jack's jacket. Hanging by a single strand of thread.

"Why don't we talk about you? The naked you. Because I'm realising that I've never seen you naked. Only in the flesh. You don't trust me. Is that it? Evie."

"I was instructed never to trust anyone. It's part of the job."

"Yes. This job of yours. I'm beginning to form a picture. I've got this picture of you dropping down from the sky. I've got this picture of you carrying a firearm in your purse."

"Now you sound like the Gestapo."

"And who is this English pilot? Did he fall out of the sky too?"

"We've got a long day tomorrow."

"What's new? Every day is long. War has changed the maths of time. Sometimes there are a damn sight more than sixty seconds in a minute and sometimes there are a damn sight less."

"Can we just go to sleep?"

"You're not going to get naked?"

"No."

There's a look in his eye. As if he is lining up a snooker shot. "I can't help being myself. What about you?"

"I'm most myself with Leopold. I was thinking that today."

"Because there's trust there?"

"Yes."

"I know I'm a bit of an actor. I know sometimes I'm watching myself even as I talk. But do I tell lies? I don't think I tell lies."

"Jack saw you talking to an SS officer."

She hadn't meant to confront him with this. But out it comes, like a hiccup, like a sneeze.

"Oh, so that is what all this is about. For all you know I could be working for the Germans. For all you know I could even be German. Heil Hitler!" he shouts. Doing the Nazi salute.

"Did you?"

"I've spoken to SS officers in my time. So what? It's part of my job."

"Your job which is largely a mystery to me."

"I suppose I must be jealous. Jealous of your English pilot. Your emotion when you first saw him went right down underneath your dress."

"You're not working for the Germans?"

"No. I'm not working for the English either. Between you and me I've never much liked the English."

"You prefer Germans?"

"Did I say that? Look, why don't I go and bring the pilot in here? I'll sleep with the kid."

"Stop calling him the kid. His name's Leopold."

"Xavier actually. As things now stand. I'm the only person in this circus who goes by his real name."

Before long he is asleep. It surprises her how quickly he falls asleep.

Unless this is an act too.

She creeps over to where his trousers lay on the floor. She slips his wallet from the pocket. His wallet makes her hands feel dirty. She doesn't believe he is working for the Gestapo. It's a relief to feel this. Something integral has been restored to her being. There was a moment's doubt while reading the note when she questioned some core part of herself. The integrity of her discernment. She takes his wallet over to the window. Even though holding it makes her hands feel dirty. To the bars of moonlight between the slats of the brown shutters. She finds nothing incriminating in his wallet. A forged travel pass. A forged official document exempting him from enforced labour in Germany. At least she imagines they are forged. Half the things everyone carries about on themselves are forged. A lot of money.

She gets back into the iron bed with its frayed yellowing sheets and scratchy prison blankets.

She doesn't know how long she has been asleep when Jack is standing at the door. His dark hair tousled. "We've got to get out of here quick," he says. "The Germans are coming. He's brought the Germans here."

12

"Sorry you're lumbered with me."

Leopold is already in bed. His face blanched by the candlelight.

Jack climbs in beside him. Feeling a bit awkward, a bit apologetic, but with a want to befriend the boy who shows him himself as a boy at frequent intervals.

"I don't mind."

"I saw you once. From my window. I made up a story about you. I wasn't allowed to leave my room, you see. So I made up stories about the people I saw outside. And one day I saw you. Strange how things work out, isn't it?"

"I don't think I know yet how things work out."

"Join the club. I suppose I was hoping we would all go to Spain together. What shall we call her? You and me. When we talk about her alone together. What do you call her in your head?"

"I don't think I call her a name. She's just there."

"How come you're here anyway? Why aren't you at home?"

"I was in prison."

"And she was in prison too?"

"Yes. I did a drawing of her. Then we escaped."

He gets Leopold to piece back together what happened. Feels it as some kind of tribute that Leopold is willing to confide in him. When he has the full story he knows Evie must have the boy and his mother on her conscience.

The last thing she needs is for you to make her feel bad that she has taken a new man into her life. Put aside childish things…

"I was in prison as well. Except we got clean sheets every week and acted in plays. What did you miss most in prison?"

"My stamps."

"I had stamps. I remember that feeling. Pasting them into the appropriate page of the album. The feeling of safety and pride they give you. All arranged in order. Like you're an emperor with your kingdom all mapped out."

At that moment he hears Jean Paul shout out Heil Hitler behind the wall.

She's told him.

His heart begins racing. He listens out for activity behind the wall. His body is tense with the expectation of a confrontation. He imagines a fist fight with Jean Paul. The image is vivid. He can feel it move through his muscles. Can feel the impact of the blows he strikes ricochet up the length of his arm. But Jean Paul is stronger than he is. In all probability he would lose any fight with Jean Paul. He would end up sprawled on the floor with blood on his face. With Evie looking on. He remembers Charlie once telling him that he always imagined fist fighting every man he met. Weighed up his chances of winning. How he might defeat his imaginary opponent. The last time he imagined fighting with someone it was with Angus. Angus is dead now. Charlie is dead. Benedict too.

All goes quiet in the room next door.

He can't sleep. His mind is racing.

One more day with Evie.

He goes outside. To smoke a cigarette. He can hear a swishing noise in the cowshed and pictures the tail of a cow brushing against the straw on which it lies. As if in the throes of an uneasy dream.

One more day with Evie.

It's almost that time of the morning when his batman would wake him and he and Benedict would get dressed together and brush their teeth at the sink, barefooted on the linoleum floor, and stumble into the twilight clatter of the mess for breakfast.

Almost that time of the morning when he would run over the grass, kicking up dew, towards Ed and Stan and his Spitfire. Whenever he looks up into the sky he is almost immediately up there.

One more day with Evie.

He is quietly talking to himself when he sees the moving black shape down in the valley. A silhouette of menace. The only conclusion to jump to. He runs up the stairs. Barges into Evie's room with the self-importance bestowed by an emergency.

"We've got to get out of here quick," he says. "The Germans are coming, He's brought the Germans here."

Jean Paul throws back the blankets. Is out of the bed in an instant. Stark naked in the grey light. He sees Evie is wearing a slip. He wonders what this means even in his urgency to get out of the house. Jean Paul throws open the shutters. But he is not looking at Jean Paul. He is looking at Evie pull on her dress over her head. Shake down its length with a little shimmy of the hips.

"It's an English motto, isn't it, to always err on the side of caution."

"What do you mean?"

He follows Evie over to the window.

"It's Pascal and Auguste. They had to move a store of arms during the night. Now can we all go back to bed?"

Before he leaves the room he looks down at the map of folds her body has etched on the undersheet of the bed. He imagines the warmth of her body still rising up from the fabric.

13

"You've changed."

"So have you. How have I changed?" she asks.

"There's more space around you now. Acres of ground where before there was an ordered enclosed garden."

"Should I be concerned?"

"Just the opposite."

"You can't imagine how strange it is to be called Evie again. I feel like we're talking about someone we both know who isn't here."

"What happened to her? To Evie."

He is walking with Evie away from the house. In a field where the scent of spring lifts up from the grass underfoot. A scent that seems to peel away protective layers inside and makes him more vulnerably hungry for happiness. Makes happiness seem the only natural response to the ripening day.

"One day she went for an interview in a basement room at the War Office and then she went to Lilywhites and came out with a khaki serge FANY uniform and before long she was learning how to silently kill people and jumping out of airplanes. None of which should I be telling you."

"You're some kind of spy then?"

"Courier. Carrying about messages in my underwear."

She must know he is now going to picture her in her underwear. Picture her in her underwear which conceals a secret message. That's how he would like to communicate with her at the moment. To write her messages and slip them inside her underwear.

"I've often thought how ironic it is. After you telling me your name wasn't your real name. That seemed to set a pattern. Afterwards no one I knew was called by their real name anymore."

"Including you."

"I was wretched for a long time, you know. Really very depressed. It was a relief to hand over control of my life to someone else. All of a sudden I was completely cut off from everyone I knew. From my old life. Reborn as someone new. A group of strangers telling me who I now was, what was expected of me. It was an odd feeling. Not entirely unpleasant. I felt guilty about you. I didn't stop missing you. I felt I had been a terrible coward. This gave me the opportunity to be brave."

"You weren't a coward. We were all getting the chop. One by one. Sooner or later it had to be my turn. It should have been but I was lucky. I didn't give you much to look forward to."

"Jean Paul isn't working for the Germans. I know when he smiles he looks like a cat that's about to scratch but if it wasn't for him I wouldn't have been able to take care of Leopold. He's my prime concern now. I'm responsible for him. It's because of me that his mother was arrested and he has no home."

"It's because of the war. Not because of you."

Now is the time to say the thing he most wants to say. There is a struggle inside, a heavy undertow of shyness jostling his resolve. The fear of rejection more intimidating sometimes than the fear of physical pain.

"Why don't you bring Leopold back to England?" he says. "Why don't the two of you come with me across the Pyrenees?"

"I've thought about that. It's tempting. But I'm under orders in a way. And once I get back in touch with a circuit here I'll have money and I'll be able to take care of Leopold. Perhaps find a woman to look after him."

"While you carry about messages in your underwear?"

"While I carry about messages in my underwear. I'm so happy you're alive, Jack. It suits you much better than being dead."

"Hey, you two."

It is Jean Paul. Standing by the well in the courtyard. Shouting through cupped hands.

"Time to go."

14

He stands by the roadside. The grass is almost waist-high. He watches Evie cycle off down the tunnelling aisle of trees into the distance. It's like a rehearsal of what is to come later. The parting. The farewell. There is birdsong in the air and the sun makes a glowing transparency of the canopy of leaves overhead. Evie is cycling up ahead to check the roads are clear. Because there are rumours of German patrols in the area.

"So you thought I was a traitor?"

There is a note of enthusiasm, a note of enjoyment in Jean Paul's voice. He smiles. They both smile.

"Maybe I was just pretending."

"Cigarette?"

Evie is right. When he smiles he is like a cat that's about to dig in its claws.

"Thanks."

Leopold has gone off behind the trees. To relieve himself probably though he didn't say this.

"A hundred years ago, less actually, I would be challenging you to a duel. Pistols or swords?"

"Probably pistols having seen you fence that SS officer with a bunch of flowers."

"Oh, so that's when you saw me. Those flowers were for Anais."

"Just as long as they weren't for Evie."

"I'll look after Anais. And the boy. You don't have to worry about that. Why not at least thank heaven for small mercies?"

"Okay. I'll do that."

Leopold now returns from behind the trees. In his short grey trousers and grey pullover.

The van just about makes it to Dijon. He walks with Evie to the square where he is to meet his contact. They sit down side by side on the steps of a church. Five minutes early. She in her blue summer dress with the violet flower patterns.

"How bizarre it is, talking in French with you. Like some party game. I'm very impressed by the way. Your accent is a bit ragged around the edges but you speak it well."

"When I was in the camp, studying, I always imagined talking to you in French. It was my motivation, that picture."

"And now here we are, making that picture."

"Not quite as I imagined. Every time I imagined you and me together we always ended up back at that river."

"When you fell asleep."

"When I fell asleep."

She reaches across and lightly takes hold of the loose button on his jacket. He thinks she is going to pull it off. But she doesn't. She caresses it.

"Don't look but there are two Gestapo agents in the square," she says.

He thought her caressing his button was a sign her feeling for him is still amorous. Now he wonders if it is some tactic she has been taught to deflect suspicion. "How do you know?"

"They make my flesh crawl. When I feel my flesh crawl I know there's one of them close by, looking at me."

"Why not not go through with this? I could stay in France. Be of some help."

"And if anything happened to you I'd have you on my conscience too. You're the first good thing that has happened to me in a long while. I want to help you reach safety."

"There is no safety."

"Don't say that. Here's our contact. The man carrying the red book."

"What do we do?"

"When you're in London go to see Katie. She works for my firm. Orchard Court. Off Portman Square. Remember that? She became a good friend of mine. I'll use her to get a message to you. It'll be in code of some sort. You'll have to decrypt it."

"What about these Gestapo chaps?"

"They're not chaps. They're monsters from hell. And nothing gives me more pleasure than getting one over on them. I don't think they're looking for us. They're just stooging around. Off you go. Good luck. And don't look at me like that or I'll start crying and draw attention to myself."

15

He is so miserable it's like being handcuffed and guarded again. Back in captivity. Not once, on the train journey south, does he feel he is edging towards freedom.

He is less fearful for his welfare. When a miserly faced, tight lipped Gestapo agent closely scrutinises his papers on the train his feigning of indifference is close to being authentic.

Orchard Court. Off Portman Square.

The loose button on his jacket is the only precious thing he owns. He touches it often. But gently. As if were it to come loose his last connection with her will be severed.

He remembers the thick grey army socks Evie wore at the farmhouse. The thick grey army socks and the summer dress.

There are two guides. He meets them in a mud-floored hut in what feels like an outpost at the end of the world. Deeply bronzed men with hard furrowed faces. Like cracked earth. He is joined by five fellow escapees. Three American airmen, a German Jewish man and a South African infantryman. He barely talks to any of them. He gains a reputation for being solitary and reserved. Secretive. Another new identity.

He is the only one not wearing boots. One of the Americans teases him about it good-naturedly. He has forgotten the man's name. Except that it sounds more like a surname than a first name.

Up in the mountains he loses his footing. Slides back down steep slopes in continuation. He pushes through thorned foliage. The needles clinging to his flesh. Pinpricking his palms and fingertips every time he closes his hands. He throws himself down, face in the dirt, whenever someone hears a noise and the alarm is transmitted along the line. He throws himself down because the others expect this of him but his heart rarely quickens with alarm. He eats with his hands. Bully beef, bread and peaches. Eating with his hands beneath the sickle moon. He tries to sleep on sloping ground. Often he wakes to find himself rolling down an incline. Wakes with feet and hands numb with cold. Clothes soaked through with dew. His hand reaching for the loose button on his jacket. The reassurance it is still there.

The physical effort of constant climbing up into thinner air, of clambering up over another rock, of pushing his way through more blackberry brambles, of wading through icy water, of pulling himself by thorny branches up slopes, of lifting his feet out of drifts of gleaming crackling snow. Evie begins to recede as a vivid presence in his mind. It makes him angry with his mind. Until he sits down to rest again, in the shadow of a sheer rock face, in the midst of a pine forest, and once more he can't believe he agreed to abandon her so soon after finding her again.

They climb another mountain. The first mountain was called the Pic du Gard. This new mountain doesn't seem to have a name. As if they are the first people in history to set foot on it. He hears the thunder of the river long before he sees it. A twist of silver smoke through the trees. He remembers that other river where he fell asleep and she emerged out of the moonlit water and his hand goes to the button, the loose button on his coat that she touched, but the button is no longer there. He turns around. For a moment he is about to double back on his tracks. He is about to go searching for the button. In the thick of night with only a thin slither of sickle moon to guide him.

"This is the most dangerous part of our journey," says one of the guides.

He forces himself to listen, to forget about the button.

"We have to cross a bridge that is patrolled by German sentries with dogs."

PART SEVEN

1945

1

It's his third visit to Orchard Court. Not that he ever sets foot inside the building. He does not have the necessary clearance. He meets Katie outside. This is his third encounter with Katie. He was initially suspicious that Evie wanted to set the two of them up. He could tell Katie was attracted to him. And it depressed him. The idea that Evie might be trying to offload him onto another woman.

Today Katie is carrying a brown paper parcel. He thinks it's something for him. Something to do with Evie. But she places it on the floor when she sits down at the table of the pub. He sees there is some strain around her mouth and light keeps leaving her eyes.

He walks over to the bar. Waits while two ARP wardens in boiler suits are served. Civilians no longer pat his shoulder or ask for his autograph. Even though he is back in his RAF blue. Decorated with a DFC, presented to him by His Royal Majesty the King at Buckingham Palace. But he is now a flying instructor at an Operational Training Unit. Telling boys what to do, where they're going wrong. For the time being. Until he is posted back to a fighter squadron.

"You said you had news," he says bringing Katie her drink. He pretends to be calm, composed, his voice is calm and composed, but inwardly he is bracing himself, inwardly he has gone into a spinning dive and is struggling to resume control of his instruments.

"Evie was back in England for a short while. She tried to call you."

He stares at Katie with his lips parted.

"Tried to call me where?"

"At your training unit I would imagine."

"I had some bloody leave. I went to see my grandparents."

"I'm really worried about her."

"Tell me why."

"I can't, Jack. Sworn to secrecy and all that."

"It's not secret to me. I was in France, remember. I know exactly what Evie's doing."

"You swear you'll never tell anyone what I tell you?"

"You have my word."

He uses his handkerchief to clean his pipe. The pipe is a new acquisition. Lends him, he feels, more credence in his guise as instructor. Adds a dash of worldliness to his performing self.

"This is difficult for me. I've been sworn to secrecy. And the words are sticking in my throat." She lights a cigarette, a Senior Service cigarette, and casts a hunted glance around the pub and its pall of tobacco smoke. "It's a long story. Dates back almost a year in fact."

"I've got nowhere else to go."

"For a long time several people in the firm have been suspicious about certain wireless messages arriving from France. These messages didn't ring true. There was something distinctly fishy about them. For one thing, the secret security check was left out by operators who previously had sent hundreds of messages without ever forgetting to include these codes. Or the fist was all wrong."

"Hang on. Fist. What's that?"

"It's what we call every wireless operator's distinctive rhythm and touch. Every operator is assigned what we call a godmother in the signals room at HQ and this godmother comes to know very well the fist of her charge. Word went round the office that there was a strong possibility that the Germans were playing back our own radios to us. Learning about all our secret operations. But these misgivings were ignored by the big cheeses in the firm. I can't, you understand, name names. But the situation went on getting more and more suspicious. We would hear a report that this or that agent had been arrested and then receive a message contradicting this. Two agents were sent out to investigate and nothing more was heard of them. The big cheeses at the firm refused to countenance the idea that any of the circuits had been contaminated. It was too close to D Day. So Evie was sent out to check two suspect circuits, one in Paris, and one in Normandy. She was warned it was dangerous but opted to go anyway. As you know she feels responsible for that boy."

"Leopold."

"Yes. The day after she arrived in France we received a new message from one of the dubious wireless sets. The message thanked us for the constant supply of arms and supplies and was signed, the Gestapo. Obviously they could no longer contain their glee at having tricked us for so long. Since then we've heard nothing from her."

"The firm, as you call it, sounds like a bloody fiasco run by incompetent buffoons."

"It is a bit tally-ho. I mean, to us, the war can sometimes seem like nothing but a board game. We're very closeted."

"And Evie has been sent straight into a Gestapo trap."

"We don't know that for sure."

"But the details of her drop in France were all transmitted through one of the contaminated wirelesses?"

"Yes."

"So the Gestapo knew exactly when and where to expect her?"

"Yes. But the hope is, they may have let her run for a while. It's common practice. In the hope of picking up other contacts. And that she will lose her tail."

"Doesn't sound like much of a hope to me. Basically your firm has been completely outwitted by the Germans?"

"'Fraid so. Or that's how it looks."

"What's in that parcel?"

"Parcel?"

"The parcel on the floor. The parcel you were carrying when I met you."

"Oh yes. I was going to ask you. It's Evie's yellow coat. I used to secretly covet this yellow coat. And because of that I feel superstitious about it. I was looking after it for her. Will you look after it? I'd feel better if you were looking after it."

He never saw Evie in a yellow coat.

2

"You have the controls."

"I have the controls, sir."

He catches the boy's eye in the mirror. This rosy-cheeked freckled boy called Higgs sitting in the rear cockpit. He gives the boy Higgs an encouraging smile. But he does not like this business of relinquishing control. Would rather be at the controls himself even if it meant dogfighting with an armada of enemy aircraft. But it fits his state of mind. This sense of helplessness. This business of having no choice but to relinquish control.

"Okay, how about we try a plum slow roll?"

The pilgrimage. Was it morbid? Back to Mrs Savage's guesthouse. Back to the same room with the same bed and the same green and gold eiderdown. Where he stayed awake all night, mostly by the window, under the eaves, as if keeping vigil. As if Evie might return from the bathroom in the hallway at any moment. He sat by the window, under the eaves, trying to remember the exact timbre and cadence of her voice. Willing her to speak to him again. To recite again the poem her father had taught her. *And wilt thou leave me thus? Say nay! Say nay!*

The next day he cycled to the river. He was never quite sure he had found the exact same spot. It seemed important he found the exact same spot. The spot where he awoke to see her pile of clothes on the riverbank. He needed to return to all the places where Evie had been most vivid. Where Evie had been alive. As if by standing where she had stood he could make her still be alive.

"Not bad, Higgs. You might though apply a touch more upper rudder. Want to have another go?"

The French section of Special Forces is being wound down. Katie no longer works at Orchard Court. But she is in touch with a woman who has taken it upon herself to track down the whereabouts of the many missing agents.

"But she's being hampered in her work by General de Gaulle."

He has come to dislike General de Gaulle. Fervently dislike him. General de Gaulle is denying the British access to all Nazi records and documents. Has forbidden the British access to the Gestapo headquarters and the prisons in Paris. As if he owes the British nothing, as if it's all thanks to him and him alone, thanks to General de bloody Gaulle that Paris is now liberated.

He looks down through the torn clouds at the chequered fields of the English countryside. Realises he has no idea how well or badly Higgs has just executed his second slow roll.

"Better," he says. "Now let's see you do a stall. And remember what I told you."

"Yes sir."

But this woman who Katie won't name has received information from a former prisoner of the Gestapo in Paris. He says there are inscriptions on the walls of the cells of the Gestapo headquarters in Paris. The building in Avenue Foch. He says he remembers them well. One of the inscriptions he remembers is signed Anais and dated, June 6. The day of the Normandy landings.

The complaining shudder of the engine haemorrhages up through the seat of his pants. The starboard wing flicks down in one swift seamless gesture. The aircraft arrowing vertically towards the ground.

"Okay Higgs, ease on the stick. We don't want to spoil anyone down there's Saturday lunch."

"No sir. I mean yes sir."

"So we know Evie was in Avenue Foch on June 6. It would appear all the political prisoners were moved not long before

Paris was liberated. There are conflicting rumours as to their destination. It might be that the women were separated from the men. One rumour is that the women were taken to a camp called Ravensbrück. No one though has heard of this camp. It's somewhere in Mecklenburg, north of Berlin. There's also a rumour that these prisoners were classified under the term *Nacht und Nebel.*"

"Night and fog."

"I didn't know you could speak German."

"Learnt it in the camp. French and German. What does it mean in Nazi terminology?"

"No one is quite sure. But we do know they were *ständig gefesselt* – permanently chained. Anyway, that's about it at the moment."

"I wish I could meet this woman. I wish I could get involved."

"I'll keep you informed. And Vera is a very determined woman. Whoops. I told you her name."

"I'm about to be posted in France. As a flight commander."

"Back to the fray?"

"Back to the fray."

He remembers he used to do this with Evie. Repeat what she had just said. With a kind of soft elegiac lilt in his voice.

3

Tom's presence calls forth Benedict's absence. You can't have one without the other. He and Tom together are somehow awkward and incomplete without the company of Benedict. Without the chatter and banter and laughter of Charlie and Angus and Hugo and Harry and George. As if passages of vital connecting dialogue are missing from the script. As if Benedict's absence has taken with it parts of his own identity. Tom's presence makes him feel a bit guilty that here he is smoking a pipe in a deckchair in the warm sunshine in the French countryside. He has to defend himself against a nagging silent accusation. As if he is to blame for still being alive. As if there is some suspicion involved that he has got off so lightly. He has to argue that his life is still at risk every day. Even though the Germans are on the run. Even though the Germans have more or less lost all control of the skies.

"Why can't I like any of the pilots now the way I liked Benedict? The way I liked Charlie and Hugo and Harry?"

"Because we've become jaded."

"Is that what it is?"

"What about the camp? No pals there?"

"Cooped up like that. Not really. A lot of them got on my nerves a bit. All the schoolboy pranks and futile little acts of rebellion. As if mucking up the roll call was a serious threat to the Nazi war effort. Just brassed off the guards who on the whole were decent chaps."

"Just doing their job."

"Don't you miss the old days though?"

"The sick feeling in the stomach."

"Falling asleep face down in your dinner."

"Being outnumbered ten to one."

"Dragged out of bed stiff necked and feverish before the cock crowed every bloody morning."

"Eyes darting about even when they were closed in bed at night."

"I suppose it's insane to miss those days."

"And yet one does. What happened to that gorgeous WAAF?"

"What gorgeous WAAF?"

"The one in the yellow coat. The one you were seeing."

"What yellow coat? I never saw her in a yellow coat."

"But you know who I'm talking about."

"What yellow coat?"

"Saw her in London once. She was wearing a yellow coat. Caught the eye. Naples yellow I think you'd call it. Ravishing. That's what I thought."

"That's what you thought?"

"So what happened to her?"

"Supposing I told you I was going to see her in Paris this weekend."

"I'd have no reason to disbelieve you."

"Except it's only in a manner of speaking that I'm going to see her in Paris this weekend. Let's get really drunk tonight, Tom, Let's get really drunk and talk to all our ghosts."

There is a gendarme standing at the entrance of the building in Avenue Foch. Jack walks up to the man. He has nothing with which he might bribe the man. So he decides to appeal to his better nature. Tell him the truth. The man does not have an unkind face. Tell him the woman he loves was a prisoner here and he is desperate to find some clue as to where she was taken afterwards. The man listens to his story. He watches a hardened layer come off the man's face. The man calls out to another man inside the building. The other man screws up his eyes. They withdraw together and begin an argument in whispers and eloquent facial expressions. Then the man with the not unkind face is leading him up the stairway.

This pilgrimage. Is it morbid?

The echo of his footsteps on the stairs. Seeming to wake up moments of the building's history. Like séance rustlings in the dark. Seeming to create a passage back through time.

"The cells were on the fifth floor."

Everything is past tense here now.

There are eight rooms on the fifth floor. Eight times three is twenty-four. The number of the house he grew up in. But what does that mean?

It is in the seventh room that his breath catches in his throat. That his feet cease to trust the ground. There is something almost supernatural about the etched words in the wall. Something not quite of this world. They are like a living tug from the spirit world. He runs his fingers over the inscription in the wall. He sits down on the floor, beneath a square window barred with iron rods in the ceiling. He feels they ought to lock him up. He feels he has got off too lightly.

4

Jack is in Germany. At the prison in Karlsruhe where he believes Evie was taken after her incarceration in Paris. The woman tells him all the prison registers have been destroyed. He doesn't believe her. But what he can do? He still sees in his mind's eye the cell he peered into on the way to this office. The slop pail by the sloping concrete buttress and, above, the tiny meshed window high in the wall. He flinches from an image of Evie imprisoned in this sordid stark cell, her feet chained.

He shows the woman the three photographs of Evie. The photographs he got from Evie's mother. He went to see Evie's mother at the end of the war.

The war is over. What is there to cheer about?

He went to see Evie's mother still wearing his slate blue RAF uniform and his DFC. Evie's mother had no idea she was in France. She thought she was in Scotland. Initially she treated him as if he was somehow to blame that Evie was in France and not in Scotland. It hadn't occurred to him that Evie would lie to her own mother. That the scale of her deception was so ubiquitous. Evie's mother kept asking him questions about how he knew Evie as if he had no right to know Evie. And there was something artificial about her speech. Too much practice in the crisp enunciation, the drawing out of her vowels. Evie's mother after all was born in France. Yet her accent was more English than the BBC. Slowly though she warmed to him. Because of his obvious concern for her daughter. His urgent desire to help find her. And before he left she told him about a dream she had had of Evie.

"She was hiding her head beneath the sheet of this makeshift bed she was in. The sheet wasn't very clean. It made my flesh crawl a bit just looking at it. She was speaking gibberish. I kept telling her to speak clearly. But I couldn't get any sense out of her. She didn't answer to her name. I then realised we were in some kind of museum. And there was a huge skeleton of a dinosaur. The bed Evie was in was by the side of this colossal dinosaur skeleton."

He shows the woman the three photographs of Evie. The stout frowning woman in her starched clothes who was a guard in this German prison. Where he now believes Evie was taken after her interrogations at the building in Avenue Foch.

"Yes. She was here."

"Are you sure?"

"Yes. She was one of the British spies."

"Where was she taken when she left here?"

"We were never told. The Karlsruhe Gestapo took these women away in the middle of the night."

"Can you remember when that was?"

"I think it was July or August of last year."

"Can you remember what she was wearing?"

"Maybe a green dress with stripes. White espadrilles. But I can't say for certain. One of the spy women was wearing a green dress with stripes. I remember because it was a pretty dress. You should perhaps speak to Frau Baecker. She was head warden. I remember she was angry because she was not allowed to give the British women back their possessions when they were taken away. Frau Baecker had to do everything by the book. She complained more than once afterwards to the Karlsruhe Gestapo."

"Where are these possessions now?"

"I don't know. You will have to ask her yourself."

He goes to the address the woman gives him. The head warden's address. The house is no longer there. The house is a heap of rubble, like all the houses on the left side of this street. Beggarly people are sorting through the rubble. They don't look at him, in his slate blue RAF uniform and his DFC. They pretend he isn't there. The air stinks of sewage from ruptured pipes. He feels some sympathy for the children but none for the adults. The adults who now cower in abject servility when he walks among them in his uniform. He imagines them in parades, cheering Hitler, cheering the SS, while he and Benedict were up in their Spitfires, while Evie was trying to keep Leopold safe and he loathes them. He is glad their homes are rubble. That they are forced to live in tents outside the town. It worries him a little, how little generosity he now has in his nature, how little inclination to forgive.

5

Otto Agger is one of the haystack men. The men who are looking for Nazi war criminals. Otto is an Austrian Jew with close cropped black hair and blackened fingernails and has taken an interest in the plight of Evie and is doing all he can to help. Jack sits in his office, at a desk with an anglepoise lamp. In an office within a razor wire fence in the German spa town of Bad Oeynhausen. Headquarters of the British army on the Rhine.

"You might want to pour yourself a drink," says Otto.

Yesterday he learnt that one of Evie's companions, Roger Vannier, field name Bruno, was murdered at Buchenwald, hanged by a butcher hook inserted at the base of his skull.

"What now?"

"A testament from a man in that camp called Natzweiler."

"The camp the *Daily Express* wrote about?"

The article caused a rumpus in Great Britain because it was the first evidence that armed British women had been deployed as agents in Nazi occupied territory. The story maintained that four of these unidentified women had been drugged and shoved into the crematorium furnace at the camp called Natzweiler while still alive.

"Yes. Their arrival in the camp caused a big stir because it was unusual to see women there. At first it was thought they might be prostitutes for the SS. Except they looked too refined to be prostitutes. The witness believes this was July or August 1944. He said they knew they weren't prostitutes when they saw flames and sparks emerging from the crematorium chimney.

The inmates knew that the furnace had been lit and these women would be murdered. Apparently the women were given soup and then locked in individual cells. Our witness says three of the women were very striking. Elegant. In their twenties. The other was older. More outspoken. He remembers her as a dark haired woman wearing a grey coat with short green socks, navy blue shoes with rubber soles. Another was dressed in a fur coat with a ribbon in her hair was carrying a suitcase. The witness said a pink stocking garter was found on the floor by the ovens which belonged to one of these women. And this is the part you don't want to hear."

"Spit it out, Otto."

"The prettiest of the girls was wearing a green stripy dress with white espadrilles."

"I can't imagine Evie in a green stripy dress. But then it was her task in France to disguise all traces of who she really was. Perhaps a green stripy dress was part of the disguise. The most fervent hope I've ever had is that Evie never bought or borrowed a green stripy dress. How surreal is that as a wish?"

Otto nods.

"At the same time I'm wishing that green stripy dress on someone else. Someone else who has loved ones out there worried sick about her."

"Hey, it's not your fault."

He knows how these four women were killed. One by one they were escorted into the doctor's surgery. They were told they needed a typhus shot but instead injected with a lethal poison. They were dragged down a corridor and placed on mortuary slabs and stripped of their clothes and then they were dumped on an iron stretcher in the furnace room. The last of the women fought back when she was lifted towards the flames. Hence the newspaper story that they were burnt alive. But he refuses to graft Evie's face onto any of these women. He refuses to merge Evie and the hypodermic needle puncturing flesh, the syringe plunger pumping poison into blood, into one and the same frame.

He sits at the desk, the telephone receiver cradled on his upraised shoulder. While he waits he shuffles through his notes - A transport left Paris for Germany on 7 August 1944. Three, possibly four, British women executed at Dachau concentration camp. Shot in the back of the head. Spies. Identities still unknown.

He is waiting for Katie to answer her telephone in London.

"Katie, when Evie was back in London, was she wearing a green stripy dress?"

Please say no, Katie.

"Let me think. I saw her twice. We went for lunch at Fortnum & Mason. What was she wearing? Do you know I'm damned if I can remember."

"Surely you'd remember a green stripy dress."

"Okay, I remember she was wearing a pair of those canvas shoes with the rope soles. I remember telling her they were a dead giveaway she had been in France and she laughed."

"Espadrilles. Were they white?"

"Yes. They were white. But I'm almost certain she wasn't wearing a stripy green dress. Though I can't for the life of me see her clearly now when she was in London."

"Can you imagine Evie wearing pink garters?"

"No. I don't think so. Not really her style, is it."

"That's what I thought."

"Why are you asking about green stripy dresses and pink garters? What have you found out?"

"Nothing definite yet."

6

"Got some news for you. Some important news. Not necessarily bad, though you might want to pour us both a drink first."

He pours himself and Otto a glass of cognac.

"Found out it was a woman who betrayed Evie to the Gestapo in Paris."

"For the money?"

"Jealousy. She's had all her hair shaved off and a swastika cut into her forehead."

"What do you mean, jealousy?"

"This is the part you might not like."

"Spit it out."

"She was in love with a man Evie was seeing."

"Do you know his name?"

"Jean Paul Berger."

"I knew he was bad news."

"You know him?"

"Yes."

"Apparently the Gestapo were trailing her for a while but she managed to slip the net. She even met with a Gestapo agent posing as a Canadian wireless operator. She might have carried on eluding the bastards were it not for this woman. I've got her address. In Paris. Want me to arrange some movement papers for you?"

"Do I want to talk to her? Could I bear to look at her?"

"She was a jealous woman."

"Meaning?"

"She will have noticed every detail about Evie."

"Including what she was wearing."

"Especially what she was wearing. A jealous rival is going to remember a green stripy dress."

Jack finishes his cognac. "Do you know I'll probably be arrested when I go back to England?"

Otto cracks his knuckles. Something he does when he doesn't know what to say. "You're not joking?"

"No. There's a warrant for my arrest."

"Why is there a warrant for your arrest?"

"Evading conscription. My poor grandparents. They don't know what to think. They thought I was a hero."

"You were a RAF fighter pilot. You've got a medal from the King."

"I pretended I was someone else. Someone not myself."

"You pretended you were someone else? I don't understand. How?"

"How? Easy. I got a birth certificate made out in someone else's name from Somerset House. A dead boy."

"So you really did get awarded the medal but as someone else?"

"That's right."

"Why? If you don't mind me asking."

"Seems stupid now. My father was shot as a coward in the last war. I was ashamed. I suppose I thought people would find out. That I'd be stigmatised in some way as a result."

"So your real name isn't Jack?"

"No. My real name is Jack."

"Well Jack, travel papers? I'd say post haste. She's not very popular where she is and may scram soon."

7

"Who are you?"

The woman has opened the door on the third floor of the apartment in Paris only a fraction. He understands this is her life now. Standing suspicious and angry and bitter behind doors fear will only allow her to open a fraction. Her face appears momentarily in the gap. He glimpses a misaligned front tooth between her lips that are parted in a kind of animal snarl. A black feathered hat pulled low over her forehead. Black feathers with blue highlights. He wonders if the disgust he can't help feeling for this woman is part of what she sees when she looks at him.

"I'm a friend of Jean Paul's. Can I speak to you?"

"You're another one of them, aren't you? Go away."

"I just need to ask you one question. About Anais."

"Anais? I don't know anyone called Anais."

"How about Monique or Aurelie?"

She slams shut the door.

"Will you just tell me if you ever saw her wearing a green stripy dress? That's all I want to know."

He stands listening for a reply outside the closed door. He can sense she is still standing there. He writes the question on a piece of paper and slips it under her door.

Out in the street he sits down on a bench and lights a cigarette. He is lost in his thoughts when Leopold says hello to him. Leopold with a bruise on his cheek and a satchel slung over his shoulder.

"I saw you."

"I was miles away." He offers his hand for Leopold to shake. "This is the best surprise I've had for a long time. How are you, Leopold? What are you doing here?"

"This is where I live now."

"Where do you live now?"

Leopold twists his neck in slow motion instalments. Points to the door he himself has recently emerged from. When he looks round he catches a glimpse of a woman at a window. It's her, Fanny, the woman who betrayed Evie. Spying on him.

"With Fanny? How did that happen?"

"Jean Paul brought me here after Monique went back to England. He told me she was going to write to me but she hasn't."

"What about your mother?"

"She's dead. She was gassed. I heard them whispering about it. But I don't really know what that means."

"The only reason Monique hasn't written to you is because she can't. You're her favourite person in the world."

"How do you know?"

"You'll have to take my word for it. She hasn't written to me either. I'm looking for her. Sit down here for a moment. There's one really important thing I need to know. How much notice did you take of her clothes? For example do you ever remember her wearing a green stripy dress?"

"I don't know."

"Can you think really hard? Close your eyes and try to picture her the last time you saw her."

"I don't really look at clothes."

"Will you try though? It's important."

"Do I have to close my eyes?"

"It might help you concentrate better."

"The last time I saw her she bought me an ice cream."

"Where?"

"In a café."

"Where?"

"I don't remember. Is it true Fanny is a Nazi?"

"Who says that?"

"Boys round here. They throw stones at me. They call me a Nazi."

"Is that how you got the bruise on your cheek?"

He wonders how angry he ought to feel with Jean Paul. Bringing Leopold to this house of ill repute. Fraternising with Nazis. Who's to say he wasn't involved in Evie's betrayal in some way too? On the other hand at least he took some trouble to look after Leopold.

"Have you seen Jean Paul lately?"

"He comes here sometimes."

"Do you like him a bit better now?"

"I suppose so. But I want to go home. I want to see if my friend Adela has come home."

Evie told him about Adela. He knows Adela will never be coming home.

8

He has been sitting on the bench all night. Passers-by take little notice of him. Another homeless wretch sitting alone on a bench. He leaves the bench only once to get a sandwich and a coffee from the café further down the street. And then to ring the bell again. She told him to go away when he rang on the bell. Didn't even open the door a fraction this time. Screamed at him to go away when he asked about the stripy green dress.

It's almost midnight when Jean Paul arrives. On foot, unshaven, dragging his feet. He holds up his hands in mock surrender when he is greeted. His formerly wavy brown hair now greasy and lifeless.

"The English pilot. What is the English pilot doing here in Rue Saint Jacques?"

"When Evie was in Paris, before she was arrested, did she ever wear a stripy green dress?"

"Have you been drinking?"

"It's a simple question. Just answer it."

"What makes you so sure I saw her in Paris?"

He wants to punch his face. His chest is tight, his breathing quick with the desire to punch his face. He keeps clenching his fist. Ready to strike. A voice says, just do it. He isn't sure he won't do it. Won't land a punch on Jean Paul's face and then grapple with him clownishly on the pavement and in the gutter.

"You didn't see her then? And yet your girlfriend was so jealous of her she betrayed her to the Gestapo."

Jean Paul walks past him. Sits down on the bench. "You know it never once crossed my mind she would do that."

"You don't seem to hold it against her much."

"Would it make you feel any better if I told you I blame myself?"

He sits down beside him. His fist unclenched. "I haven't come here to apportion out blame. I just need to know if you ever saw Evie wear a green stripy dress."

"In my head I don't call her Evie."

"Well?"

"I don't really remember. What does it matter if she ever wore a green stripy dress?"

"What was she wearing the last time you saw her? When was the last time you saw her?"

"The last time I saw her was at a fair, believe it or not. Swings and roundabouts and painted porcelain ponies. I took the kid on the dodgems. There were two SS soldiers in another car and that was the car I kept molesting. Monique or Anais or Evie if you like, was watching. I made her laugh by continually bashing the SS car. What was she wearing? I don't know. I can only see her smile."

He too can see her smile now. He wipes his nose with his sleeve.

"One thing you don't understand is that my feeling for her is not like yours. If it were she would not have had anything to do with me. I didn't tangle her up the way you did. She liked me because I didn't like her too much."

"You know she's probably dead."

It's the first time he has ever pronounced this idea. Not even in his own secret thoughts has he ever formed it into words. For a moment it's as if his head has been pushed under water.

"I only saw her three times in Paris. The Gestapo was hot on her heels and she needed a safe house. I introduced her to Fanny. I take it you've been to see Fanny?"

"She wouldn't speak to me."

"The only thing that keeps her going is the kid. She's looking after him, you know."

"I spoke to Leopold earlier."

"What's your real name by the way?"

"Jack."

"That Nazi you saw me with in Nancy. You must be curious about him."

"I told you, I'm not here to apportion out blame."

But he is curious about the Nazi he saw Jean Paul with in Nancy.

"Believe it or not I fenced with him before the war. My club went to Germany. A tour of exhibition matches. I met Karl Heinz in Karlsruhe. Then met him again in Nancy."

"I went to Karlsruhe. That's where Evie was in prison."

"He beat me. In our match. That's why he liked me so much. You know the communists in Nancy want to lynch me because of him. Just as well some of my fellow Gaullist chums will attest that I helped blow up a viaduct and a power station, eh? Tell you what, why don't you come up and we'll ask Fanny if she ever saw Evie wear a green stripy dress. A women is more likely to notice these things."

"You go up. I'll wait down here."

When Jean Paul lets himself into the apartment he walks away. Walks off down the wide Parisian street. His footfalls the only sound for a while, echoing with a hollow clarity in his wake.

He no longer wants to know if Evie was ever wearing a green stripy dress.

9

"The more I think about it, the more certain I am that Evie wasn't wearing any kind of green stripy dress in London."

"I'm not sure the dress matters anymore, Katie."

"Why do you say that?"

"Because there are now what, twelve women known to have been murdered. Even if Evie wasn't wearing a green stripy dress she could still be one of the other eleven dead girls."

"Which still leaves six or seven unaccounted for. Don't forget there are also two British women who got out of the camps alive. And that's just so far. At the moment there are hundreds of thousands of refugees wandering over Europe or in transit camps or in hospitals. There are prisoners so ill they can't talk or remember who they are. You don't know Evie isn't one of them. You said yourself you can't imagine anyone killing Evie in cold blood."

"I said that before I knew what went on in those camps. Now it's so much harder to believe the opposite. Now it seems the best I can hope for is to learn the details of how she died. Otto said one of your agents who got out of the camps has been debriefed."

"Yes. She was in Ravensbrück concentration camp. She was kept in solitary confinement the whole time so she doesn't know who else was there."

"There isn't much logical continuity, is there? Why were some sent to this camp, others to that? Why were some executed almost immediately on arrival and others allowed to live?"

"That's what gives me some hope."

"Did you know the four girls killed at Natzweiler were given soup before being killed? Probably thought, why would they give us soup if they are going to kill us? You can imagine the sense of relief they must have felt when the soup arrived. After arriving in that camp with the merciless lights and the dogs and the watchtowers and the chimney which must have seemed like the end of all history."

"At the end of all history some of the prisoners find themselves back in prehistory."

"What are you talking about?"

"I'm going to speak to the Swedish Red Cross again tomorrow. Some of the prisoners released from Ravensbrück have been taken by bus to Malmo. Apparently the only place they have to put them is with the dinosaurs and tyrannosaurus rex inside the museum of prehistory there."

"Katie."

"What is it?"

<h1 style="text-align:center">10</h1>

He keeps telling himself mothers have these kind of psychic intuitions. He keeps telling himself that it is too much of a coincidence not to be an oracle.

He arrives at Malmo railway station with Leopold. He has kidnapped Leopold. It was something he felt inspired to do. Going first to Paris allowed him to postpone the moment of truth too. Another seventy-two hours in the suspended zone of wishful thinking that predates knowledge. He did the same thing as a child. Always opened the most exciting looking present last. To spend as much time as possible with a swill of hope in his breast. To delay for as long as possible the scouring brutality of disappointment. He likes to think bringing Leopold is some kind of altruistic act. But he knows he has brought Leopold for his own protection. In the event she isn't here. So that he doesn't have to bear the crushing disappointment of her not being here alone. Leopold, he hopes, will give him something to be strong for.

"Let's call her Evie from now on. Okay?"

"Okay."

"I think it's time everyone went back to the name they were born with, don't you?"

"If she isn't here does that mean she's dead?"

"I'd like to say no. That it just means she's somewhere else."

"But that would be a lie?"

"Yes. That would probably be a lie. Thanks for coming, Leopold."

"If she's not here will I have to go back to Fanny?"

"I don't know."

He keeps picturing the moment when he and Leopold walk into the museum. The moment that is getting closer and closer. The moment that is already close to being a memory. Sometimes when he and Leopold enter the room in the museum there is a huge model of the skeleton of a dinosaur. Sometimes when he and Leopold enter the room of the museum there is no model of the skeleton of the dinosaur. He knows if there is no model skeleton of a dinosaur Evie won't be there. He is tempted to ask someone on the way, this bearded old pioneer-like man selling newspapers, this preoccupied hatless woman pushing a pram, if the museum has a model of the skeleton of a dinosaur. But he doesn't ask anyone. To spend as much time as possible with a swill of hope in his breast. To delay for as long as possible the scouring brutality of disappointment.

"Last week everything depended on a stripy green dress; now everything depends on a dinosaur."

"Do you mean she will only be there if there is a dinosaur?"

"Yes. Look. Here's the museum."

He avoids the nurses. He wants to make this discovery himself. He puts on an air of having the authority to walk around the museum at will. It's like a return to the days of eluding the suspicion of the Gestapo. His heartbeat urgent with the imminence of an emergency.

There are rows of mattresses on the floor. No iron beds. A detail Evie's mother got wrong. The eyes of the people on these mattresses frighten him. Frighten him and make him ashamed of his health. There is so little personality in the eyes of these people. So little hope of recovery. The smell of disinfectant is overpowering. As if these people with the hollow staring eyes have had their identities scrubbed away and disinfected.

There are rows of mattresses on the second floor too but no model skeletons of prehistoric beasts.

Is there a third floor? He looks about anxiously for another stairway, for an elevator. Surely they can climb higher. All the glass cabinets he passes, the ordered and annotated exhibits, are like pages in a dossier. It occurs to him that the Gestapo would have had a dossier on Evie. That there was someone working for the Nazis who took as much interest in her as he did. He is wondering about this man when Leopold shakes his arm and points. Another set of stairs.

They pass a nurse on the stairs. She says hello and smiles kindly at Leopold. He looks up at the ceiling. Following with his eyes the echo of their footsteps. A fresco of some burgeoning heavenly celebration in lime greens and grapefruit pinks and rinsed chalky blues.

At the top of the stairs he and Leopold stop and look at each other. He has never seen Leopold so openly express wonder. The smile they share grows so wide he feels his face can no longer contain it. The dinosaur is smaller than he imagined. Caught as if in the act of stepping leisurely over a vanished terrain of unknown vegetation. Jaws loosely open. There are skeleton models of other prehistoric beasts and birds too but he leads Leopold over to the dinosaur. Between the double row of mattresses. Not everyone is in bed. Some of the patients are sitting and talking to each other with one or two nurses hovering.

It is Leopold who sees her first. Lying on her back not far from the skeleton tail of the dinosaur. She too has the hollow staring eyes. Her hair very short. She stares up at him without recognition. He tries to change the expression on his face. Give her a clue as to his identity, as to his name. To not be recognised by her dissolves all the weights in his body. It's as if he melts into a puddle on the floor.

"Evie? It's Jack."

She can't see him. There is a kind of film over her eyes. She looks almost like a yellowing marble effigy of herself. But as if the sculptor gave her cheekbones too severe a definition. As if the sculptor failed to get an expression of life in the line of her lips.

"Is that her name, Evie?"

He turns to the woman on the mattress beside Evie who has spoken.

"Yes. Her name is Evie."

"It's no good you talking to her. We've all tried. She doesn't say a word. Where is she from?"

"England."

"We thought she was French."

He doesn't like this business of talking about her as if she isn't there. When he bends down close to her she flinches.

"And wilt thou leave me thus? Say nay! Say nay!" He recites the lines as though they are a secret mantra, a fairytale spell. But the spell doesn't work.

"It's no use," the woman says. "Poor thing."

"Look, Evie! I've brought Leopold."

He pushes Leopold forward. Leopold's head twists round at a heartrending angle on his neck. His eyes staring, his mouth hanging open, seemingly in supplication.

"Try saying something, Leopold."

Leopold shuffles his feet.

Evie is looking up at Leopold. She closes her eyes. Screws them tightly shut. Then Jack watches her open her eyes again and this time there is a flicker of Evie in them, a highlight of response.

Acknowledgements

For inspiration, sustenance and feedback, thanks to:

Charles Cecil, Freddie de Rougemont, Georgiana Calthorpe, Emily Pennock, VJ Keegan, Rupert Alexander, Vanessa Garwood, Antonia Barclay, Justin Sparrow, Anna von Kanitz, Jessica St. James, Lucy Corbett, Tom Lumley, Talitha Stevenson, Charlie Warde, Paola Rosà, Gina Monaco, Tim Binding, Alex Preston, Judith Kinghorn, Annabel Merullo, Charlie Campbell, Hamid Khanbhai, Christabel Brudnell-Bruce, Charlotte Raymond, David Flusfeder, Tim Atkins, Tiarnan McCarthy, Sarah Haybittle, Chiara De Cabarrus, Lisa Andris, Kim Macconnell, Rachel Webster, Stuart Bridgeman, Linda Fleischman, Hugo Wilson, Eloise Anson, Caroline Scott, Marc Dalessio, Paolo Cristellotti, Mark Roberts, Richard Burton, Katie St. George, Charlotte Cecil, Josephine Rea, Bill Liesegang, Ebba Heuman, Cristina Zamagni.